MURDER IN GROSVENOR SQUARE

CAPTAIN LACEY REGENCY MYSTERIES BOOK 9

ASHLEY GARDNER

JA / AG PUBLISHING

CHAPTER 1

March 1818

I had an appointment on Lady Day, not half a week away, to face a man in a duel.

My opponent was one Lord Andrew Kenton Stubbins, known to his intimates as Stubby. The reason for the appointment—I'd come across him beating a young woman he'd hired for his pleasure. I'd indicated to him, by snatching the strap from his hands and giving him a taste of it, what I'd thought of his choice of pleasures.

Stubby had subsequently challenged me, Lucius Grenville had agreed to be one of my seconds, and I'd been fitted with a new suit for the occasion. I thought it ridiculous to waste new clothes on what was certain to be a messy business, but both my wife and Grenville, the most fashionable man in society, assured me it was the done thing.

Being a man of Mayfair now, with servants at my beck and call, I could have sent one of them to do my errand today, but I used the excuse to go out for a bit of exercise. I made my way via hackney to the Strand to fetch a walking stick I'd sent for repair. During my adventures in January, the stick had been stolen from me only to turn up again next to a corpse in my old rooms in Covent Garden. The stick had been exonerated of any wrongdoing and returned to me by a Bow Street Runner, but I'd discovered eventually that the sword inside was bent.

I did not use the sword much, and so did not hurry to repair it. But I complained of it until my wife, Donata, in exasperation, told me to please get the blasted thing fixed.

I'd taken the walking stick to its birthplace—a shop in the Strand—explained the problem, and left it with them. This morning, I'd had word that the sword was now in good repair, and I'd come to collect it. I was particularly fond of that walking stick, as it had been a gift from Donata, who only two months before this had done me the honor of becoming the second Mrs. Lacey.

After I retrieved it, I decided to walk a while before returning home. Spring was easing over London, kinder winds replacing the harsh ones of winter. March meant green creeping mist-like over trees in the city parks, bulbs pushing their leaves through the ground. It meant rain and fog as well, but also days like this, blue skies with a promise of sweeter weather to come.

March also meant a whirl of soirees, supper balls, musicales, dinners, at-homes, and other such functions beloved of Donata, formerly the Dowager Viscountess Breckenridge. She was a hostess to be reckoned with. Now that she had a husband to stand beside her in his well-kept regimentals, she doubled her efforts to best every other lady in Mayfair. Hence my eagerness to run an errand to the Strand this afternoon, and my excuse to linger and enjoy the first flush of spring.

"Captain?" A voice at my elbow pulled me from my airy contemplations.

The young man who'd addressed me had brown hair and small brown eyes set rather close together. He was well dressed in an expensively cut coat and kid gloves, his hat as fine as any Grenville would own.

"Mr. Travers," I said in true delight, taking his offered hand.

I'd met Gareth Travers while investigating the affair of Colonel Westin, a murder with roots in the Peninsular War. Travers was the close friend of Leland Derwent, whose family invited me to dine with them once a fortnight, where they'd beg me to entertain them with stories of my army days. Now that I was married, they'd extended that invitation to my wife as well.

The Derwents were a family of innocents, looking upon the world with benevolence, never noticing its darkness. Travers had a bit more cynicism in him, but I imagine he enjoyed their unworldly companionship as much as I did.

"Well met, Captain," Travers said. "I am pleased to have been walking along this same stretch of pavement. I've been meaning to call on you."

"Have you? What can I do for you, Mr. Travers?" I liked Gareth, who seemed intelligent and sensible, though I did not know much about him.

He hesitated. "There is tavern not far from here. Perhaps …?"

"Of course," I said politely. A chance to stop for a good pint would delay me further from returning home. Donata would hold a soiree tonight, and the house was currently in an uproar preparing for it. My role would be to stand with her at the top of the stairs and shake hands with the crush that shoved their way toward us. A friendly ale at a pub was just the thing to fortify me for the task.

We walked along the Strand toward Charing Cross, Travers leading me to whatever tavern he had in mind. As we neared St. Martin's Lane, a strange roar rippled through the spring air. The sound grew and built, flowing down the street to us like a sudden river. A cart horse shied, hooves clattering on the cobbles while the driver tried to calm it. Travers stopped, as worried as the horse.

"A mob?" he asked, his young face drawn in concern.

I sincerely hoped not. Riots at times tore through these streets, mobs crushing, breaking, beating, anything in their way. I could not blame those who protested the cost of bread, which seemed to rise out of all proportion to anything sensible. In these times after the war, so many had returned from the army to no work and no wages, cast upon the shores of their native land without recompense. Add to that the cost of grain and men unable to feed their families, and anger built to the breaking point. Houses and shops were demolished during the violent rioting, with soldiers called to fire into the crowds and restore peace.

A strained peace, with desperation boiling just below the surface.

If a mob came this way, we'd have to take refuge in a shop or house. I could not outrun a riot on my injured leg, though I had little doubt that Travers, young and healthy, could sprint to safety.

After listening a moment I said in relief, "I do not think so." The crowd was excited, but missing the sharpness of fury. "Someone in the stocks, possibly."

Travers relaxed a bit, but only a bit. "Poor bastard."

I agreed. The stocks were for those convicted of crimes of a lesser degree than murder, robbery, and other heinous things. While the convicted might not be hanged, he could lose his life if the mob grew incensed enough. If the person had the crowd's sympathy, he would fare little worse than stiff limbs from the ordeal, but if the crowd despised him or her, the man or woman could be battered to death.

It became clear as we neared Charing Cross that the fellow in the stocks today did not have the crowd's sympathy. The unfortunate man was already covered in filth from rotted vegetables and dung. His head hung down, and he shuddered when another missile burst upon his back. My pity for him stirred.

I could not get close enough to read the placard that proclaimed his crime. The crowd was chanting, but it was difficult to hear what they said. I turned to a coffee vendor who'd decided this a good place for business today. "What has he done?" I asked.

The vendor looked pointedly at the rather dented bulbous silver coffee urn in front of him, so I politely handed him a coin and bought a cup. He took a cracked mug from his cart, turned the spigot to release thick, steaming coffee into it, and handed it to me.

I took a sip and tried not to make a face. I was going soft, being served the finest brew at Lady Breckenridge's table every day. Then again, my former landlady had made coffee better than this in her little backstreet bakeshop.

"Buggery," the vendor grunted. "So they say."

"Ah." While a hanging offense, sodomy had to be proved with a witness. Gentlemen who engaged in the practice usually were wise enough to make certain they were completely private. But a charge of unnatural behavior could be made and tried. Conviction meant a day in the stocks, at the mercy of the mob.

"Poor bastard, indeed," I said.

"He'll last." The vendor, a large bull of a man, showed no compassion. "Resilient. He'll be happily poking away at some other bloke in a week or so."

I had no wish to stand and watch the man confined by his hands and feet be kicked in the backside by youths who found this good fun, so I finished a few more sips of coffee, handed the mug back, and signaled Travers to lead me on to his tavern.

The public house was north on St. Martin's Lane, the interior dark with aged wood, the atmosphere quiet. Travers must be a regular, because men greeted him with nods instead of hostile stares.

"Brutal." Travers looked a bit white about the mouth as we dug into good, thick ale the landlord brought us. "But so many laws in England are."

"Stocks are a bit harsh for the offense, I always thought," I said. "I knew two soldiers during the war who spent the night with each other before every battle. We all knew it but said nothing, because the two in question always fought the more fiercely for each other the next day. I believe the Spartans did much the same."

Travers listened to this revelation in surprise. "You are a reformist then?" A hint of a smile touched his lips. "A radical perhaps?"

"A realist, I would say," I said with a shrug. "I've learned to take things as they come." Or perhaps I had been sanguine because the two gentlemen had never tried to seduce *me*.

However, injustice always enraged me, and I was known to take matters into my own hands. Hence, my forthcoming appointment with Stubby Stubbins.

It was difficult for me not to rush back to Charing Cross, unlock the stocks, and let the pathetic man out, but I knew that such an act could result in my death and his. No, he'd finish his sentence, go home, nurse his wounds, and be more careful the next time.

I took another drink of ale and let the bitter taste of hops soothe me. "Why did you wish to call on me?" I asked Gareth. "Something for which you seek my help?" I was gaining a reputation for assisting those in need.

"Nothing so dire," Gareth said easily. He sipped his ale, licking a droplet from his pale upper lip. "I simply thought to have a conversation."

This surprised me. I had nearly twenty years on Travers and never thought him interested in conversation with a fortyish ex-army man. Whenever he and I both attended the Derwents' dinners, he rarely spoke to me at all, preferring the company of Leland and Leland's widowed cousin, Mrs. Danbury.

For all his professed interest, Gareth Travers did not seem to know what he wanted to say to me. He began a ramble about the Derwents—his amusement about how unworldly they were and his admiration for them at the same time, and his worry for Lady Derwent's health. I nodded at intervals, waiting to discover his true purpose in speaking to me.

When he started to appear at a loss, I broke in, "You've known the family a long time?"

Travers seemed relieved I'd taken charge of the discussion. "From years back. Eely—Leland, I mean—and I were at school together, but you knew that. I spent all my holidays with the Derwents, practically lived with them. My own father's a bit threadbare. Clergy, you know. He was happy to have the Derwents look after me."

Travers dressed well to be the son of threadbare clergy, I thought. But while his father's living might be minuscule, Travers could have come into trust money or been left a legacy by a friend. Money didn't always travel in a straight line— except in my family. Our line of wealth had gone directly to my father and then straight into the ground.

"You are fond of the Derwents," I said.

Travers looked embarrassed. "I am. They have been very good to me."

"And they've been good to me. They enjoy taking in strays."

"Too true. Eely is an ass about it sometimes. Once at university, Leland tried to help a bloke he found in the street. Took him in, let him stay in our digs, gave the man his clothes, his money, tried to find employment for him. I warned him, but Leland is stubbornly blind sometimes. Of course the chap up and robbed us of almost everything and disappeared into the night. Leland was only sad we hadn't helped him more. He even offered to recompense me for my losses. And then he wanted to go after the man and try again."

Travers laughed, sounding genuinely amused. I imagined, though, that he hadn't been much amused at the time.

"Some people resist being reformed," I said. Well I knew this. I'd tried last year to help a street girl called Felicity, with mixed results. She was the lady in question Stubbins had been beating when I'd discovered him.

"Well, Eely won't hear of it. Bless the boy."

Travers called him *boy*, when the two were the same age. "Leland is a kind young man," I said. "Heaven help him."

Travers nodded. "Good thing he has me to look after him. His father is as kind, and sometimes as foolish."

"But Sir Gideon is a man of much power, and he's reached that state by being a philanthropist," I pointed out. "Perhaps Leland will do the same."

Travers tapped his ale tankard, shaking his head in mild exasperation. "Perhaps, but until then, it falls to *me* to keep the lad out of scrapes."

"He is lucky to have such a friend," I said in all sincerity.

Travers glanced at me a moment, his brows drawing together. Then he drained the rest of his pint and rose with restless energy.

"Pleased to have met you, Captain." Gareth stuck out his hand as I got to my feet, and I shook it. "I look forward to dining with you at the Derwents next time. Good day."

As he started for the door, I had a thought. "Mr. Travers, a moment."

Travers waited for me as I grabbed my hat and then walked with him out the door. When we stepped into the fine weather, I spoke to him in a low voice. "How do you feel about settling questions of honor?"

Travers raised his brows but gave me a shrewd look. "Why do you ask, Captain?"

"I need a friend," I said. "One to stand by me, with Grenville. Next week, on Lady Day, early in the morning."

"I see." Travers set his hat on his head. "Should I speak to Mr. Grenville about the particulars?"

"Indeed. That would be best." I hesitated then said delicately, "Perhaps Leland and Sir Gideon do not need to know of your plans."

Travers shot me a sudden grin, the look in his eyes one of satisfaction, almost triumph, which puzzled me a bit. "I believe I understand you." He shook my hand again, squeezing my fingers warmly. "Well met, Captain." With that Travers gave me a nod, and walked away into the crowd, whistling.

I SURVIVED DONATA'S SOIREE THAT NIGHT WITHOUT TOO much damage. She was always very careful with her guest list, and I could not fault the time spent talking with people I truly liked and respected.

Things were rather tense, however, in the Lacey household for the next few days, the knowledge that I would meet an unsavory gentleman early on the upcoming morning for a dangerous act keeping us terse. To that end, my daughter Gabriella, who was staying with us for the Season, had been sent to spend a few weeks with Lady Aline Carrington, at her country house and at Bath, to prepare for her come-out ball Donata planned for later in the Season. I missed Gabriella, and wanted the duel over with so I could return to my newfound domestic bliss.

Donata was all for me teaching Stubby a lesson, but she was worried, I could see. She did not say much, but her look told me everything.

Grenville and Travers paid a call on me to go over the particulars of the duel. Though Grenville spoke with his usual sangfroid, I could sense his anxiousness. Travers, on the other hand, was excited, and quite flattered I'd chosen him as my other second.

Whatever Travers had wanted to say to me in the tavern, I never learned. With much on my mind, I did not pursue it.

And so we came to Lady Day, and my appointment.

CHAPTER 2

*F*og shrouded the green deep in the middle of Hyde Park, blotting out the rest of London. I blessed the mists which closed around us like clinging fingers. No one would be able to see us here, and by the time the noise reached a watchman or foot patroller, we'd be finished and gone.

I wore my new suit, a black affair of thick cashmere, my waistcoat ivory satin. It was the finest suit I'd ever owned, and I would waste it on a duel.

Stubby Stubbins and his seconds arrived moments after I did. Stubby was tall but rail-thin, with light brown hair he'd slicked with pomade. His eyes, a shade of blue so pale that they washed out into his face, fixed on me in burning anger. His coat's shoulders were padded wide as was the fashion, making his torso a severe upside-down triangle.

Grenville, who'd brought me here in his carriage, did *not* wear the padded shoulders in his silent condemnation of the latest craze. I had no doubt that, without his approval, the fashion would quickly disappear.

Grenville opened his box of finest dueling pistols. They were made by Wogdon, dull black with silver inlay on the hammer and barrel. They'd been so masterfully wrought, it was difficult to believe they were lethal. I chose one, hefted its weight, tested the trigger, then handed it back to Grenville.

One of Stubbins' seconds, Chetterly, I remembered his name was, came forward. He threw me a nervous glance but spoke only to Grenville.

"His lordship brought pistols. He would be honored if Captain Lacey were to use one of them."

I took a step back, pretending to adjust my coat and survey the ground. The logistics of the duel were entirely the purview of the seconds.

"Captain Lacey respectfully declines, though we thank Stubbins for the offer," Grenville said. "Each combatant will use his own weapon, as we previously decided."

Chetterly nodded, looking happy not to pursue the matter. "Very well. The ground is to our liking. Two shots, one from each, will satisfy. Signal me when ready."

As the challenger, Stubby had the right to name the time and place, and I'd agreed with it. I had to admit he'd chosen well—or rather, I suspect his seconds did for him. We were in the heart of Hyde Park, early in the morning, spring fog obligingly obscuring us. The stretch of grass was well tended, making footing good. No one needed to die because someone slipped.

Grenville watched Chetterly in dislike as the man walked away. "I do *not* trust Stubbins not to have mucked about with the pistol he'd offer you, to make it jam, or fool your aim, or even blow up in your face."

"Not very honorable," I said dryly. "In this affair of honor."

"Stubby is a cheat at heart. I've known him a long while, unfortunately. I hope he remembers which is his good pistol and doesn't choose the one he meant for you." Grenville laughed, but his laughter was tight.

I caught his gaze, keeping mine steady. "I'll not die this day, Grenville."

"I hope not, my dear fellow," Grenville said, his words

light. "I haven't finished telling you the tales of my travels, and I do like an attentive audience."

The fog parted like a billowing curtain to admit another man, obscured by shadow. Grenville straightened up, putting his body in front of the box of pistols he'd set on a folding table, which his valet had brought for the purpose. The man who emerged from the mists, however, was Gareth Travers, dressed in a suit almost as fine as mine.

He gave me a nod as he approached. "Captain. Well met."

I returned the greeting, shaking Travers's offered hand. His grip was strong, but I could feel him trembling.

"I've fought battles of honor before, gentlemen," I said, releasing him. "And here I stand."

Grenville shot me a look, as though I were not appreciative enough of my own luck, and turned to Travers. "Right. This is the point where we speak again to the seconds and try to resolve this without bloodshed."

He sounded hopeful, but I knew better. Stubbins' friends were as pigheaded as he was.

I watched Grenville and Travers walk to the middle of the green to meet Danielson and Chetterly. The four men looked much alike in their dun-colored greatcoats, tall hats, and dark trousers.

Grenville and Travers returned. "I'm afraid you're carrying on with the appointment," Grenville said. "Stubby believes he has the guidance of angels." His look turned grave. "Watch yourself, Lacey."

I intended to. Grenville loaded the pistol himself—I wanted someone who knew what he was about to do it right. He tipped fine black powder into the barrel through the muzzle, so skillfully that the March breeze took nothing away. He tamped it down with the ramrod, added a cloth wad, tamped that down, then finally slid in a ball and another cloth, repeating the tamping. Grenville half-cocked the gun and primed the pan with a small amount of powder—when the hammer struck the pan, the resulting spark would set off the gunpowder inside the barrel and discharge the pistol.

Grenville checked that all was solidly inside—no ball rolling out before I could fire—and offered me the pistol, butt first. I shucked my greatcoat and my frock coat, Grenville's valet coming out of the shadows to take them from me. I handed him my walking stick, preferring to balance without it for shooting.

As Gautier, the valet, scuttled away again, folding the coats over his arm, I took the pistol from Grenville.

All was ready. Time to walk out and meet Stubbins.

Stubbins wouldn't look me in the eye when we met in the middle of the green, though I stared straight at him. Stubby's chest heaved with agitated breath, but I did not read fear in him so much as determination. He was anxious to kill me.

"Gentlemen," Chetterly said. "Walk twelve paces, turn, and fire when ready."

I gave Stubbins a curt bow and put my back to him. I didn't wait to see whether he had pivoted around to begin his walk, I simply went, counting my paces.

As I made my way to my mark, I noticed another man in the mists, standing far enough back in the fog to shroud his features. I had no need to see him clearly, however, to recognize the bulk of James Denis's man Brewster—one of the pugilists he employed as guards. Brewster had been told to watch, I assumed, and report the outcome to his master.

When I reached my twelfth step, I turned and brought up my pistol.

Stubbins swung around at the same time, and he fired.

I saw the flash of his powder, heard the roar of the gun a bare moment later. Death headed straight for me, but I didn't move. To dive to the ground, to run, would mean Stubbins would win the day, his honor satisfied.

I continued steadying my aim in the hanging time from the flash of Stubby's pistol to the outcome of the shot. Everything stilled—then propelled forward very fast. One moment I was sighting down my barrel, the next, I was dancing backward as a wad of earth exploded at my feet, spattering mud up my new trousers and shirt and into my face.

Bloody man. The ball had plowed into the ground inches from where my right foot had been. No doubt he'd been aiming for my head, but his miss had nearly crippled me.

I lost my temper. I raised the pistol and sighted down it again, calculating how much to compensate for the wind and the distance, ready to teach the idiot a lesson.

At the other end of the green, Stubbins began to gibber. He assessed my straight body, my rock-steady hand, and knew he was about to die. I sensed Grenville and Travers, on either side of me, tense, waiting to see what I'd do.

Stubby's gibbering turned to wails of distress. His seconds quavered, clearly wondering whether to dart forward and stop the duel or let me proceed.

I could always delope; that is, fire into the air, declaring the contest over. Honor fulfilled. After all, I'd been the one who'd beaten Stubbins down, the one who'd insulted him.

I thought of Felicity, crouching in the dingy bedchamber above a taproom, terrified and in pain, and Stubbins slashing at her bare back with a strap. She'd been crying, pleading, and Stubbins had gone at her, enjoyment in his eyes. He'd sealed his own fate.

I completed my aim, and pulled the trigger.

A loud *bang* sounded as my pistol went off. Smoke curled in my nose, and powder stung my face like grains of fine sand.

Stubby's pale lawn shirtsleeve erupted in blood, crimson coating the fabric. The bullet, traveling true to my will, entered Stubbins in the fleshy part of his right arm.

The man stared at his red sleeve for a split second, then he started to scream. He collapsed to the ground, clutching the wound, his screams escalating. His seconds swarmed around him, shouting at him to lie still, to let them see the wound.

I turned away and handed the spent pistol to a white-faced Grenville.

Travers was watching me, open-mouthed. "Did you miss?" he asked in a strained voice.

Grenville was already shaking his head before I answered.

"No," I said. "He'll hurt, and he'll be scarred, but he'll live." Every time Stubbins undressed, he'd see the scars on his upper arm and remember me.

Travers only stared at me. A swallow moved down his slender throat.

As I tried to scrape mud from my ruined shirt, Gautier came hurrying forward. "Sirs!"

He pointed to the bottom of the green, where the mists were yellowing with the coming day. Several men strode out of the fog, led by a man in a black suit who walked with an arrogant stride. I recognized the Bow Street Runner called Spendlove.

I calmly took my coat and greatcoat from Gautier. "Go," I said to Travers. "Now." I had no doubt that Spendlove was coming to arrest me for shooting Stubbins and would happily arrest Grenville and Travers as well.

Travers looked indignant. "And leave you hanging? What kind of friend would I be?"

"One who doesn't come up before a magistrate," I said. "Go on."

Travers gave me a stubborn look in spite of another swallow bobbing in his throat. He squared his shoulders. "I'll not desert you."

I ignored him and beckoned to Brewster, who came forward without concern. Grenville calmly wiped down the pistol, emptied the remnants of the powder from the pan, and returned the pistol to the box. He was not going to save himself either.

Brewster reached us. I caught Travers by the arm and pushed him toward the pugilist. "Take him home," I said.

Brewster nodded, putting his beefy hand on Travers's shoulder. Travers sent me an unhappy look, but I noted he didn't bother trying to fight the giant at his side. "You too, sir," Brewster said in his deep voice. "Mr. Denis said be sure you wasn't arrested." "I'll look after myself," I said. "Please take Mr. Travers out of here."

Brewster looked me over, shifted his gaze to Grenville, who was stoically putting away the gun, then watched the approaching Spendlove. At last he gave me another nod and marched the young man away.

Spendlove quickened his pace. Two of his foot patrollers peeled away to approach Stubbins, and the remaining man and Spendlove flanked me and Grenville.

"Good morning, Captain," Spendlove said, his expression a mixture of amusement and self-assurance. "And what have you been getting up to, so early on a spring morning in Hyde Park?"

CHAPTER 3

Spendlove kept his gaze on me, his light blue eyes hiding deadly glee. He had dark red hair that he tried and failed to tame, and the pale skin that went with his coloring, though his freckled face was sun-bronzed.

Timothy Spendlove wanted me under his thumb, he'd told me when I'd first met him. He wished to grind me for information about James Denis, who controlled much of the underworld in London. He'd use me until he had Denis in the dock, never mind what happened to me in the meantime.

I didn't answer his question. Grenville laid the final piece of the dueling set back into its resting place and shut the inlaid mahogany box.

"We were testing my pistols," he said smoothly as he locked the box. "Captain Lacey did not believe they were the finest he'd ever shoot, and wanted to try them himself. Unfortunately, one of the pistols went off too early and hit Mr. Stubbins."

Spendlove lifted one red brow. "Who happened to be walking by with pistols of his own?"

Grenville shrugged. "This spot is a grand place for shooting, so early in the morning. No one around to get hurt. Except, of course, Mr. Stubbins,"

"What do you say, Captain?" Spendlove asked. "You're very quiet."

"It is early," I said in clipped tones. "I'm not my best in the morning."

"I see." Spendlove spent a long moment studying me with eyes that missed very little. He flicked a glance at Stubbins, who was complaining loudly about me and Grenville to the patrollers.

Spendlove could arrest the lot of us on the moment, for attempted murder, or for brawling, or for discharging weapons in a public park—anything he could think of. I saw him debate whether it would be more to his advantage to see me up before a magistrate today or let me walk away. Perhaps if I faced a charge of attempted murder—even true murder or manslaughter if Stubbins took ill from his injury—I might promise Spendlove anything in exchange for my life and freedom.

No, Grenville would not leave me to dangle in the wind. He had an army of solicitors he could call upon to help me out of trouble and so did Donata. Spendlove knew that.

But I saw in Spendlove's eyes as he fixed me with his gaze, that he did not care what friends I had. When he got me, and he would, his expression told me, all the expensive solicitors in London wouldn't make a blind bit of difference.

Spendlove gave me a sudden and beatific smile. "Then good day to you, Captain." His tone was polite, but I glimpsed his buried rage. "Mr. Grenville."

Spendlove tipped his hat to us. I expected him to stride away, but he remained where he was, waiting for us to leave first. He said nothing more, not dismissing the event or admonishing me or vowing to have me in the end. He only watched, waiting to see what I'd do.

Grenville tucked his pistol box under his arm, and Gautier

folded the table. "Time for a spot of breakfast, eh, Lacey?" Grenville suggested, then without another word started around Spendlove and into the mists, heading for the path where he'd left his carriage, Gautier in his wake.

I gave Spendlove a brief nod, which he did not return, took up my walking stick, and walked after Grenville, leaving the field of battle.

———

MY WIFE WAS AWAKE, RECLINING ON A CHAISE IN OUR upstairs sitting room, when I returned after declining Grenville's invitation to breakfast. I was surprised to see Donata out of bed, because she rarely bestirred herself until well after one in the afternoon.

But there she was, drinking coffee and reading a newspaper, her thin peignoir flowing over legs. I smelled of gunpowder, and my face was filmed with the stuff along with the mud Stubbins had splashed over me.

Donata looked up from her newspaper at me and raised her delicate brows. "Well, I see you are in one piece," she said. "If a little worse for wear."

I unbuttoned my damp coat. "Stubbins is as bad at shooting as he is good at being a bloody nuisance." I let Bartholomew, my manservant, who was hovering like a worried maiden aunt, peel off the frock coat and waistcoat beneath.

When he wanted to strip me to the skin and scrub me down, I told him irritably to go away. "I'll bring a bath, sir," Bartholomew said. He blinked a few times, as though he had something in his eyes, then turned to carry my coat and waist-coat to the dressing room.

"No, you'll wait until I send for it," I called after him. I was suddenly exhausted and weary of the whole business.

When the door closed behind Bartholomew Donata

languidly put aside her newspaper, rose, and came to me. She laid her hand on my chest, her fingers resting over my heavily beating heart, never mind the mud on my new lawn shirt.

"I am pleased to see no holes here," she said, tracing a pattern across my pectorals.

Her hand flattened on me, then her cool assuredness evaporated, and she half-fell against me, hands clutching the muddy ruins of my shirt. Her dark head bowed to my shoulder. I smelled the lavender rinse she used on her hair, the warmth of woman under the peignoir.

Her body shook against mine—with sobs, I realized.

My brave Donata, who never cried, was clinging to me, weeping. I wrapped my arms around her and pulled her close.

"There now," I said, kissing her hair. "I was in no real danger. Stubbins is a terrible shot."

"Don't be stupid," she said, her words muffled against my chest.

I turned her face up to mine and kissed the tears on her face. That this beautiful woman wept for fear of losing me was astonishing.

I kept one arm around her waist as I led her to my bedchamber. I closed the door, turned the key in the lock, and took Donata to bed. The bath and all its luxuries could wait.

THE DUEL GAINED ME RESPECT IN SOME QUARTERS, notoriety in others. *No honor,* a few of Grenville's acquaintances at White's said. *He should have shot into the air. Stubby was the aggrieved party. Lacey had humiliated him, after all.*

Grenville's closer friends were more apt to congratulate me on a job well-done. *Stubby needed to be potted. Good to see his comeuppance.*

My visit to the Derwents the next week was trickier. Sir Gideon Derwent, my host, did not hold with duels, or violence of any kind. He admired me for being in the army, but blood and death in war was inevitable, he'd say, and necessary to put down those who would oppress. Shooting a man in cold blood in a park was a different thing.

His large home in Grosvenor Square could have been overly ostentatious had not his family made every corner cozy. Vases of flowers arranged by the hands of the Derwent ladies were placed next to marble statuary, baskets of plain mending rested next to damask chairs.

Nearly every room was strewn with books piled haphazardly on top of one another, bookmarked with ribbons, scribbled notes, pressed flowers, a folded piece of sheet music. The Derwents—Sir Gideon and his wife, his daughter Melissa, his son Leland, and the various and sundry friends they brought home—read these books, discussed them, debated them, laughed at them, praised them.

But for all their knowledge and appreciation of books, art, music, and conversation, they remained the most innocent family I'd ever known.

Gareth Travers was there that evening, as well as another couple who arrived with a daughter the same age as Melissa Derwent. Melissa and the young lady—Miss Braithwaite—knew each other, but instead of going off into a corner to whisper and giggle as young ladies do, they remained politely with the family, staying silent until spoken to directly.

I contrasted the two young ladies to my daughter, Gabriella. Gabriella would have joined in the adults' discussion and given her opinion freely. I'd overheard Donata's friends say that Gabriella was too forthright and needed to learn to concede, but I preferred her openness. Gabriella's mother, my former wife, had been meek to the point of exasperating me to harsh words. My fault for my impatience, but I would not like to see my daughter give way before a man of hard temperament.

Gabriella was learning how to be a woman from Donata

and Lady Aline—a spinster with decided opinions no one dared contradict—and Louisa Brandon, wife of my former commander, who had a backbone of steel. Gabriella was, I concluded, in good hands.

I did note that at the gathering after supper—ladies and gentlemen together, no male withdrawing for port and cigars—care was taken to seat Miss Braithwaite near young Leland, while Gareth Travers was manipulated to be near Melissa Derwent. The parents orchestrated the moves of this dance, while the young people were oblivious, or pretended to be. I did see Melissa blush when Gareth spoke to her, and a starriness appear in her eyes. Perhaps Gareth would be connected to the Derwent family in yet another way soon.

I noticed Donata watching the young people sharply, but when I caught her gaze, she turned away with a neutral expression.

Lady Derwent seemed in good spirits. The lady was dangerously thin, consumption wasting her. Sir Gideon had taken her for a short holiday to warmer climes after New Year's, but Lady Derwent insisted on returning to London for the Season. Studying her, I surmised it might be her last. She had the bright-eyed, animated look consumptives took on when they were nearing the end.

I was sad for them. These people were too kind, too gentle, for the sort of tragedy they were rushing headlong toward. I only hoped I could help when it struck.

My adventure in the park was not discussed. Not the thing in front of ladies, of course. Perhaps that was why the Derwents worked hard to keep this evening pleasant and harmless, so that such topics did not darken the door of their grand home.

When my wife and I returned to her Adams brothers' decorated house in South Audley Street, Donata shed her politeness as she shed her clothes, and bathed me in cigarillo smoke and her opinions.

"Miss Anna Braithwaite as a match for Leland Derwent?" Donata said as she reclined on her chaise, clad in her favorite peignoir. She wore a turban woven through her curls and had a cup of tea and glass of brandy at her elbow. The idea that ladies should drink nothing stronger than ratafia, or perhaps sherry, was absolute nonsense to her.

I sipped from my own glass of brandy as I lounged in a Bergere chair, comfortable in my dressing gown. I'd grown fond of these sessions with my wife late at night, shut away from the world, listening while she dissected it.

"Quite a bad idea," Donata went on. "Leland Derwent needs a woman with backbone. Heaven knows he doesn't have one of his own. Not the lad's fault, with his upbringing."

"The Derwents are the kindest people in England," I said, a bit stiffly. "I like them."

"Everyone does," Donata answered, unworried. "That does not mean they are the *wisest* people on earth, or that they would not do well with a little bolstering of their blood. If Leland is paired with an insipid female, the two of them will be crushed underfoot, especially with Lady Derwent dying. Sir Gideon will collapse without his wife, and *someone* will have to hold up that family."

I hated to think of the day when Lady Derwent left them, but I knew Donata spoke the truth. "They have Mrs. Danbury," I suggested.

Mrs. Danbury was Sir Gideon's niece, a woman twice widowed, with much more experience of life than the sheltered Derwents. She had not been present tonight—the explanation offered was that she dined with dear friends.

"Ah, Mrs. Danbury." Donata took a long pull of her cigarillo and let smoke trickle out with her words. "I forgot, you have a *tendre* for her."

I blinked. "I beg your pardon. I have never had a *tendre* for Catherine Danbury."

Donata's eyes glinted. "And yet I recall one afternoon how

you, far gone on the fumes of an interesting gas, threw away your walking stick and danced and danced with Mrs. Danbury. Laughing. You would have kissed her, had you not remembered yourself in time."

She was not wrong. My face grew hot as I recalled the day. I'd made a complete and utter fool of myself, having breathed in an intoxicating gas offered at an afternoon society gathering. The gas had, amazingly, taken all pain and soreness from me, and had apparently taken away my reason as well. My only excuse for partaking of the gas was that I'd been investigating a murder with connections to the gathering's host. Donata had been present, observed me closely, and had been quite critical. She'd also been very helpful, after that, in my pursuit of the killer.

"Blame the concoction," I said. "I would have danced with you instead, but you were rather off-putting that day."

"I didn't know you." Donata waved away smoke and took a sip of brandy. "Even if I had been friends with you then, I certainly wouldn't have let you waltz me about a drawing room full of rather tawdry people."

I raised my brows. "Your friends and acquaintance, I'd thought."

"Tawdry all the same." One dark curl had escaped her cap and rested like coiled silk on her shoulder — I grew distracted watching the candlelight play upon it. "I enjoyed the gas — a new sensation and good for the humors. A pity Inglethorpe had to get himself skewered."

We both fell silent as we remembered the dire circumstances of that case. During that investigation, as well, had been the first time I'd kissed Donata.

"I have been pondering the matter of Leland Derwent," I said after a time. I took a deep drink of brandy, savoring its rich, burning taste. "I am thinking of him as a match for Gabriella."

Donata froze in the act of lifting her tea, the cup hovering in the region of her bosom. "You are joking."

"Not at all." I rolled my glass between my palms. "You are right that Leland is unworldly and naïve. Gabriella has also been sheltered, thank God, but she has a great deal of common sense. Leland is a fine young man, his parents are of impeccable stock and reputation, and Sir Gideon is wealthy. Gabriella would be well provided for."

Donata only pinned me with an amazed stare. Steam rose from the tea, curling around her face like smoke. Then she abruptly set down the cup.

"Well, I never thought of you as a man of ambition, Gabriel."

I gave her a perplexed look. "Ambition?"

"Indeed. I'd thought you fond of the Derwents, the only explanation for you craving their company."

It took me a moment to understand her implication. "You think I have simply been cultivating them for my daughter?" I asked, offended. "You believe me to be that sort of man?"

"Either that or you have run completely mad. Gabriella and Leland Derwent?" Donata shook her head. "There are only two explanations for the idea, Gabriel—either you are ambitious or you are mad."

"I am thinking of Gabriella's future," I said, spreading the fingers of one hand. "I have nothing to leave her—no money, and only a rundown house in Norfolk that will go to the next Lacey heir, whoever he might be. Sir Gideon's fortune could ensure Gabriella's care for the rest of her days. The family is generous and, as we have agreed, kind. I can't think of a better place for Gabriella than in the bosom of the Derwents."

"A fine idea if you want her to be great friends with them," Donata argued. "But she cannot marry *Leland*, Gabriel. She would die of the tedium. She might be well provided for, but she'd be miserable."

"Miserable? Isn't that taking it a bit far?"

"I remain firm to the adjective," Donata replied. "Gabriella has a lively mind. She questions, she speaks, she does not meekly wait to be told what to do as does Melissa Derwent. The Derwents read and converse, yes, but only on very safe topics. The music of the Bach family, Sheridan's dreary comedies, the lovely landscape paintings of the East Anglians. Nothing controversial or challenging. Gabriella will become as stiff-necked as Hannah Moore and her manuals of morality. I would rather your daughter remain old-fashioned and forthright. It's refreshing in a world of growing insipidity."

We studied each other, Donata resolute, I, troubled. I understood Donata's objections, and in fact, shared them myself. But I was a father, one catching up on many years of watching and worrying. I needed to make certain that Gabriella, poised on the threshold of womanhood, would be safe.

Donata had plenty of money, it was true, but her six-year-old son was now Viscount Breckenridge, holder of the vast Breckenridge properties and wealth. Donata was well provided for through trusts from her parents, but her fate, mine, and my daughter's if she remained with us, would be entirely in the hands of Peter when he came of age. He might grow up to be as boorish as his father, refusing to help the daughter of his stepfather.

Peter had no obligation to me—I was only the army captain who'd married his mother. In fact, if he chose, he could turf Donata and me out of this house and any other he owned. Peter was a pleasant lad and fond of his mother, so the event seemed unlikely, but he'd not yet been launched into the terror that was English schools. I'd survived them by being quick with my fists and a bit of a bully. Peter would either have to do the same, or be crushed, as boys like Leland had been.

The best thing a girl child could do was marry well. Donata was determined to bring Gabriella out and make a good match for her with the son of a respectable English family.

Her good intentions stirred my greatest fears, however. What if Gabriella was paired with a sprig of the gentry who beat her, broke her spirit, demanded she wait on him hand and foot, and left her destitute in the end? Donata was wise enough to weed out the worst of the prospects, but one never knew. Unfortunately most women realized their mistake in a marriage *after* the wedding.

"Who then?" I asked her. "What about Gareth Travers? A fine young man, with a mind more open than the Derwents, and his father a clergyman."

The snort from my wife indicated her opinion. "Travers? Now you *have* run mad. He hasn't got two coins to rub together."

"Who is being ambitious at this turn?" I asked, but with good humor. "Leland is insipid but rich; Travers of a good mind but no means. What is my daughter to do?" I took another thoughtful sip of brandy and balanced the glass on the arm of the chair. "Truth to tell, I do not know Travers's circumstances. He says his father is poor, yet he dresses almost as well as Grenville."

"Fashion, my dear Gabriel. A young man has to turn himself out well, even if he is in hock to every tailor, hatmaker, bootmaker, and glovemaker in Bond Street. And probably up to his neck with bookmakers as well, trying to raise cash to pay off the others." My wife, ever cynical.

"A man who lives off gambling would not be much of a catch," I admitted.

"I would wager Leland gives him some of the money," Donata said, lifting her goblet of brandy. "Leland is generous, too much so. Or perhaps Leland sends Gareth to his tailor, and Gareth supplements his meager funds by selling pieces of his wardrobe. Most young men of ambition and little money learn to be resourceful."

I remembered Gareth's tale of Leland trying to help an indigent man with money and clothing, and the ungrateful man stealing more. Leland was more generous than sensible. I wondered about Gareth—I'd had no money to speak of when I'd been young, and others, like Colonel Brandon, had helped me. But I'd never have dreamed of taking base advantage of their generosity or selling what I was given.

"But I admit I know little about Mr. Travers," I finished my thoughts out loud. "Nothing but that the Derwents recommend him."

"Now you are learning, my dear," Donata said, giving me a warm smile. "Matchmaking is not an easy task. It is a careful thinning of the herd, and then making certain the young people in question believe the match all their own idea."

"Is that what happened to you?" I asked gently.

"Not at all," Donata answered. "My father owed Breckenridge money, and Breckenridge wanted me." She shrugged, hiding pain I knew lingered. "A match made in hell, but here I am."

And I was glad of her presence. The vile Breckenridge was dead, leaving Donata for me.

I sighed, surrendering. "It is enough to make one's hair gray."

"You have a thread or two." Donata set aside her glass and cigarillo, rose, and came to me. Her fingers in my hair were distracting, as were the scents of tea and spice that clung to her.

"I am surprised you did not accompany Gabriella to Bath," I said. "Surely you feared she'd get herself married to an aging squire with bad breath without your supervision."

Donata rested her hip on the arm of my chair. "I preferred to remain in London, with you." *To know whether you lived or died*, she did not say, but I read in her eyes. "I would never have let Gabriella out of my sight, of course, if she hadn't gone with Aline. I trust Aline's judgment completely."

"Do you?" I thought of the tall, white-haired, loud-voiced

Lady Aline. True, any aging squire with bad breath wouldn't stand a chance against Aline and her stout walking stick.

"Of course I do." Donata kissed the top of my head. "Aline likes *you*."

I snaked my arm around my wife's waist, overbalancing her until she landed across my lap. My glass of brandy, which had rested on the other arm of the chair, fell to the carpet in a wave of pungent alcohol, but at the moment, I couldn't be bothered to notice. The brandy tasted better on Donata's lips, in any case.

AS WAS HER HABIT, DONATA LAY ABED FAR INTO THE NEXT day while I, restless, had to be out and about, riding, walking, or tending to business. I rose at daylight, sliding quietly from the bed so as not to disturb her, and made for my dressing room to wash and dress.

Bartholomew put me into yet another new suit, this one with leather breeches and a warm coat, made solely for riding.

"If her ladyship keeps on in vein," I said to Bartholomew, "I'll have more clothes than Grenville, and we'll be obliged to hire another house in which to store them."

"A gentleman should have a suit for every occasion, sir," Bartholomew said, somewhat haughtily.

He had begun his career as Grenville's footman, but now as my valet, Bartholomew was becoming quite the snob. He brushed my coat to an inch of its life and sent me off.

Hyde Park in the morning was fairly empty. Only the robust of Mayfair climbed out of bed and rode this early—the fashionable hour was much later in the day.

I preferred riding at this time, when the paths were clear. A good gallop woke me up better than sedate trots, and I put my horse through his paces. The gelding belonged in truth to young Peter, but the understanding was that I took him for exercise whenever I liked. Peter was currently staying with Donata's parents in their elegant house in Oxfordshire—sent away as Gabriella had been in light of my duel—and I looked forward to riding with the boy again upon his return.

The park looked very different today from when I'd stood on the misty green and shot Stubby Stubbins. The air was clear, slightly warmer with gathering spring.

"Well met again, Captain," a voice called out to me.

CHAPTER 4

I slowed my mount to a walk as Gareth Travers, riding a large bay mare, came trotting toward me, his high hat moving up and down as he rose and fell with the horse's gait. Gareth pulled his horse to a walk, guiding it next to mine, and gave me a cheerful grin.

He wore a riding habit of skilled tailoring and gloves that hugged every finger. The hat, which he tipped, spoke of expense. I'd restrained Grenville's tailor from making my coat too ostentatious, but Travers obviously hadn't stopped his man from adding throat-stabbing collar points, wide lapels, and an unnaturally tight waist. He wore the ensemble well—I suppose the exuberance of youth made what would look ludicrous on me rather natty on him.

"Good morning, Mr. Travers," I said, giving him a polite bow. "A fine day for a ride."

"It is indeed." Travers took a long breath and gazed up at the sky. "I always enjoy an early canter."

I had never seen Travers out at this hour, and I'd been coming every day, but I held my tongue. He was young, and the young believed that doing a thing once made it the habit of a lifetime.

Travers was alone. No other horse followed us, not Leland, who was generally at his side. The Row, in fact, was quite deserted.

"You could not persuade Mr. Derwent out at such an hour?" I asked with good humor.

"Ah." Travers lost his smile. "Leland and I have begun a coolness, as you no doubt noticed last evening."

I hadn't noticed anything of the sort; they'd seemed as cordial to each other as ever. "You do surprise me, Mr. Travers," I said. "But I am certain it will pass. You and Leland have been friends for many years."

Gareth sighed with all the aggrieved weight of the world. "We had words. Strong words. Perhaps unforgiveable ones."

"Now, that would be unfortunate," I said. "Close friendships do not happen as often as one thinks. Do not throw it away because of words."

As I spoke, I thought of the times I'd been a pigheaded fool with Grenville, who'd proved himself a good friend by not dropping me altogether. Friends had to forgive each other. I thought myself wise, but Travers gazed at me as though I had no idea what I was talking about.

"I'm afraid this will be unforgivable," he said, his tone deceptively light.

I cast about for an inkling of what had happened between them. I thought about Miss Braithwaite, a young lady I had not paid much attention to, but she'd be the right age to upset a long-standing friendship between single gentlemen. "Beware of letting friendship turn to rivalry over a lady, Mr. Travers," I warned. "It can have dire consequences." Well I knew.

Travers looked puzzled. "Over a lady? Oh." He burst out laughing. "No, indeed, our quarrel is one piece of an ongoing and long-lived argument, a point on which Leland and I have disagreed for years. Recently, it has flared into impossible tediousness. And as a final thrust, Captain, we fell out over you."

I blinked. "Over me? What on earth could *I* have done to cause a wedge between you and Mr. Derwent?"

"You asked me to be your second," Travers said, and something flashed in his dark eyes I could not read. "Instead of Leland."

I took in his words, growing more perplexed. I never would have thought to ask Leland to help me with anything so dangerous. Leland, alongside his father, spoke in a loud voice against violence. I had noticed that Leland had been uncomfortable with me last evening, which I'd put down to him being unhappy with me for dueling.

"Why should he take offense I did not ask him to be my second?" I asked, as the cool breeze ruffled my hair and my horse's mane. "The last place Leland Derwent should be is a duel. If he'd been arrested, his father would never have forgiven me."

Travers shrugged. "Eely felt betrayed. By you. And by me for accepting."

Damn and blast the boy. I liked Leland, but he had the delicacy of a virgin schoolgirl. "I see. Would you like me to speak to him?" I did not look forward to such a conversation, but nor did I want the guilt of coming between two boyhood friends.

Travers looked amused. "I would be pleased if you did, though I doubt it will do any good. Eely has these ideas, you know. We've fallen out before. I imagine we'll mend."

"See that you do." I adjusted my crop and the reins, and my horse came alert. "I do not wish to spend the rest of my life thinking my ridiculous duel ended a friendship. Make it up with him. Today."

My words were meant to make Travers contrite and say, "Yes, sir, of course I will." Instead, he laughed again. "I will tell him you wish to speak to him," he finished. "Then I will leave things up to him."

I had no idea how to respond. Perhaps I *had* forgotten what it was like to be young, when trifles became drama, and lives changed with a few ill-chosen taunts. "As you wish," I said stiffly.

"Please, do not form a coolness to me as well," Travers said, flashing a quick smile with his small mouth, his spirits still high. "Let us ride on together. Teach me how to be a cavalryman."

I bit back annoyance and nudged my horse to a faster pace. I decided to show Travers a few cavalry moves, to wipe the smug grin off his face, which it did. He left the park breathing hard and subdued, but he lifted his hand in a good-natured wave as he went. I shook my head and got on with my ride.

I PUT THE MATTER ASIDE AS I WENT ABOUT MY BUSINESS OF the day, but I'd keep my word to Travers and talk Leland out of his temper. I was curious about the long-standing disagreement, but I would not pry. I'd do what I could to heal the rift and then let the two make it up on their own.

I had no time to pay a call on Leland that day, however, and that evening, Grenville hosted one of his popular soirees, which I attended with Donata. Grenville's fine house was full to bursting, with the top of society crushed into every corner. Donata was at her element here, her slim body garbed in a shimmering blue-gray silk with gathered cap sleeves on her shoulders, loops of applique that ran down the skirt from the high waist, and a pattern of appliqued and embroidered leaves around the hem. Gloves skimmed up over her elbows, and a single peacock feather adorned her hair, defeating the overly garish headdresses other ladies had worn in imitation of Donata's usual ones.

My wife was a lovely woman, and I felt a pride in her as she paraded in, head high, to be surrounded by friends and admirers. I, merely the husband, drifted away to amuse myself while she held court.

Grenville had provided a card room where gentlemen were busy gambling for fortunes. I enjoyed cards and other games, but I had no wish to accidentally lose Donata's house, or her son's horses, or the services of Bartholomew, or something equally foolish by the wrong turn of a card. The gentlemen at these tables were worse than any sharps in a gaming hell.

I did what I usually did at Grenville's soirees, spoke to my circle of acquaintance for a time then turned my steps to his upstairs sitting room, my refuge.

I liked Grenville's private retreat, which held spoils of his travels—gold trinkets from Egypt, ivory from the Orient, carpets and a silk tent from the deserts of Africa, wooden carvings from the Americas. The scents of sandalwood and tobacco, beeswax and old paper hung in layers in the air. A man could journey around the world in Grenville's sitting room, from the Japans to the Ottoman Empire, from the heat of Africa to the strange jungles in South America. Grenville stored his most precious books in this room, rarities that other collectors envied. He also purchased modern books, and I looked forward to an evening with the latest volume of the *Description de L'Egypte*.

I made my way to the *Description's* special bookshelf, a carousel case with wide horizontal shelves ready to hold each volume when completed, when I heard sniffling. I turned to a shadowy corner, and beheld Leland Derwent seated on a leopard-skin and ebony chair, his elegant leather shoes planted next to the chair's gilded claw and ball feet.

Leland had fair hair, cut short in the back with long waves on top, the height of fashion—Grenville wore his hair thus. Leland had thin side whiskers, but his hair and skin were both so pale that the whiskers faded into his face. He wore a suit of black superfine with an ivory waistcoat, his coat's cut almost an exact imitation of Grenville's tonight, but not quite. To wear the *exact* suit would never do. The diamond in Leland's cravat pin, I knew, was quite real.

As I debated whether to give Leland my speech now or steal away and leave him to his sorrow, he looked up and saw me. "Captain. Good evening." He removed a handkerchief from his coat pocket and unashamedly wiped his eyes. "No, please, do not go. I would like not to be alone at the moment."

Leland was in obvious distress, and in spite of my discomfort with weeping young men, he stirred my compassion. I kept my voice gentle as I answered. "You sought out this room, I presume, to be alone."

"I *thought* I wanted to be," Leland said, wiping his eyes again before stuffing the handkerchief carelessly into his pocket. "But I would prefer your company, sir. Please stay. I wish to speak to you."

I hobbled to a chair near his and seated myself, stretching out my leg, which was growing sore. I propped the walking stick on the chair's side. "What's this all about then, Leland? Your argument with Travers? Your anger that I did not choose you to second me on Lady Day?"

Leland looked startled, his gray eyes, as clear as the diamond in his cravat, widening. "You know?"

"I had the pleasure of riding with Mr. Travers this morning." I stifled a groan as the back of my knee unlocked, and I decided to dive into the heart of the problem. "Leland, my friend, I did not ask you to second me, because if I'd killed Stubbins, as I'd half a mind to, I'd have been arrested, and you would have gone to Newgate along with me."

"I would have been honored to," Leland said, his chin up.

"Honored to spend the night at Bow Street nick? Or wherever the Runners dragged you? To stand in front of the magistrate in the morning? To be sent to a lovely room in Newgate prison to await trial? What would it do to your father to have a son hanged or imprisoned as an accessory to a murder?"

Leland's mouth hung open, showing moist redness against

white teeth. "Would it have come to that? A duel is an affair of honor."

"Not if I'd killed him. That would have been manslaughter at the very least. Mr. Spendlove would have sped you to the magistrates with glee. He very nearly took me there on the spot, and I'd only grazed Stubbins' arm. I was protecting you, lad."

Leland blinked a few times before he gave me a faint smile. "I hadn't thought of it that way."

No, he hadn't, and my scenario was extreme, but possible. Spendlove disliked me, and he'd happily humiliate and discommode my friends in order to teach me who had the upper hand. "Stay home and keep out of duels," I said, hoping I sounded enough like a headmaster.

"You asked Gareth to be your second," Leland pointed out. "And Mr. Grenville. You did not think to protect them?"

"Mr. Travers is of different mettle," I answered, choosing my words carefully. "And I have no control over Grenville."

Leland pondered all this a moment. "I do see, I suppose. Gareth does have more nerve than I do—in fact, he can be a bit ... reckless."

"Good," I said. "Make it up with him, then, won't you?"

"Oh, no." Leland's mouth set in determination. "Mr. Travers and I are finished."

I rose and moved to a marble-topped console table whose gilded legs had been carved into the shape of fantastical sea creatures. I lifted the brandy decanter that rested there and poured a substantial measure into a waiting glass. "Why?" I asked. "Do not toss away a friendship for so trivial a disagreement."

"It was not trivial, Captain."

I turned to find that Leland had left the chair and now stood at my elbow, his expression fierce. I thought to politely offer him a brandy as well, then remembered his family practiced abstinence from strong drink. Good wines were fine, but no spirits.

"No?" I asked.

"No." Leland's eyes held deep anger. "Mr. Travers has made it plain that he is tired of me and wants the company of someone more worldly. A man like you. So he said."

"Leland." I set down the decanter and glass, though I longed to toss the brandy down my throat. "It is not unusual, as you grow older, to seek out new friends. Travers has been a bit rude to you, I agree, but I would not fret about it. He'll come around."

I tried to sound reassuring, but Leland shook his head. "I am not being clear, Captain. Gareth did not mean he would look for a friend in a man similar to you. He meant you specifically. *You* are his new confidant, the one he will turn to now, not me."

Oh, Good God. I thought of Travers hailing me in the park this morning, appearing at an hour when I'd never seen him before. He'd sought me out on the Strand last week, then looked stunned but pleased when I'd asked him to second me. I truly wanted the drink.

I'd observed such occurrences in the army—I'd seen, time and again, younger lads develop a hero-worshiping interest in competent officers or good sergeants. The interest usually faded in time, or else either the lad or hero was killed in battle. Not pleasant memories.

"I am flattered," I said—more because it was the polite thing to say than because I, indeed, felt flattered. "But I am far too busy these days to cultivate a new friendship. Travers will tire of the idea, turn to you again, and all will be well."

"No," Leland said with more emphasis, and even triumph. "I am at the end with Gareth Travers. I told him you'd want nothing to do with him."

I held on to my patience. "I didn't mean it quite like that, Leland ..."

"Gareth is a fool," Leland said. "You have always been my friend, always understanding. Always there for me." He reached out and clasped my hand. "I told Gareth, in a way he would not mistake, that *I* had met you first."

I stared, nonplussed, at Leland's soft but determined face. I was a very slow thinker, in many ways, and I could not fathom how I had become the bone of contention between two lads who'd been friends since they'd been mites at school.

That is, I was slow, until Leland caressed the back of my hand with his thumb. The scales, as they say, fell from my eyes, and the world became crystal clear.

CHAPTER 5

*L*eland," I said sharply.

Leland's thumb drifted across the sensitive skin on the back of my hand, a gentle contact, tender even. He dropped his gaze to where he touched me.

My ideas of his innocence evaporated like boiling mist under sunshine. Here, in Grenville's private sanctuary, I was confronted with the truth.

"You have always been kind to me, Captain," Leland was saying. "Not disparaging, like so many." He gave me a shy look from under his lashes. "Gareth told me the tale you gave him — of the two soldiers."

I couldn't breathe under the bath of cold water he'd just thrown on me. "Two soldiers?"

"Who were lovers," Leland said. "And did better in battle for that. He told me how you admired them."

Oh, for God's sake.

I closed a hard grip over Leland's fingers and firmly moved his hand from mine. "Leland," I said clearly. "You are mistaken."

He stared at me, confusion in his young eyes. "But … Gareth said …"

"Then *Mr. Travers* was mistaken."

Leland's confusion grew, his pupils narrowing to black dots of panic. His chest rose with a harsh breath, and his face suffused with red. "He told me … He told me …" He began to gasp.

"Sit down," I said, my voice firming.

Leland's breath grew wheezing, but he didn't obey. I seized him and marched him back to the leopard chair, pushing him down into it. Leland clutched the gilt and ebony arms, his breathing rapid and clogged. I returned to the console table and poured another brandy.

Leland didn't want to take the glass, but I waved it under his nose until the brandy's fumes made him jump. He seized the goblet then and drank down its contents in desperation. His gasping quieted, but his face remained blotchy red.

While I waited for him to calm, I thought back over my two-year acquaintanceship with Leland and Gareth Travers, and saw things in a different light.

Leland and Travers, inseparable. Travers dressing far beyond his means, likely funded in whole by Leland, as Donata had speculated. Grenville had once told me of rumors of more than friendship between the two young men, but I hadn't paid much attention. Such things were often said about gentlemen who were close friends—I imagined people said them about Grenville and me. But in the case of Travers and Leland, the whispers appeared to be true.

Leland coughed, choking on the liquid. Then he swallowed, his throat cleared, and he took a long breath.

I slid the empty glass from his slack fingers. "Better?"

Leland looked up at me, eyes wide, but his pupils had begun to spread darkness through the gray. "Gareth told me … He told me you were lovers. I was so *angry*. And he laughed."

"I assure you, Leland," I said in a hard voice, "that is not the case."

"But he described it. In great detail. He said—"

I held up my hand, stopping him before I could hear anything discomfiting. I would need to have a few choice words with Mr. Travers, and I hoped to God he hadn't related his tale to anyone else. Teasing Leland was one thing; spreading it about that I was a molly would be something else entirely.

"Leland, I am *married*," I said. "You know my wife well. Why would you believe him?"

"Many of … us … marry," Leland said. "Have to, don't we? It's our duty."

"A bit hard on your lady wife, wouldn't you say?"

He looked puzzled. "Her duty too, Captain. Most marriages are thus."

I could not argue. Upper-class marriages were made to fund an estate, to bolster a family with good connections, to hang more heirs on the family tree. Cousins married, pairing the daughter of the house to the male heir so she'd not be tossed aside when the heir inherited her father's estate. Marriage became a business transaction, not a love affair.

The son of Sir Gideon Derwent, the extremely wealthy philanthropist, would be a catch for any young woman. Leland would marry the lady who snared him, siring children with her as he needed to.

Indeed, I'd been thinking of pairing him with *my* daughter. Thank heavens for Donata's percipience. I wondered if she knew of Gareth and Leland's affair. If so, she had let me babble on like an absolute fool.

"Put this idea out of your head," I said. "I have never shown Mr. Travers or any other gentleman the slightest interest. I married for esteem, not convenience—you slight Lady Breckenridge if you believe otherwise."

Leland's flush deepened. "Forgive me. I had no wish to offend her." He hadn't, I could see. Hadn't realized he would. Many gentlemen married for pedigree and took mistresses for love—why should Leland think me any different?

He took another breath and looked around, blinking, like a man waking. Leland seemed to realize that he'd been sitting in Grenville's private room, spilling out his deepest secrets to a man he'd assumed would be of like mind. His anguish and embarrassment grew.

"You won't tell my father, will you, Captain?" Leland asked in a near whisper. "He doesn't know. He would die of shame."

I hardly wished to repeat this conversation to anyone. "No fear," I said. "What in the world made Travers claim I was his molly mop?"

"He wanted to upset me." Leland glanced at the empty brandy goblet in my hand as though wishing for more. "He and I had a flaming great row about ..." He flushed anew. "Many things. I suppose he was trying to make me jealous."

"So you contrived the idea of making him jealous in return?" It was so ridiculous I was torn between laughter and outrage. "You both might have stopped to get your facts straight before you made the attempt. There are other gentlemen you could have chosen."

Leland looked at me in genuine surprise. "Of course I could not have. Gareth was not trying to make me jealous because he'd simply been with another gentleman. He was taunting me because he'd bedded you before I could."

Now I needed the brandy. I returned to the console table, took up my glass and drank it as though it were heavenly elixir.

Perhaps I should be flattered that two young men fought over my favors, but it was too bizarre. I could have understood better if they'd had Grenville in their sights—he often did attract such attention—but *me*? The injured war horse who preferred a night before a fire to more social activities? I, with unruly dark brown hair and brown eyes in a weather-beaten face, saw only harsh cragginess when I looked into the mirror, not the smooth features of a man like Grenville.

Travers and Leland had known me long enough to understand that I preferred the company of ladies. Very much so. But perhaps they'd seen only what they wished.

I would keep my word and not tell Sir Gideon—if Leland and Gareth wanted to be lovers and be happy, it was hardly my concern. I wished them well. A dangerous pursuit, however —as shown by the poor fellow in the stocks at Charing Cross I'd witnessed with Gareth. The sympathy I'd shown, I supposed, followed by impulsively asking Gareth to second me in the duel, had given him the wrong idea.

I set aside the remainder of my brandy and took up my walking stick.

"I give you my word that I will say nothing of this beyond you and Mr. Travers." I pinned Leland with a severe look. "But tell Mr. Travers I would like to speak to him." Shake him, more like. "He may meet me at the Gull in Pall Mall tomorrow afternoon at three. Now, I suggest you rest here until you feel better, then go home."

Leland swallowed, his eyes wet, but he nodded. "Yes, Captain."

My sanctuary here was at an end as well. "Good night then," I said, and without further speech, left the room.

The landing was dark, Grenville's private chamber near the top of the house. Grenville ordered no lights here during his soirees, to encourage the guests to remain below. I paused in the darkness, hanging on to the railing, taking deep breaths.

I was angry. Travers dragging me into a personal quarrel with Leland, each of them purporting to want to be the first to be with me was ridiculous. Unnerving. Disturbing.

Suddenly weary, I went back downstairs to the light and noise, but the clamor combined with the wash of perfume made my head ache. I quickly had enough and quit the house, heading home alone.

I THOUGHT I'D DISMISS THE INCIDENT AND CARRY ON, BUT IT
bothered me as I rose the next day and went on my morning
ride. Not because Leland had offended or disgusted me. He
and Gareth were by no means the only gentlemen in London
who'd formed a passion for each other, and as long as they
were discreet, they might be all right.

But I worried about Leland—he was open and honest, and
if he put forth his needs to the wrong person, as he had last
night, disaster could befall him. While many people looked the
other way at such things, there was a contingent who did not.
Sodomy was punishable by death, and I doubted Leland would
be able to endure exposure, imprisonment, and trial.

I knew from Pomeroy that many trials at the Old Bailey for
"unnatural behavior" ended in a verdict of *not guilty*, usually for
lack of evidence. The act had to be reliably witnessed, or else
anyone could accuse anyone of sodomy and thus rid themselves of an inconvenient person.

If Leland stood trial, however, no matter what the outcome,
he'd be ruined, and his family with him. Travers and his clergyman father would be ruined as well.

Blast the bloody fools.

I hoped I'd see Travers as I rode and get the meeting with
him over with, but he never appeared. Donata, who'd found
nothing odd in me retreating from a soiree early and going
home, was still abed when I had an early dinner and left in a
hackney for Pall Mall.

The Gull was sparsely populated at this hour, the better for
my errand. It was an older tavern, left over from the days of
coffee houses, out of fashion now, where the political decisions
had truly been made. I'd chosen it because Leland's friends and
Grenville's would likely not enter and interrupt us—fashionable men were now at the clubs in Jermyn and St. James's
Streets. I took a seat in a private corner, and waited.

And waited. Travers missed his appointment of three, and
he hadn't arrived at half past, nor at the three-quarter hour. I

was ready to leave and to hell with him, when he sauntered in at four.

I rose, waiting impatiently as he crossed the room, his dark gaze darting about in some distaste. The barman caught my eye and brought over another tankard to place in front of Gareth as he took a seat.

"I did not realize such places still existed," Gareth said as he glanced at the bowed beams, the scarred trestle table, and the thick pewter tankard filled with ale.

"They do," I said, a trifle coldly, resuming my seat. "I will surmise that Leland told you about his conversation with me last night?"

"Yes, the silly young ass." Travers laughed as though he had years on Leland, when, in fact, Leland was a few months older. "I am sorry he pulled you into our quarrel."

"You both pulled me into it," I said, annoyed. "Please cease to do so."

Gareth laughed again. He sipped the warm ale from the tankard and made a face. "Foul stuff. I must beg your pardon, Captain. You are in the right—it was bad of me to use you so. I have been quite impatient with Leland of late. He is determined I should have no independence of him, which becomes rather galling. One has one's pride."

I was still angry with him for his presumption, but I did understand what he meant. How often had I grated when Grenville paid my way or gave me gifts I could never hope to repay? Even now, when I had a bit of blunt at my disposal, the idea that it was Donata's and her son's money did not make me happy.

"Be that as it may," I said. "It was not well-done. Dangerous, even."

Travers continued to smile. "I know I ought to have asked your leave and told you what it was all about. I simply grew so angry at him, and when you told me the story of your army chaps ..."

"You thought I would at least be sympathetic." I hardened my voice. "And I am. However, lying about another gentleman impinges upon his honor. What if Leland had spread the tale of your fictitious tryst with me? It might have ruined me and hurt my wife, her family, and my friends. Think on this."

Gareth's smile began to fade, worry entering his eyes. Likely such a thing hadn't occurred to him—he hadn't thought at all, in fact. He'd wanted to anger his lover, without weighing the consequences.

"I have begged your pardon," he began.

I leaned forward, knowing that if I were to shut his mouth, I had to be harsh. "If I took your actions as deepest offense, instead of the imprudence of youth, I should call you out. Would you like to face me across a green, Mr. Travers?"

His face paled as he remembered Stubbins, on his knees on the grass, screaming as he clutched his bleeding arm.

"No," Travers said, more quietly. "I believe I would not."

"Then we will say no more about it. Whether you make it up with Leland or continue to quarrel with him—that is your affair. But do not drag me into it. Understand?"

My sternness finally quelled him. Travers's head bowed slightly, and he nodded. "I am sorry."

"Good." I returned the nod and lifted my tankard. "No more words about it, then."

Travers remained where he was, fingers moodily twitching on the dull but smooth pewter.

I sipped my ale, liking the rich, bitter stuff. Much better than the thin wines and sherries served at some of the soirees I attended in Mayfair.

Travers heaved a long sigh and looked across at me again. "May I ask you one thing, Captain?" When I indicated with a flick of my hand he should go on, he said, "What am I to do about Leland? He does not understand that he puts me in a cage, and he is shocked when I suggest a means to leave it. I do not mean leave *him*. But I am four-and-twenty years old. The

Derwents have cared for me for years, but it is high time I was my own man."

I did understand. Families were known to adopt close friends of sons or daughters and care for them for life, and some gentlemen would envy Travers his position. I, with my independence and pride, however, had empathy for Gareth's frustration.

"Do not pull against it too much," I advised. "Make certain you are voluble in appreciation for what the family has done for you. Indicate that being able to live independent of Leland does not slight the Derwents in any way. In fact, explain how much you would be able to help *them*, perhaps—with whatever is this means you speak of …"

"A windfall," Gareth said quickly. "A fine one."

He was not going to tell me, but I could speculate. He could have received a bequest from a distant relative—Gareth could be charming; perhaps he'd charmed an elderly auntie to leave him a sum in her will. Or he'd found a job of some sort, a way to make a living. It was ungentlemanly to work for pay, and perhaps this rankled Leland.

I continued. "Explain to him how you wish to use this windfall to show your appreciation. With a donation to one of Sir Gideon's charitable projects, perhaps."

Gareth brightened. "Ah, now, that might be just the thing." He moved in his seat, as though anxious to jump up and run out on the spot to carry out my advice.

"Go," I said, barely hiding my exasperation. "I am content to sit here alone." Refreshingly alone.

Gareth surged to his feet. His brown eyes were bright, his face flushed with hope. He held out his hand. "Thank you, Captain. And I am truly and deeply sorry for offending you. I shall never do such a thing again. It was foolish."

Gareth was young, and had plenty of time in his life to do something equally as foolish, but I only shook his hand, accepting his apology.

He leaned close. "You'll say nothing, will you?" His eyes held anxiousness, and I remembered his white-faced horror at the man in the stocks.

I released his hand and sat back. "I have already said there would be no more words on the matter. That means no words to anyone."

"Yes," Gareth said, a bit breathlessly. "Thank you, Captain. Thank you very much."

He snatched up his hat, shot me a grin, and spun for the door, his coat whirling. He hurried out and banged the door behind him, earning the disapproving looks of the other patrons over their newspapers.

I sat back and enjoyed my ale, bloody glad the mess was over and done with.

THAT EVENING, I RETURNED TO MY ROOMS IN THE LANE OFF Covent Garden, still working on putting things to rights there. Donata had gone out with some of her close friends for a light supper and gossip before moving on to the opera, and I left her to her feminine delights.

Covent Garden market was crowded when I reached it, though the sun had already gone down. Vendors loudly called out their wares, and women and girls, servants and boys swarmed the place, bargaining, arguing, shouting. I purchased an apple that looked as though it had sat in a barrel all winter, and munched it as I moved through the market.

As I walked, I reflected upon how much more pleasant it was to stroll these lanes when my boots were whole, my body fresh from a bath, and with the knowledge that I could return home to a welcoming wife. Even the blustery wind that started to blow, bringing rain, didn't dampen the effect.

I tossed my apple core to a stray dog as I turned from Russel Street to the cul-de-sac of Grimpen Lane, where I rented rooms. I fumbled keys out of my pocket and unlocked the door next to a bakeshop. Behind this door was a flight of stairs, which led to the chambers that had housed me since my return to London in 1814.

The rooms were a bit bare now—I'd moved many of my things to Donata's house—but I kept the writing table, armchair and footstool, small shelf of secondhand books, and the chest-on-frame, which was an old-fashioned but useful piece of furniture. I had begun using the front room as an office, where I could meet friends in private, or help those who had begun coming to me with problems they felt they could not take to the magistrates.

I'd also kept my bed, which would be nothing but a bare mattress. So I was surprised, when I entered the bedchamber, to see it spread with quilts and occupied by Marianne Simmons.

She sat with her back against the headboard, propped against a pillow, her blond curls flowing loosely to her dressing gown. A small ivory snuffbox was open on the bed next to her, and she had a glass of ruby port in her hand. Newspapers were strewn across the covers, from the clean pages of the *Times* to the ink-smeared single sheets of more dubious publications.

Marianne was crying. She'd swiped at her tears with ink-stained fingers, resulting in black dappled cheeks.

I stopped when I saw her, my hand on the door handle. "What the devil?" I exclaimed.

"Oh, it's you, Lacey," Marianne said, as though me finding her reclining in my bed was of no consequence. She sniffled, swiped one hand across her eyes, and took a long drink of port.

"Why are you here?" I asked, then softened my tone as she turned wet blue eyes up to me. "And what on earth is the matter?"

Marianne shoved a paper across the covers. "*That* is the matter. I'm such a bloody little fool."

I eased myself to the edge of the bed, my sore leg happy

with me for resting it, and reached for the paper. The sheet contained a drawing of Lucius Grenville in profile, exaggerating his dark eyes, sleek dark hair, knotted cravat, and high collar points. Facing him, also in profile, was a woman with frizzy black curls, a pointed nose, a long neck, and diamonds at her throat.

The caption read: *Signora C— , a talented and very lucky soprano, native of Venice, has caught the eye of our own Mr. G—. She now wears jewels from his household. Can he be thinking of handing her the plate?*

CHAPTER 6

*A*h," I said.

For the past few weeks, Grenville had begun squiring about an opera singer called Paola Carlotti, the newest sensation to reach the Covent Garden stage. The two were well matched in looks, and newspapers had begun depicting them together. *The handsomest pair in Mayfair*, they'd been labeled.

Grenville had scarcely spoken to me of Signora Carlotti; in fact, he'd scarcely spoken to me about much in the last weeks, except arrangements regarding the duel.

He and Marianne, with whom Grenville had been carrying out an *affaire de couer* since May last, had begun a coolness earlier this winter, after the incidents surrounding Drury Lane at New Year's. Marianne had expressed the wish not to see him anymore, and Grenville had complied. She'd retired to Berkshire for a time, and I hadn't known until walking in here this evening that she'd returned.

Grenville, the most famous dandy in all of Britain, now that Mr. Brummell had removed himself to France, was not one to rush after a woman, pleading for her forgiveness. Nor would he flee to his country estate to sulk. Indeed, his reputation forbade such things.

So he'd taken up with Signora Carlotti, giving the newspapers much enjoyment. Signora Carlotti, already famous for her voice on the Continent, was now gaining great repute in London. I'd heard her, and I agreed with the assessment that she was brilliant.

Handing her the plate was the journalist's speculation that Grenville meant to marry her. Many families passed part of their wealth down in the form of heavy silver dinner services that retained their value through the years. A woman "getting her hands on the plate," meant getting her hands on the family's money, usually through marriage.

"This is trash, Marianne," I said, shoving the papers aside. "You cannot credit everything you read in a scandal sheet."

Marianne sniffled again, much liquid in her nose. She swiped it away with her hand, and I yanked out a large handkerchief and passed it to her.

Marianne took the handkerchief, not too proud to accept. She blew her nose and dabbed her face with the fine lawn square. "Don't be stupid, Lacey. Signora Carlotti is beautiful, sings like an angel, and is a novelty. I imagine he believes himself madly in love with her."

"As a point of fact, I have no idea."

"Truly? And I thought the pair of you so chummy."

"I hardly live in his pocket. I've been busy."

"Playing house, yes." Marianne smiled through her tears. "With Lady Breckenridge. Are you weary of her shrewishness yet?"

"Keep a civil tongue," I said, trying and failing to sound severe. "You never answered my question of why you have purloined my apartments and my bed."

Marianne shrugged. "More comfortable than mine. And I hardly expected you this late."

"Wanted a good wallow, did you?" I began folding the

papers. "You could apologize to Grenville and ask to be friends again. Wouldn't hurt you."

She cast me a pitying look. "I doubt he remembers my name. He gave me a decent amount of money at our parting, but it will only last so long. I will have to crawl back to Drury Lane and beg for a place, I suppose. But I'm getting too old for it, Lacey. The rich gents like them young, and I have lines on my face."

Marianne, a few years younger than me, had no lines that I could discern, but I did not disagree with her. Gentlemen who looked for mistresses on the stage tended to pick out those with fresh faces and youthful steps.

"It was bound to happen," Marianne said, dispirited. "I will find another means, don't worry about me. I have before, and I will again …"

Her words faltered, her bravado crumbling. Marianne closed her eyes, fighting tears, then she gave up and hunched over, face in her hands, letting sobs come.

I set aside the papers, moved around the bed to her, then sat down and pulled her close. Marianne clung to me and cried into my shoulder, her body shuddering as I stroked her hair.

She was right that Grenville was likely done with her. He was a proud man and had been hurt at her rebuff when he'd tried to apologize to her. He'd first been contrite, then stiff, then began squiring about Signora Carlotti.

I heard a step in the doorway, and a retreat. Not the heavy tread of Mrs. Beltan, but someone lighter, quicker. I gently extricated myself from Marianne and stood up. She huddled down again, my handkerchief to her face.

I emerged into the sitting room in time to see the front door close. I crossed to it as quickly as I could, having left my walking stick in the bedchamber, and threw open the door.

The man on the top step froze, as though surprised I'd come after him. I did not recognize him. He was not a young man, nor had he reached middle age. He wore a well-fitting

dark suit, but his cravat was sloppily tied, as though he'd
dressed in a hurry or had a thoughtless valet. He wore gloves
of an expensive variety, and shining, well-made boots that he
stood in uneasily. He had a round face, riotously curly black
hair, and shock in his blue eyes so deep it pulled me away from
irritation at his interruption.

"Are you Captain Lacey?" he asked uncertainly.

"I have that distinction," I answered.

The man looked me up and down a few more times, his
agitation growing. "Yes. You'd better come."

I did not move. "Where? Who are you, please?"

"I ..." For a moment, I had the impression the fellow didn't
remember. "Mackay. Nelson Mackay."

"Mr. Mackay." I gave him a polite bow. "Where am I to
follow you?"

He chewed on his lip, his face pale, his blue eyes full of
anguish. "He asked for you. He said to fetch you. *Please*,
Captain."

I felt a draft as Marianne came out of the room behind me,
her dressing gown straightened and face clean but her hair
hanging down her back.

"Good heavens," she said, studying the man from red-
rimmed eyes. "He seems in a right state. You'd better go with
him, Lacey, hadn't you?"

I GATHERED UP MY GREATCOAT, FETCHING MY WALKING STICK
from the bedchamber, and followed Mr. Mackay into the dark
dampness of the March night. He led me through Russel Street
to Covent Garden, the vendors in the market now closing
down for the night, which meant the criminal element would
be emerging to play.

The street girls knew me and grinned as I passed, but they
stared at Mackay, who was as out of place as a tropical bird in

brickyard. He walked carefully, as though he rarely took a step in his too-shiny boots, which made me wonder—where was his coach, hired or otherwise? Why was he tramping, alone, in the environs of Covent Garden?

I had no chance to ask. He began a brisk pace after we turned to James Street and so on to Long Acre. Beyond that, we headed toward Seven Dials, not the most salubrious part of town. I kept my walking stick ready and looked about me, but Mr. Mackay seemed oblivious to danger. I'd never seen a man so nearly beg for ruffians to set upon and rob him.

As Mackay turned down a narrow and noisome passage, I wondered whether *I* wasn't the man asking to be set upon. I'd followed him here, knowing nothing about him, and I now willingly walked after him down the lane. I was a lame man armed only with a sword, which I'd have to extricate from my walking stick. I'd never manage against a crowd of Seven Dials toughs.

Mackay stopped in the middle of the passage and let out a noise of despair. I caught up to him and found him peering at a swath of mud on the hard-packed cobbles.

"He was here." Mackay put his hands on top of his head and made another moaning sound. "He was here. What has become of him?"

I liked this less and less. I loosened my sword and studied the stones, finding not only mud but something dark and glittering in the faint light from a window above us. I crouched down, wincing at the pain in my knee, stripped off my glove, and touched my fingers to the wet patch.

The dying light showed a dark red substance clinging to my fingers, kept damp by the mud. Blood. And much of it.

"Who?" I asked, rising with difficulty. "Who was it?"

"Where did he go? Who took him?" Mackay's words came fast with the beginnings of hysterics.

"Mr. Mackay." My voice cut sharply through his cries. "You must tell me. What did you find here?"

He couldn't answer. He'd be no more help to me, I could see. I wished for a lantern, but I'd brought none, having no idea Mackay had meant to lead me into these warrens.

I left him there and went back to the main street. People were hurrying home, ready to put walls between themselves and the night. I followed a man who ducked into a nearby house, and caught the door before he could shut it.

"I need a light," I said into his frightened face. "A lantern, man. I need one."

He hesitated, so I pushed inside his house, unhooked a lantern I found hanging beside the door, lit the candle from one his equally terrified wife had already lighted, and made my way out.

"I'll return it when I'm done," I promised as I went.

The wife recovered her shock and screamed at me "'Ere! You!" before her husband slammed the door, muffling the sound.

Back in the alley, Mackay was leaning against a wall, his breath coming in hoarse gasps. At least he'd stopped wailing.

I returned to the blood and lifted the lantern over it, quickly finding smears that led farther into the passage. The smear died to droplets after a time, but the candle picked them out.

I'd hoped Mackay would follow me, but he remained behind, in the dark. I stooped as I went along, supporting myself with my walking stick, flashing the lantern across the ground.

I came upon a boot print in the middle of the blood trail, then another, but the boots were of different sizes. Two men, one perhaps supporting the other. If they were seeking help, they were going the wrong way—deeper into the darkness.

I found them not many steps later. Clouds had gathered thickly above the city, rendering this closely confined passage utterly dark. The lantern, however, told me all I needed to know.

Two men lay stretched out upon the ground. They wore the boots whose tracks I'd seen, but the rest of their clothes were in disarray. One was missing his coat and waistcoat, the front of his long trousers open. The other's breeches and drawers were down around his boots, though he'd retained his waist-coat and cravat.

The one with breeches fallen down was dead, his eyes open and staring into the night. The other, his pale hair smeared with black blood, was still breathing, his heart beating under my palm as I pressed it to his chest.

The dead man, his brown eyes open to the sky, was Gareth Travers. Next to him, his head bloody, lying beside the body of his lover, was Leland Derwent.

CHAPTER 7

*M*y strength left me. My legs folded up, and I found myself sitting against the dirty wall next to the two young men.

"Leland," I whispered. "What happened to you?"

He didn't answer. His eyes were closed but not tightly, a gleam of white orb showing in the lantern's light.

I prayed. I hadn't in a long while, but I begged God with harsh words to please make this scene not what it was. Make Leland Derwent not be here, beaten in an alley next to Gareth, who was dead.

God didn't answer. He didn't change anything in that dark alley. Nothing stirred at all, not even the rats that were wary of my light.

Strength returned to me with my rage—at Leland and Gareth for being here at all, at whoever had beaten these lads so thoroughly that one had died and one still might.

Had they been caught together in the passage? Performing an act that was so vile to whoever had found them that they'd been beaten down? And why the holy hell had Leland and Travers chosen a passage near Seven Dials for their tryst? Why not somewhere soft, private, and safe?

"Leland," I shook him, then pried open one of his gray eyes and shone my lantern into it. Leland didn't move, didn't moan.

"Mackay!" I called back down the passage.

He did not respond, and I started cursing the man. What the devil had *he* been doing here? Why hadn't he helped?

I shouted again for Mackay then went back down the passage to where I'd left him, hoping he hadn't run away.

I expected so much that he had, that I was surprised to find him leaning against a wall, a folded handkerchief at his mouth. Mackay rocked a little, breathing in uneven gasps.

I shone the lantern in his face, making him blink. "Go back to my rooms," I told him. "Fetch Marianne if she's still there, and tell her to send for Grenville."

Mackay's eyes rounded in distress. "Mr. Grenville? You can't ... he can't ..."

"For God's sake, man—Leland will die if he's not looked after. I need Grenville's coach to get him home. Now go."

"But ..."

I suppressed the urge to punch him. "Then are you willing to sit by them and wait until I return?"

Mackay's eyes went even wider, and he shied from my light. "I can't stay *here*."

"Then go fetch Marianne. She's the woman in my rooms. If she's not there, check the rooms above. If you can't find her at all, tell Mrs. Beltan in the bakeshop to send someone to Grenville—if you're such a milksop that you can't go yourself."

Mackay managed a nod. "The woman in your rooms. Yes. I'll ... go."

Handkerchief once more at his mouth, Mackay stumbled down the passage to the street. I wondered if he'd make it to Grimpen Lane.

Leland needed to be home, needed a surgeon. Grenville's carriage could carry him there in some comfort. I knew Grenville would respond quickly to a message from Marianne, never mind her conviction he'd forgotten all about her. I knew better.

I supposed I could have sent for Donata's carriage, but I knew she was using it tonight to take her from friends' abodes to the theatre, and truth to tell, I couldn't remember exactly where she'd gone. I only knew that Grenville, once found, would put things together in a rapid and efficient manner.

I made my way back to the two men and sank down beside Leland. His blood was black on his face, and I lifted his head to my lap. I patted his cheek, but didn't have much hope of waking him. His breath grated, but at least he still breathed.

Travers lay a foot beyond us, his eyes staring at nothing. The lad I'd admonished so harshly in the tavern earlier today, who'd grinned at me in the end and sprang up with such exuberance, was dead.

I knew I ought to have sent Mackay running to Bow Street, or shouted for the Watch myself—though I doubted any night watchman would be brave enough to venture down here.

But the two lads found like this would raise too many questions. I did not want Pomeroy, or even worse, Spendlove, to see them like this, to reveal to the world that the two had been lovers. I might not be able to save the lad's lives, but I could spare them that.

A strong voice came out of the darkness behind me, making me jump. "Captain."

The word was followed by a man who strode toward me with the confidence that nothing in this place was more frightening than he was. I'd have been alarmed by his size and the fact that he carried a cudgel, if I hadn't recognized him as Denis's man Brewster.

"Do you have a conveyance?" I snapped at him without greeting.

Brewster took in the two young men, their clothes open and missing, and me sitting next to them, my legs sprawled. He gave me his usual stoic look from his great height and said, "I'll take care of it, Captain," then turned away and walked firmly back down the passage.

I had no need to wonder how Brewster had happened to turn up here. He'd been following me. Denis always kept watch on me, and Brewster had no doubt been haunting my steps since I'd made for Covent Garden this evening.

Once Brewster was gone, I came to myself, shaking off my stupor. Leland was too cold. I slid off my greatcoat and wrapped it around him.

I groped about in the dark and flashed the lantern around, but I could not find what had become of Leland's coat and waistcoat. He wore a lawn shirt, so light it was almost silken to the touch, but the shirt gaped open, Leland's collar and cravat gone.

The killer might have taken the clothes, or perhaps a person who'd come upon them had decided to steal a good coat rather than help the two young men. Leland's coat and waistcoat could fetch a good price with a secondhand clothier who didn't ask questions.

I gently buttoned Leland's trousers, hiding the pale patch of skin and his flaccid member. I didn't like to move him too much, but I laid him on his back then rose and made my way to Travers, restoring his clothing the best I could.

I sat down again, returning Leland's head to my lap, the lantern a dim beacon next to us. I brushed Leland's hair back from his face, examining his wounds, but I had not much doubt how he'd come by them. Someone had beaten the back and side of his head, but it was too dark to tell more than that.

Travers had been beaten even more severely.

I passed one of the longest hours I'd ever passed, alone in the dark passage with the two young men. I felt helpless and limp, aching.

After a time, I heard rattling at the end of the alley and the sound of a horse's hooves on cobbles—a large draft horse, not the light stepping of a dandy's carriage horses.

A flat-bedded dray wagon came to a halt at the passage's mouth. The driver didn't dismount, but Brewster dropped off the back. "You *stay* there," he said in his rough voice.

The driver glanced about nervously, but he kept the reins slack in his hands and made no move to pull away.

Brewster came to me with his lumbering gait. "Where do you want 'em shifted to, Captain?"

"What do you make of the wounds?" I asked him instead of answering. While I had much experience with injuries made by pistols, carbines, bayonets, knives, and various forms of artillery, I'd never learned about the art of bludgeoning.

Brewster bent over the bodies with an air of a professional. "Hard to see in this light. But I'd say a piece of wood. One with nails in it." He touched the side of Travers's head where the blood was blackest. "He was smacked with the club, and the nails sticking out of the end went right in."

I swallowed a sourness in my throat. "What the devil kind of man would do such a thing?"

Brewster shrugged. "I can see any number of coves around 'ere doing for 'em. They'd want to keep mollies, especially rich ones, away from their boys."

"I very much doubt Mr. Travers and Mr. Derwent had any interest in the lads around here," I said. "Which returns me to the question—what were they doing *here*?"

"Can't say as to that," Brewster answered, though I'd spoken mostly to myself. "Need to get 'em away, though, before the Watch stumbles on 'em."

He had a point. I could not wait any longer for Grenville's carriage—I'd have to apologize for the summons later.

I tried to lift Leland, but my leg was sore from being folded up on the pavement in the cold. I couldn't hold him.

Brewster took Leland's slack body from me with surprisingly gentle hands. "Let me, Captain. You get 'em tucked in all comfortable on the dray and leave the carrying to me."

His suggestion was sensible. I stayed with Travers, while Brewster carried Leland away, hoping without much hope that Gareth would blink his eyes, laugh, and tell me he and Leland had played a fine joke on me.

He didn't. Travers lay still, dead, and would never joke again.

I WASN'T CERTAIN WHERE TO TAKE THEM. IF I ROLLED UP IN a dray in Grosvenor Square and carried two bodies inside Sir Gideon Derwent's house, it would be in every newspaper the next morning. If I took them to Grenville's, not far from the Derwents, the same thing would occur.

I contemplated taking them to my rooms in Grimpen Lane, but I had gossipy neighbors, none more than my landlady. Mrs. Beltan often stayed late in her shop, preparing for the next day, and the ladies across the street would visit her, knowing Mrs. Beltan sold her leftover bread at half price and sometimes even gave it away.

"I know a place, sir," Brewster said, when I'd voiced my dilemma. "If you need to hide 'em for a bit."

"Leland needs a surgeon," I said.

"No matter. We'll get 'em stashed away, and a surgeon can be fetched."

Not ideal, but I wanted them out of the rain. "Lead on," I said wearily.

Brewster gave me a nod and climbed up onto the seat with the driver. I settled in the back next to the tarp-covered bundle that was Leland and Travers, commending us all to the hands of a man who made a living committing murder for James Denis.

CHAPTER 8

rewster took us to a house in a tiny lane off High Holborn. Not the most affluent address, but the house was private. The narrow abode, the width of one room and a staircase hall on each floor, rose four stories to a ceiling lost in shadows.

The house was dark, no lights but a candle in a lantern Brewster held. I'd insisted on returning my lantern to the man I'd taken it from, much to Brewster's amused disdain.

Brewster led me up two flights of stairs to a front bedroom. I could tell it was a bedchamber only when Brewster's lantern cut through the vault of blackness to illuminate pale hangings around a large bed. I laid Leland on the bed's coverlet, ignoring the blood and mud both of us smeared on it. "It's bloody freezing in here," I said over my shoulder. "Get a fire going."

Brewster grunted, not liking to take orders from me, but he saw the sense in doing so. Soon he was banging around the fireplace and had a blaze going. He lit fresh candles in silver candlesticks, lighting up the small room.

The bedchamber was sparse, with only a bed, a washstand, and a night table. No curtains hung in the many-paned window, though they were draped heavily around the bed, which told me it was used. The washstand was from the past century, polished mahogany, the top with the washbowl made to swing open to reveal the slop bowl beneath. Grenville had one like it in the guest room in which I'd often stayed.

Leland was breathing, but that breath was labored. His lids were half-open, his eyes unmoving. "We need to find a surgeon," I reminded Brewster. "A good one, not a quack."

Brewster didn't answer and started to trudge away.

"Wait," I called. "What about Travers?"

Brewster paused in the doorway. "Still in the cart. He's dead, inn't he?"

"Bring him inside. Give him some dignity."

The man did not hasten to obey. "He needs burying. He's going to start stinking."

"Then we will have to live with the stink. Put him in a ground-floor room and keep the mice away from him."

Brewster scowled. "I can't do everything, Captain. And Mr. Denis won't like a corpse in his front room."

I looked at him in surprise. "This is his house, is it?"

"Aye. He keeps it for business. Sometimes a ladybird."

The idea that the ice-cold Mr. Denis ever did anything as sentimental as tuck a mistress into a discreet house was absurd. I nearly laughed, but the laugh would have been tinged with madness. I supposed every man needed to satisfy his bodily needs—God knew I enjoyed it—but Denis seemed to subsist on cold air alone.

"Perhaps he will know a surgeon who can be discreet," I said. "You can send word to him?"

"Oh, aye, he'll know you're here." Brewster's voice was hard, his annoyance apparent. "Anything *else*, sir?"

"Yes, hunt up Grenville. He will be racing to my summons at Seven Dials."

Brewster didn't bother to answer; he strode noisily out of the room and left me.

I heard him slam the front door of the house, but I also heard movement in the lower floors, presumably the driver carrying Travers inside.

I hunted up cloths from a cupboard in the hall, but I'd need to climb down the stairs for water or shout for the dray's driver to bring it up. That assumed there was any water below, and the man wouldn't have to run to the nearest pump.

I could at least wipe the mud and grime from Leland's face. Leland remained insensible, making no noise or movement as I touched his bloody wounds.

All the while questions continued to whirl through my head: Why had Leland and Travers been in that dirty passage? Or had they been attacked elsewhere and carried there, arranged to be found as they'd been? The large quantity of blood suggested Travers had bled out on the cobbles where Mackay had first taken me. But who had moved them between the time Mackay had found them and I'd returned with him? Had Leland been conscious enough to try to get Travers to safety? Or had the killer returned and tried to hide them?

As to who had attacked the two, Seven Dials had no shortage of toughs and men who lived on anger. A street gang who'd come upon two toffs on their own, no matter what they'd been doing, wouldn't mind giving in to violence. Discovering that they were mollies would have lent fuel to the fire. But where did Mackay come into it?

I would have no answers until Leland woke. I worried he'd never wake at all.

I do not know how long I sat in the dim light, cleaning Leland's face, but presently I heard Brewster return. His heavy tread sounded on the stairs, combined with a lighter, more nimble one.

The man Brewster ushered inside was short of stature but had muscular arms, like a blacksmith's. This gentleman said nothing to me but went straight to Leland's side while Brewster lit more candles.

The surgeon—I assumed that was who he was—demanded water and clean towels. Brewster moved to oblige, far more quickly than he'd ever obliged me.

The surgeon had sallow skin and a fringe of brown hair around a balding head, but eyes that brooked no foolishness. Surgeons would never be given the status of doctors, since they worked with their hands—setting bones, cutting off limbs, taking out bits of a man's insides—but the best ones saved more lives, in my opinion, than any doctor I'd met.

The surgeon turned Leland's head to study his wounds, peeled back Leland's eyelids, felt him for fever, and loosened the shirt I'd laboriously done up. "How long?" he asked me, his words clipped.

"I am not certain," I said. "He was struck down at least an hour before I found him, I would say. And it's been the better part of two hours since then."

"You a surgeon?" the man snapped. "How do you know it was an hour?"

I was too tired to be offended. "I'm a soldier, or used to be. I'm guessing from the state of the wounds and the pallor on his friend, who did not survive, that they were struck down about an hour or so before I found them. Though I suppose Travers could have taken some time to die."

The surgeon shook his head. "The man in the kitchen? He was dead minutes after he was hit. This one wasn't so lucky." He gestured to Leland.

Cold bit me. "You are saying he will die as well?"

"Depends on his constitution. He's young. I'll do my best for him."

The man's accent put him from outside London, somewhere in the west I'd say, though not as far as Cornwall. I'd had a Cornish man under my command in Portugal, and whenever he'd spoken in his native dialect, I hadn't understood a bloody word he'd said. He'd understood me well enough, though, and survived many a battle to sail happily home to his wife and brood of Cornish children.

Brewster quickly returned with the water, so perhaps the house did have a working pump, or one close by outside. The surgeon began to clean away the dried blood, revealing many gashes in Leland's head, face, and neck.

The man had brought his own needles and thread, and he sewed the larger wounds closed. I reflected that it was a mercy Leland was oblivious at the moment. The surgeon worked with admirable skill, but didn't bother softening his stabs with the needle, his tugs on Leland's raw flesh. I'd seen many a hardened soldier screaming as a surgeon held him down to stitch him back together.

When the surgeon finished, he rubbed an ointment on the wounds, then looked at me without expression. The man's face hadn't changed expression at all, in fact, since he'd entered.

"Have someone stay with him," he said, packing up his things. "He'll have a fever, and thrash, and he needs to be still, or he'll open the stitches. Tie him to the bed if you have to. Send for me if he needs tending again."

"Thank you," I said. I didn't have much money with me, but I pulled a handful of coins from my pocket and held them out to him.

The man studied the silver in my palm then met my gaze with those unemotional eyes. "Mr. Denis pays me. Good night."

"Will Leland survive?" I asked, dropping the coins back into my pocket. I felt I knew the answer already, but I couldn't help asking.

"Time will tell," the surgeon said. "He's young and strong, as I said. He either will, or he'll catch a bad fever and won't."

A man not willing to commit an opinion. I could not blame him — life and death was never certain. Without further word, the surgeon walked off down the stairs, out of the house, and into the night.

I NEEDED TO SEND WORD TO SIR GIDEON. HE MIGHT LOSE his son tonight, and the family deserved the chance to tell him good-bye. I did not want to risk moving Leland again so soon, and so Sir Gideon would have to come here.

I was on the verge of telling Brewster to deliver a message to Grosvenor Square, when Grenville arrived.

"Dear God, Lacey, what the devil?" was his greeting as he strode into the room.

Grenville stopped at the foot of the bed and gazed at Leland in shock. He was dressed for an evening on the town, in one of his most elegant suits, his cravat pin a glittering emerald. Diamonds winked white fire on his fingers, and his cravat was tied in a complicated but perfectly symmetrical knot. All this refinement contrasted sharply to the fear on his face.

"Forgive me for disturbing you," I began, my voice cracking.

The fear flared to anger. "Bloody hell, Lacey, do not become prim with me. Matthias came running into White's with a message that I must go to you in a dark passage in Seven Dials. If it had been any man but you, I'd have flat refused, but I knew you'd have good reason for me to rush there. Except, when I arrived, there was nothing but a foul stench and blood, and then one of Denis's men found me and sent me here. Who the devil beat Leland over the head, while you do not have a scratch on you?"

I waited until his words ran out, and then I quietly explained.

Grenville put his hand to his already rumpled hair and dropped to the nearest chair. "Good Lord, Lacey. Does Sir Gideon know?"

"Not yet. I was about to send for him."

Grenville shook his head. "I'll go, of course, my dear fellow. My apologies for lighting into you like that. This is appalling."

"I do not know what to do with Travers," I said, my words heavy. "I don't know who his people are, where he's from ..."

Grenville got to his feet, his commanding personality taking over. "Do not move." He strode out the door. I heard him giving orders to Brewster and whoever else was below, though I was too tired to comprehend them.

In a few minutes, Grenville was back, carrying the box he kept in his carriage that contained brandy and glasses. He poured a substantial amount of liquid into a glass and shoved it at me.

"Get that inside you," he said. "Then we'll decide what to do."

I WAS NEVER MORE GRATEFUL TO HAVE A FRIEND LIKE Grenville than I was that night. His brandy burned a trail of healing fire down my gullet, but his help went far beyond that.

Grenville knew I was in shock, and he was putting aside his own to handle the situation. He'd known Leland and the Derwents far longer than I had, and yet he turned away sorrow to do what had to be done. He told Brewster to find more blankets and pillows to make Leland as comfortable as possible, to stock water and tonics in case of fever, and to build up the fire to chase away the chill the rain and wind had brought. Brewster did it all without complaining, his expression as emotionless as the surgeon's had been.

Grenville had never met Travers's family either, it turned out, but the Derwents would know who they were. He made sure I was all right, told Brewster that he should not leave me alone, and departed.

Brewster had no intention of going anywhere. "Mr. Denis's orders," he said when I asked him if he didn't want to return home, despite Grenville's instructions.

Mr. Denis had long had the habit of assigning men to

watch me. Since our return from Norfolk, it had been Brewster most of the time. The fact that Grenville wanted the man to stay with me attested to his worry about both me and Leland. Grenville thoroughly distrusted and disliked Denis and everything connected with him, so his insistence on Brewster remaining spoke volumes.

It was not long before Leland began the fever the surgeon had warned me of. He did thrash, and I held him down. I was strong, but so was he, and I had to recruit Brewster to help me. After the better part of an hour of this, Leland sank back to the pillows in exhaustion. I hoped he'd open his eyes and look around, but he drifted off again, finding whatever comfort in his darkness.

More time crawled by—there were no clocks in the room, and I seemed incapable of pulling out the watch Donata had given me to check the time. At long last, Grenville returned with Sir Gideon, and I could put off my sorrowful tasks no longer.

CHAPTER 9

*M*y boy." Sir Gideon sank to the chair at the side of Leland's bed. "My poor dear boy." He clasped his son's hand, tears running unashamedly down his cheeks.

I stood awkwardly nearby, letting Sir Gideon have a private moment. His round back shook and his white head bowed over Leland's too-pale hand.

"How did this happen?" he asked in a broken voice. "Who did this, Captain? Why should anyone want to hurt *Leland*? He is the kindest of us."

I agreed with him. Leland had no harm in him at all, and as far as I knew, Travers had not had either.

"You will find out, won't you?" Sir Gideon mopped his damp face with a large handkerchief, but didn't release his son's hand. "You will find who did this and bring him to justice?"

What could I do but agree? I only hoped Sir Gideon's trust in me wasn't badly misplaced.

Sɪʀ Gɪᴅᴇᴏɴ ᴡᴀɴᴛᴇᴅ ᴛᴏ ᴛᴀᴋᴇ Lᴇʟᴀɴᴅ ʜᴏᴍᴇ. I ᴅɪᴅ ɴᴏᴛ like to move him, but Grenville had brought his traveling chaise, whose rear seat slid down into a makeshift bed. He'd had the seat fashioned to ease his inclination toward motion sickness, and I blessed Grenville's thoughtfulness in bringing it tonight.

Brewster carried Leland down the stairs and out to the carriage, Sir Gideon and I coming behind them. Brewster laid out Leland on the bed, careful of his injuries, and tucked blankets around him. Grenville thanked Brewster and helped a shaking Sir Gideon into the carriage.

Grenville paused with one booted foot on the step, one hand on the side of the carriage. "I've made arrangements to transport Travers to the Derwents' house as well," he said in a low voice, wind moving the tails of his coat. "Sir Gideon wishes it. He also told me how to find Travers's family. In Bermondsey." He briefly gave me the directions to a vicarage there.

"Thank you," I said. Grenville was a good man to have at one's side in a crisis. He gave me a nod and swung himself inside the carriage.

Brewster shut the door for him. The carriage jerked and rolled away, leaving Brewster and me in foggy darkness, Travers dead in the house behind us.

Bʀᴇᴡsᴛᴇʀ ᴀɢᴀɪɴ ʜᴇʟᴘᴇᴅ ᴍᴏᴠᴇ Tʀᴀᴠᴇʀs's ʙᴏᴅʏ ᴡʜᴇɴ ᴛʜᴇ smaller carriage Grenville sent for the purpose rolled up soon afterward. The coachman refused to come down off his box, not at all happy about having to transport a dead body, but we got Travers settled, and I pulled a sheet over the lad's silent and graying face.

The carriage moved away, wheels grating on the cobbles. I found my knees bending as I nearly collapsed in reaction.

Brewster held me steady and got me inside to the dusty, empty drawing room on the ground floor. He thrust a glass filled with more of the brandy Grenville had left into my hand, and I drank it down.

"Thank you," I said, wiping my mouth. "You've been a great help, Brewster."

"Mr. Denis's orders."

"I know that," I said impatiently. "But there's carrying out orders, and there's carrying them out well. I understand the difference."

Did Brewster grovel in the face of my thanks? No, he grunted and sat down on a striped damask sofa, pouring himself some of the brandy. My new friends in Mayfair would be horrified to see a man like Brewster sitting in the drawing room with me, drinking the finest brandy France produced from an elegant crystal goblet. I saw no reason for him not to, and drank with him in silence.

"What will you do now?" Brewster asked after a time.

I sighed. "Hunt up Mr. Travers the elder. Though I do not relish the task of breaking this news."

"Maybe you should leave it to Mr. Derwent's father."

I thought of Sir Gideon, a man of feeling who hid none of his emotions. Reverend Travers would end up comforting Sir Gideon instead of the other way about. "No. I'd better do it," I said.

"I'll come with you, sir."

I glanced at him in some surprise. "No need. I doubt an elderly clergyman will pose any danger to me."

"All the same. Mr. Denis says I'm to see you want for nothing and follow you everywhere. So that's what I do."

I knew I would not persuade him otherwise, and I was too weary to try. I drained my glass. "Very well, then. He lives in Bermondsey. It is very late, but if it were my son dead, I'd want to know right away."

Brewster nodded. He finished his brandy more leisurely, then rose. "I'll fetch a hackney."

I tucked Grenville's box with flask and now-dirty glasses under my arm and left the house with him. Brewster carefully locked the door with a large key, and then led me back out to High Holborn and a hackney stand.

———

BERMONDSEY WAS A PLACE OF DOCKYARDS AND WHARFS, where waterways cut into the land, expanding the unloading areas. In spite of the newer dockyards that had sprung up farther east along the Thames, the wharves here were lined with tall ships in a crowd of masts, the place teeming with activity.

The vicarage Grenville directed me to was tucked into a lane far from the wharves, behind a church with a high, square steeple. The lane, narrow and cobbled and squeezed with houses, dead-ended not far away into an open field. Some places in London could be like that, city giving way to country in two steps.

I was not certain what to expect as I knocked on the door of the vicarage. It was midnight, the church clock behind me chiming serenely. The dockyards at the other end of town had been a hive of activity, even in the darkness, but in this lane all was quiet.

A maid jerked open the door, her pale-eyed glare raking us in distrust. I could not blame her—splattered with grime and dried blood, Brewster and I resembled nothing less than street toughs or madmen. "They've gone to bed," she snapped. "What you want?"

I removed a card from the silver case in my pocket and handed it to her. "Please tell your master I need to speak to him at once. It is a matter of some urgency."

"Are you a constable?" The maid took the card and glanced

at the writing on it, but her eyes didn't move, nor did her face show any comprehension. She couldn't read.

"My name is Captain Lacey. I'm a friend of Reverend Travers's son Gareth. Please."

She studied me then Brewster again and seemed to make up her mind. She stalked back inside, then returned after a few minutes and beckoned me to follow her up a narrow, creaking staircase to the next floor. She gave no invitation to Brewster, but he came anyway.

We were shown into a sitting room furnished with leftovers from the last century. Tables with delicately curved legs stood here and there, a wing chair faced the fireplace, and the footstool in front of the chair sagged with use. Next to the chair was the most modern piece of furniture in the room, a Canterbury filled with large books. A tea table stood at the ready, as did a sideboard in the Chippendale style, with a decanter of sherry and crystal glasses on its top.

The door opened behind us, but instead of the middle-aged and portly vicar I expected, I was confronted by a fairly young woman with a trim body and oval face. She was fully dressed in a long-sleeved, plain gown of gray cotton, with a high ruffled collar modestly outlining her throat. A few strands of hair were out of place beneath her cap, but other than that she was neat and alert enough to receive afternoon callers.

I pulled myself out of my surprise and made her a polite bow. "I beg your pardon," I said. "I came here to speak to Reverend Travers."

"Who is asleep," she answered in a crisp voice. "He retires at ten precisely every evening. I am Mrs. Travers. May I help you …" She glanced at the card in her hand. "Captain Lacey?"

"It is a matter of delicacy," I said, my throat tightening. "Bad news, I am afraid. Your husband ought to hear it."

"Then he will hear it from me."

She stood firm, obviously having no intention of rushing off to rouse her husband. Mrs. Travers could not be much older that Gareth himself—I put her a year or two younger than Donata, who had reached her thirtieth year last spring. The hair beneath her cap was light brown, and she had very blue eyes. Her youth and comeliness contrasted acutely with her gown of drab and respectable gray, and she stood with her hands folded over my card.

"It concerns his son," I said. "I'm afraid he's been hurt."

Mrs. Travers blinked once, then she lifted her chin and said frostily, "I must inform you, Captain, that Reverend Travers has nothing to do with his son. We wish him a speedy recovery, but bid you good night."

I saw I was going to have to be blunt. "It is much worse than that. Mr. Travers will not recover. He's been killed."

Mrs. Travers stilled, her gaze on me. Her body was so motionless that a wisp of her hair moving in a draft seemed a wild gesture. I read stunned disbelief in her eyes, astonishment so strong she did not know what to do.

Brewster had moved to the sideboard and the sherry, prepared to deal with a swooning lady. Mrs. Travers, however, exhibited no signs of falling to the floor. She remained rigid and upright, staring at me.

"How?" she asked, the word loud in the sudden hush. The only other sounds were the trickle of sherry into a glass as Brewster poured it and the pop of the fire. "You said Gareth has been *killed*. What do you mean? Run down in the street? Fallen from a horse?"

"Perhaps we should sit?" I gestured to an armless lady's chair in muted green and gold that was only a few steps behind her.

Mrs. Travers conceded to lower herself into it. She kept her gaze firmly on me, as though conveying that she sat because *I* needed her to, not for any weakness on her part.

I pulled a straight-backed chair to face hers. The lady's chair had been made to accommodate the wide panniers of forty years ago—Mrs. Travers looked lost in it with her very narrow skirt and prim, high waist.

"There is no gentle way to state this," I began. "Mr. Travers was struck down—cudgeled—and died of his wounds."

Mrs. Travers's eyes widened slightly, but she again made very little movement. "Do you mean he was fighting?"

"At the moment, it is impossible to tell what happened," I said. "I suspect they'd been set upon by thieves, or toughs who simply wanted violence. It was very dark, and I had difficulty viewing the scene of the crime."

I heard my voice tremble with exhaustion. Perhaps Mrs. Travers was correct that I was the one who needed to sit.

"*They?*" Mrs. Travers pounced upon the word. "*They* who?" Her face tightened with rage.

"He was with his friend, Mr. Derwent. They were both hurt. Mr. Derwent—"

I got no further. Mrs. Travers sprang from her seat, fire in her eyes. "*Derwent?* I might have known that lot would be involved." She clenched her hands, bending my card in two. "Tell me, Captain, what has become of Mr. Leland Derwent? Are you breaking the news to *his* father, that his son has been set upon and killed?"

I had come to my feet as soon as she had. A gentleman did not sit when a lady stood, no matter the lady's manners. "Mr. Derwent was injured, but is alive. For now." Leland's wounds were severe—it was by no means clear whether he would survive. "Sir Gideon has taken him home, Mr. Travers's body as well. Mr. Travers can remain there until you and your husband send instructions—"

"You gave him to the *Derwents*?" she nearly screeched, as though I'd announced I'd left Gareth to the murderers' care. "The Derwents, who were the ruination of our boy? Why did you not bring him home at once?"

My temper stirred. "Madam," I said in a hard voice. "First, I had no idea until an hour ago where Gareth's home *was*.

Second, I had no wish to trundle him across London and sling him to your doorstep without preparing you or his father. Third, Sir Gideon quite kindly offered to give Gareth a place to lie until you could collect him. I can think of no more respectable house for him to stay in, no more considerate family to tend him."

Mrs. Travers's cheeks burned red. "That is because you cannot possibly know the Derwents and what they are capable of. Thank you for informing me, Captain. Now, please leave my house."

Neither I nor Brewster made any move to go. I found it interesting she named it *her* house, not that of her husband upstairs in his bed. Ladies invariably referred to property as *my husband's*, often proudly—even if a lady came into property, unless complicated trusts surrounded it, it would go to her husband the day they married. And since this house was a vicarage, it was owned by the parish.

Mrs. Travers's eyes widened while we stood in place. "Did you not hear me?" she demanded. "Take yourselves away at once."

The door opened, as if in response to her anger. The maid stood on the threshold, ready to usher us out.

I nodded to Brewster, who clicked the untasted sherry to the sideboard and walked to the door. The maid ducked aside for his bulk, her look sour.

"Please convey my condolences to Reverend Travers," I said, bowing to Mrs. Travers. "I believe you will send instructions about Gareth to Sir Gideon?"

"Of course I will," she snapped. "I take care of everything, don't I? Why should this be any different?"

"I am sorry to come here with such sad news," I finished. I bowed to her again, and took myself out the door.

Mrs. Travers's voice floated after me. "I am sorry too, Captain. You cannot understand how sorry I truly am."

Brewster raised his brows at me, and we left the house. I

saw a shadow in the window of the room we'd left, then we climbed back into the hackney we'd asked to wait.

Brewster let out a long breath as the carriage rattled forward. "What a termagant," he said. "I'd take the back of me hand to her, was I her husband. S'pose a vicar wouldn't, though. Mebbe that's why she married him."

I gave him a stern look. "I will not stand for disrespect for a lady, Brewster," I said, though I privately agreed with his assessment. "Nor any thought of violence toward them, no matter how they behave. Ladies are weaker than we are, and deserve our protection."

Brewster snorted a laugh, unabashed. "Only shows you've not known some of the ladies I have, Captain."

Still chuckling he leaned back into the seat and closed his eyes, and we made our way to Blackfriar's Bridge and over it in silence.

WHEN I REACHED MAYFAIR AGAIN, THE COACH LEFT ME AT the house in South Audley Street. Brewster did not descend, saying he was going on to Curzon Street and Denis's home. I suspected Brewster would be back soon to watch over me, but I only bade him good night before I ducked into the house.

It was half past one. The hour surprised me—I had assumed it much later. Donata was still out, the butler, Barnstable, informed me. He looked me up and down, taking in my state, and suggested a hot bath.

I was more inclined to leave again. I wanted to rush to the Derwents' great house and discover whether Leland had survived the journey home. But for some reason, my feet would not move me out the door.

My melancholia tapped at me, wanting me to indulge in it a while. It was insidious, that melancholia. Action was the best response to the tendrils of lowering thought, but my sudden fatigue wouldn't leave me.

I gave in to Barnstable and his need to tend to my aches. Looking satisfied, he ordered hot water to be brought to my dressing room, and offered his hot-cloth remedy for my hurt leg.

I succumbed to his ministrations. At least, I thought as I lowered myself into the scalding water, the scent of mint and eucalyptus wafting through the room, I had made one person happy this night.

———

I FELL ASLEEP IN MY BED WAITING FOR DONATA TO RETURN. My dreams were sharp, images swooping upon me out of the darkness. Strangely, it wasn't Travers's body or Leland's bloody face I saw, but Sir Gideon and his sorrow, Brewster hulking along to lift and carry, and Mrs. Travers with her strange anger.

The pictures dove at me, over and over, until I was the one in the passage with no light, a crushing blow falling on me in the darkness.

I cried out and grabbed the hand that came toward me. A startled gasp jerked me out of sleep, and I saw that I'd clamped my hand around Donata's soft wrist. She watched me with wide, startled eyes, her loose dark hair hanging about her face.

Instantly I relaxed my hold, but instead of releasing her, I pulled my wife down into the bed with me.

The concern left Donata's eyes, and she came to me, brushing back my sweat- and bath-dampened hair. She had changed into her nightrail, but that was soon gone.

Donata didn't speak, and for that I was grateful. Words could do nothing for me at the moment.

I'd left the house cheerfully this evening, and had been unexpectedly thrust into death and sorrow. Now I wanted life to fill my soul, and I found it in my wife. Her acerbic tongue was stilled as I kissed her, our bodies warming each other's as the blankets fell away.

When I slept again, my dreams continued but were more distant, as though I watched them through thick panes of glass. I was surrounded by Donata's warmth and scent, and I woke with my nose pressed into her bare back.

I touched her hip, and she murmured and shifted. I knew she'd never wake this early, so I kissed the curve of her waist and left the bed.

It was difficult to stand up in the cold after her warmth, but I reached for a dressing gown and went to find my clothes and something to eat. My stomach, always healthy, rumbled to be filled.

Bartholomew took care of me with regard to clothing, and I went down to the dining room to be served by Barnstable and a footman.

The newspapers Barnstable had stacked by my plate made no mention of the attack on Leland Derwent or Gareth Travers. Nothing at all, in fact, about anyone being hurt near Seven Dials. Strange indeed. The London press loved sensation, but though I scoured all three newspapers, I found nothing about the tragedy or even speculation on a disturbance in the area.

My melancholia had receded, thanks to sleep, my wife, and being surrounded by those determined to look after me, but this did not mean I intended to forget the entire affair. Someone had set upon my friends, with dire consequences, and I and Sir Gideon wanted to know who.

After breakfast, I walked north along South Audley Street to Grosvenor Square and the Derwents' large house. I had hope that receiving no word from the Derwents meant Leland was well—surely Sir Gideon or Grenville would have sent me a message if Leland had not lasted the night.

I breathed a sigh of relief when I reached the house and

saw no closed shutters or blinds, only a residence that had been opened for the day as usual. A footman waited at the door, his purpose to assist visitors into and out of carriages.

When the footman saw me, he looked both eager and mournful at the same time. "They'll be glad to see you, Captain," he said when he opened the front door and followed me in to take my coat and hat. "Mr. Derwent, he woke this morning. He's still sore hurt, but he's asking for you."

CHAPTER 10

J'd never been upstairs in the Derwent's large house. Theirs was enormous for a London townhouse, with substantial rooms on both sides of the central staircase, and more chambers behind the stairs, stretching well back into the garden. The house wound five stories above me, with plenty of space on each floor.

Halfway up to the first floor, I paused on a wide landing with a tall window as a lady came down to me—Mrs. Danbury, Sir Gideon's niece.

While Catherine Danbury had the same light-colored hair and gray eyes as the rest of the family, she did not possess the air of unworldliness they did. Though not yet thirty, Mrs. Danbury had been married twice before. Apparently her last husband had been something of a scoundrel, dying in scandalous circumstances that the *ton* hadn't quite forgiven. Mickey Danbury had run through his wife's money, and Catherine had retreated here after he'd broken his neck.

She'd not become a recluse, however. Embraced by the Derwents, who treated her as lovingly as they did their own daughter, Mrs. Danbury enjoyed a vibrant social life. She was friends with everybody—her agreeable disposition and dimpled smile making her well-liked.

Her vibrancy was dimmed this morning, her smile absent. Her face was starkly pale, and she was almost to me before she realized I waited on the landing.

"Captain Lacey." She halted and backed to the railing, her hand reaching out to steady herself. She did not look happy to see me. "Why are you here?"

"To inquire after Leland," I answered. Her abruptness worried me. Surely she should be rejoicing that Leland was alive? "I heard he'd asked for me."

"Oh, he did. He did." She gave me an odd look. "I hardly know how to behave with you, Captain. He says you are the only one who will understand. He refuses to speak to the rest of us about what happened, and why he was in such a foul part of London. He asks for you, and only you."

Mrs. Danbury's anger was strange, but I thought I understood as she continued to glare at me. For whatever reason, she blamed me for Leland's predicament.

"I assure you, I will do everything I can to find out who hurt him and Mr. Travers," I said, trying to sound consoling. "Leland will have justice."

Catherine took a step toward me, her breath coming fast. "Will he? You will see to it, will you?"

"Yes," I said, puzzled. "I will do whatever I am able."

"I think a magistrate will not do for this." Her words were clipped. "You cannot possibly imagine how this will destroy a good man and a good lady. In fact, I will thank you not to interfere."

I curbed my impatience. "It is a bit late for that, is it not? I found them."

"Yes, you did. And how you happened to be convenient, I'm sure I do not know. Nor do I wish to. By all means, look in on Leland, and then leave and let them be."

She started to pass me, but I stepped in front of her. "I have

come here only to help. What have I done to earn your
displeasure?"

Mrs. Danbury looked momentarily uncertain as she met
my gaze, then her hesitation fled. "You have been no friend to
Leland. This house cannot withstand a firestorm, Captain
Lacey. *They* cannot withstand it. I beg you to leave them be."

With this she swept past me, skimming down the steps and
into one of the sitting rooms. The slam of the door echoed up
the staircase.

Nonplussed, I continued my journey upward.

I found Leland's bedchamber by following the flow of
servants coming and going with towels, blankets, pillows, and
trays of food and drink. Inside the grand room, Lady Derwent
sat at her son's bedside, his hand in hers. Leland's sister,
Melissa, reposed on a couch on the other side of the bed, but
her look at her brother was fearful, and she picked at the sash
of her gown.

Lady Derwent's greeting was entirely contrary to Mrs.
Danbury's. She began to rise as I entered, her look one of relief
and joy. "Captain, how wonderful to see you."

I motioned her back to the chair, and kept my voice low.
"Do not bestir yourself. How is he?"

Lady Derwent sank back down but reached for my hand.
"I am so glad you've come. So glad."

I covered her cold fingers with mine. "He is better?" I
asked.

Lady Derwent's clear gray eyes brimmed with tears. "He
woke," she said, glancing at Leland, who lay insensible, his
breathing even. "He asked for you—no, begged to see you. We
dreaded explaining that Gareth—Mr. Travers—had not
survived, but he already knew, poor boy. He must have
witnessed it. Horrifying. I cannot imagine ..."

"Then do not," I squeezed her hand again, wishing I could
pass my strength to her. Though age and consumption had
diminished her, Lady Derwent must have been a ravishing

beauty in her youth. The bones of her face, the softness of her eyes, still carried the prettiness she'd had. Her daughter was lovely too, though Melissa's timidity prevented her natural beauty from shining through.

I went on, "If Leland saw who did this, then we can seize the culprit and bring him to justice. The villain should be made to pay."

Lady Derwent nodded. "Yes, we will prosecute. Gideon has already said so. But Leland, he said he will only speak to you of it." She bit her lip. "And then he drifted off again, and has not wakened."

My concern returned, but perhaps the best thing for him was sleep. "Shall I come back later?"

"Not at all." Lady Derwent released me to lever herself to her feet. I was beside her again in an instant, my steadying hand under her elbow. She gave me a grateful look. "He asked me to beg you to stay when you arrived so he could speak to you the moment he woke. But I'm afraid I must ..." She put her fingers to her mouth as though she could press back the cough that began to lift her chest. "Gideon is finally in bed, and I—"

She broke off, her breath faltering. Melissa came to her other side without a word, but she would not look at me in her shyness.

"Have a rest," I told Lady Derwent, and included Melissa in the admonition. "I will look after Leland."

Lady Derwent's voice was a whisper. "I know you will. Thank ... I beg your ... " Another cough threatened.

"Save your breath for the steps to your chamber," I said quickly. "Good morning, Lady Derwent. Miss Derwent."

I made them a bow, and mother and daughter left the room, daughter supporting mother. One of the maids who'd come to assist Lady Derwent shut the door behind them.

As soon as the latch clicked, Leland's eyes popped open. "Captain?" he whispered.

I went quickly to the bed. "Leland?"

He hadn't been sleeping at all, I saw. His eyes didn't have the vacant, bleary look of someone just roused, though they were moist and filled with pain.

"Gareth." The word rasped from him, filled with grief.

"I know."

Leland groped for my hand. I sank to the chair Lady Derwent had vacated and clasped Leland's fingers as comfortingly as I had his mother's.

"I am so sorry," Leland said in a croak. "I was such a bloody fool. I—"

"Stop," I said. "No recriminations."

Leland's head moved on the pillow, then he winced and stilled. "I feel as though the devil is dancing inside my skull. It bloody hurts."

The fact that he used such strong words told me the depths of his anguish. "You were coshed, lad. Of course it hurts. Can you tell me what happened?"

"Would that I knew." Leland's voice was weak, but held conviction. "I did not see who did it, if that is what you mean. All of a sudden, I was on the ground. Gareth was beside me. He looked at me, gave me a little smile, and then ... then ..."

Leland squeezed his eyes shut, his lashes moistening, the lad too weak to sob. I stroked his hand, wishing I could be of better comfort.

His eyes drifted open again. "Forgive me. I can't seem to stop."

"You will receive no censure from me, Leland."

"It was always Gareth and me," Leland said. "We never needed anyone else."

"I know."

"He was always there for me." His voice scraped, but he lurched on, his eyes bright, as though he needed to get the words out. "From the time we were eight years old, at school. I was terrified. All those boys, watching me, taunting me. Gareth laughed at my fear. Said it was a grand adventure, wasn't it? We were explorers, and the other boys were wild natives. We started having meetings of what he called our Explorers Club. Membership—two. It was very exclusive." He broke off to laugh, which brought fresh tears.

I continued to hold Leland's hand, knowing nothing I could say would help. "Can you tell me anything at all about what happened?"

He drew a few breaths before he could speak again. "I wish I knew. It's all a horrible blank. The last thing I remember is agreeing to meet Gareth at my club, at Brooks's. I have the idea we were going to do something else from there, but I cannot remember what. I do not know whether I even went to Brooks's."

"Easy enough to determine." I tried to sound cheerful. "Your valet will know. So will your coachman."

"That is true." Leland looked more hopeful. "All I can remember is opening my eyes in the pitch dark with cold cobbles beneath my cheek, and pain, so much pain ..." His chest moved. "I somehow got to my feet. I got Gareth up. I tried to help him out of there, but I was lost. Our clothes were half off—I couldn't stop to find them. Then I fell. Gareth was next to me ... lying there, giving me that smile he used to. As though he were telling me, *Keep your chin up, Eely, you'll be fine.*" Leland faltered, and wet his lips. "Then I woke here. I thought at first it had been a dream. That it was time to rise and meet Papa for breakfast. But my head exploded with pain when I tried to lift it, and Mama came rushing in. She told me ... told me ..." Tears tracked his cheeks. "*Damn* him. Why is he dead? Why did he leave me alone?"

I had lost loved ones in my life—most people I knew had— but for Leland to lose someone who understood him as no one else had, and so young, had to be terrible. The person he'd had by his side all those years was suddenly gone, the world emptier without him.

Their exclusive club had just diminished to membership
—one.

"Leland, I am so very sorry," I said. "I will find who did
this. I promise you."

"Won't bring him back to me, will it?" Leland released my
hand and rested his on the coverlet. "Do you know, I keep
expecting him to come bouncing in the door, laughing at me,
saying it has all been a joke or a dream. But my mother
confirms that he is gone." Leland stopped, going silent for a
long moment. When he spoke again, his voice was thin. "Mr.
Grenville helped bring me home, she says. Does he know?"

I understood what he meant. I shook my head. "I have not
told a soul."

Leland let out a breath of relief. "I think I could bear the
whole world knowing, even my mother and father, but not Mr.
Grenville."

"I cannot think why," I said, trying to reassure him. "Mr.
Grenville is a most understanding gentleman."

Leland blinked at me. "I have seen Mr. Grenville reduce a
gentleman to tears by giving a look of asperity to his cravat."

"I have seen him do that as well. But I've learned that while
he will ridicule pompous fools, he is kind to those he respects,
and amazingly compassionate. It took me a long time to understand this. I wronged him when I first met him."

"Even so." Leland flushed again. "I would not like Mr.
Grenville to know my secrets."

"I will not tell him unless you give me leave to. What about
Mr. Mackay? He was there."

Leland began to frown, then his brows drifted apart as
though he found the effort too tiring. "Who is Mr. Mackay?"

"He came to find me, to lead me to you." I described him.

"Oh." Leland drew a ragged breath. "I remember. I sent
him to you. He was gone a long time, or so it seemed, and I
knew I had to move Gareth …"

I put up my hand to still his tormented thoughts. "Was he one of Gareth's friends? Did he see what happened?"

"I did not know him. I spied him there, begged him to go to Grimpen Lane and find you. I didn't remember until he ran off that you no longer lived there."

"He was lucky, as I had just arrived. But anyone at my lodgings would have known how to send for me. You did right."

"Please give him my thanks," Leland said, his voice cracking. "And beg him to say nothing."

"If I can find him," I said. "And I will—he may know who did this terrible thing."

"No." Leland started to shake his head. "Do not try to find out. Please. We must have been set upon to be robbed, that is all. You'll never find the men in the warrens of London, and it doesn't matter." He trailed off, voice weakening.

"It does matter," I said. "I dislike seeing my friends hurt. I will find the man who did this and take him apart."

Leland gave me a wan smile. "You are a soldier. I always wanted to be like you. But it doesn't matter. Not to me. Nothing does anymore."

His voice faded, his eyes drifting closed again, and I grew alarmed. He was so weak, and the distress was doing him no good.

I stood. "Would you like me to send in your father?" I asked as gently as I could. "Or Mrs. Danbury?"

"No," Leland said in a near whisper. "I'd like to be alone, Captain. I need to get used to it."

CHAPTER 11

$\mathcal{I}$'d hoped to speak again to Mrs. Danbury before I left the house, to discover why she was so adamant about me staying away, but when I looked into the room she had entered on the ground floor, it was empty. The footman hovered near, wanting to escort me out the door, so I let him.

Clouds covered the sky, and a misting rain began to fall. I waved away the footman's offer to have the Derwents' coach brought around for me, and walked from the square to Grosvenor Street, and thence to Grenville's.

I found Grenville awake. He was in his dressing gown in his sumptuous bedchamber, imbibing coffee, his hair mussed from sleep. When Matthias ushered me in, Grenville waved me to a chair and bade the young man bring me coffee as well.

"Nasty business," Grenville said as soon as I was sipping the fragrant brew. "I thought to stay with Leland all last night, but Lady Derwent sent me home. She might seem frail, but that woman has a will of iron."

I had to agree. "Leland has woken, which is a good sign, but at this point, I have no idea whether he will live or die." I paused, unhappy. "He's a resilient lad, but head wounds …"

"Yes, it looked bad." Grenville's optimistic demeanor was considerably dimmed. "The Derwents are taking it hard."

"They'll take it harder if he dies," I said.

We reflected on this gloomy prospect. "The question is," Grenville said after a moment, "is what the devil were they doing in that unlit passage in Seven Dials? I had thought them discreet enough to stay indoors, and pampered enough to wish a soft bed in which to couple. Good Lord, I would."

I nearly choked on my coffee, and quickly set the cup aside. "Not a half hour ago, I was promising Leland I'd not breathe a word to you."

Grenville lifted his brows. "Everyone knows, Lacey. Or at least has guessed. Leland Derwent and Gareth Travers have been fused as one since they were children. They've taken no interest in ladies, they lived in the same rooms at university, Gareth runs tame in the Derwent household, and neither have made any obvious move to enter the marriage mart."

"*You* have not entered the marriage mart," I pointed out. "Not every man does."

"Ah, but there is a difference. My *affaires* are talked of—incessantly—and no one has observed Leland or Gareth so much as casting a woman a longing look. We *know*. We simply do not speak of it. Nor did we expect them to do anything except happily grow old together."

"And now they cannot."

"No, poor lads," Grenville said, heaving a sigh. "Which returns me to the point—why on earth did they meet in a back lane in the middle of a rookery?"

I tried to press aside anger and worry to look at the problem clearly. "Perhaps they did not. Perhaps they were found in the act, somewhere comfortable, as we speculate, struck down, and carried there. Or, they were not in flagrante at all but were arranged to be found like that."

"A very elaborate scheme," Grenville said. "For what purpose?"

"To humiliate the Derwents? To intimate that all was not as moral and upright in Sir Gideon's house as it seemed?"

"Surely, in that case, they'd have been found in a more public place," Grenville said. "As it was, they were lucky to be found at all."

"That is true." I said. "If the motive were to ruin the family, there was great risk in it not coming off."

"And it won't." Grenville's reply was quick and resolute. "*You* know how they were found, but we can keep it from others. That they were struck down as they were robbed and then left for dead will be the story. Who else knows about them being in dishabille?"

"Brewster," I said. "The man Denis has sent to be my nursemaid. He carried the lads from the passage, but I'd redressed them by then—though I never found Leland's missing coat. The cart driver Brewster hired saw nothing."

"Denis's men are a close-mouthed lot," Grenville said. "Though it might be worth speaking to Denis to make certain." He took a sip of coffee. "Anyone else see them before you put their clothing to rights?"

"There was the young man who came to fetch me. Mackay. Nelson Mackay. A little older than Leland and Gareth. Black hair. Blue eyes. Good clothes, soft hands—not a laborer. Haven't seen him at the clubs."

Grenville's brows came together as he thought. "I've not the heard the name." He shook his head. "No, I can't place him. I will ask Gautier. He has more knowledge of who is who in London than Debrett's."

I let amusement trickle through my foul mood. "I thought *you* were the font of all knowledge."

Grenville contrived to look modest. "I do know an extraordinary number of people—far too many I sometimes believe. But Gautier knows them from all walks of life." He sighed. "I do feel the crowd pressing on me a bit these days, Lacey."

I resumed my coffee. "Are you going to speak longingly of Egypt now?"

"Of course I am. I have mentioned putting together an expedition for next winter. Now that you are safely married—with your daughter perhaps ensconced in the bosom of matrimony herself by then—we can be off."

The thought of my daughter married so soon brought a pang to my heart. But, after all, that was the intent of her debut Season. Donata and Lady Aline were working to interest the best young English gentlemen in her, but I was not yet ready to let her go.

"I am not certain my wife will take well to me leaving for several months to remote lands of the Ottoman Empire," I said.

Grenville waved that away. "By next winter, she will likely send you off with enthusiasm. Newlywed bliss palls, you know."

"Oh? You have experienced it?"

Grenville gave me a look of feigned horror. "Of course not. But I have watched many of my friends go through it, and every single one says the same. Why do you think I avoid the parson's trap?"

So he could do what he pleased, I knew, without having to answer to anyone. I'd learned that Grenville prized, above everything, his freedom.

I would have thought Marianne his perfect mate, in that case. She was not a clinging woman, and she too prized her liberty. They might rub on well together, if they were both not so pigheaded.

"Do ask Gautier about Mr. Mackay," I said. "Why *he* was on the spot is a mystery. We must find him and put a few questions to him."

"Sir Gideon and I have managed to keep the story of Gareth's death and Leland's injuries quiet for one night, but it will get out, one way or another," Grenville warned me. "Bow

Street will want to investigate the crime. Shall you inform your former sergeant? Set him on the track with his usual zeal?"

"No," I said at once. Pomeroy had the knack of turning up embarrassing information, smiling all the while. And if Spendlove got hold of this, who knew what hell he might rain down on the Derwent family? "I will find out as much as I can as quickly as possible. If Pomeroy or Spendlove ever believe I think it anything but a robbery turned deadly ..."

"Then Pomeroy will not let it rest." Grenville nodded sagely. "I understand you wanting to protect the Derwents from a full Bow Street investigation. However, there isn't much to go on, is there?"

"Which is why we must return to Seven Dials." I drained my cup and set it on its saucer with a decided click. "At once."

"Ah, I feared you'd say that."

He hated rising early, but I could tell he was eager to be investigating. Though he kept up appearances by grumbling, Grenville was ready to depart in half an hour. He called for his carriage, and we set off, with Matthias and Bartholomew, who'd come in response to his summons, in tow.

THE LANE IN SEVEN DIALS LOOKED DISMAL BY THE LIGHT OF day. Darkness had hidden the grime on the cobbles and the crumbling bricks of the buildings around us, but sunshine breaking through the clouds illuminated the passage in all its squalor.

I'd expected to find more blood on the cobblestones. I'd sworn the place coated with it last night, but it had been pitch dark, and my heart had been hammering in shock and fear. There hadn't been much rain in the night to wash the cobbles. But except for a stain a few feet wide and the smears leading to where I'd stumbled across Leland and Gareth, I could find no other blood.

Grenville held a handkerchief to his mouth, the stench of the lane far from pleasant. Matthias and Bartholomew moved up and down the passage looking for whatever they thought might help.

"Does the scarcity of blood confirm your theory that they were attacked elsewhere?" Grenville asked when I voiced my findings.

"I am not certain," I said, looking over the cobbles again. "Head injuries bleed quite a bit, but the villain might have brought something with which to sop up the blood. Or they did not bleed as much as I think they should have. I am no expert."

Grenville crouched to look at the dried blood, his handkerchief moving as he grew interested. "Whether they were attacked here or not, how did that chap Mackay find them?"

"A good question," I said. "How did he so conveniently turn up? Not the sort of gentleman who would be wandering these streets. We must lay our hands on him."

"Sir." Bartholomew's voice came from farther down the passage. Grenville and I walked to him, avoiding puddles of noisome filth to find him holding a chunk of wood he'd pulled from a pile of rubbish, his brother Matthias examining it closely.

It was a stout piece used for building, once hewn smooth, now broken off and jagged. A half dozen nails poked out of it about an inch from its end. Grenville brought out his quizzing glass, fixing his gaze on the nails as Bartholomew held the wood steady in his gloved hands.

"Blood, if I'm any judge," Grenville pronounced.

"It's a good cosh," Bartholomew said. "This kind of beam's not easy to come by—would be expensive at a builder's yard."

Nails would not be easy to come by either, in this part of town. Everything that could be sold would have been.

"Doubtless the murderer threw it away here, hoping it wouldn't be found," Grenville said.

"But it turned up as soon we looked for it," I pointed out. "Anyone who took the trouble to hide Leland and Gareth back here would surely rid himself of the weapon in another place. I believe he *wanted* this to be found."

Grenville could not take his eyes from the nails. "You make too much of it. He panicked. He'd just struck down the sons of rich gentlemen and could not afford to be caught. He drags the bodies into the passage, then remembers he still has the cudgel, and hastily buries it among other rubbish."

"Do you really believe that?" I asked in a mild voice.

Grenville straightened up and dropped his quizzing glass into his pocket. "I have no idea. That is what your friend Pomeroy would say, though. An agitated man who'd acted rashly and then tried to hide what he'd done, rather clumsily."

"Sir." Matthias spoke this time, jerking his chin back down the crooked passage.

A man, hulking and menacing, stood at the opening to the street. I observed him without alarm and beckoned him closer.

"Please tell Mr. Denis that I am well protected by Matthias and Bartholomew," I said to Brewster when he reached us. "You had no need to follow me this morning."

"Tell 'im yourself," Brewster said. He picked something from between his front teeth, and spat. "His nibs gives me an order, and I carry it out. No questions. Besides." He sent an amused glance at Bartholomew, who had moved protectively next to Grenville. "This one got himself shot several times trying to protect you, didn't he?"

"Better I was shot than Mr. Grenville," Bartholomew returned heatedly. "I healed quickly."

"Heh. Then your Mr. Grenville got hisself stabbed good, didn't he? Where were you then?"

Matthias went red. "Keep a civil tongue, and don't talk about your betters. Mr. Grenville is worth twenty of you."

I admired the brothers' courage, but Brewster was a killer.

I started to step between them, but Brewster only laughed. "Loyalty's a good thing, lad. Is this the cosh?"

"We think so." I took it from Bartholomew before he decided to test it on Brewster, and showed Brewster the nails.

"Thought so. Stupid of him to leave it here. He should have tossed it in the river."

"Which is what I would have done," I said. "So our killer is either a fool or very clever."

Grenville tore his gaze from the club again, looking not at all ruffled at Brewster's and his servants' discussion of him. "You are speculating that the attacker went to great trouble to make it look as though ruffians had set upon Leland and Gareth in this passage."

"Yes," I said. "They were setting a scene—Sir Gideon's son and his lover decide to engage in a bout of passion in a street in Seven Dials. For the excitement of it? They are set upon by robbers and coshed. Found partly undressed, Leland's fine coat and waistcoat stolen. Shock ensues. Whether the villains intended death or not is unclear."

Mackay had scuttled their plans by coming to find me. Had he just happened by, or was he part of the killer's plan? If Mackay had been a witness, why hadn't he tried to prevent the attack, and why hadn't he been hurt himself?

"We must find Mackay," I repeated.

"Undoubtedly," Grenville agreed. "Where did he run off to, after he led you here?"

"I sent him back to my rooms to get word to you, but he never returned."

"Hmm. Perhaps Mrs. Beltan spoke to him," Grenville said. "She's the motherly sort—when she saw that this Mackay was upset she'd have plied him with bread and coffee. She might have ferreted something out of him, such as who he is and where he lives."

"Possibly," I said. "Except that I did not send him to Mrs.

Beltan. I sent him to Marianne, who was using my rooms at the time. I knew she'd be able to get word to you the quickest."

"Ah." Grenville's face went still except for a tightening around his eyes. "I was aware only that the summons came from you. Then it seems we must ask Miss Simmons what became of Mr. Mackay."

"I can do that," I said quickly. "No need for you to accompany me."

"Not at all. I'll not cower here or in my carriage while you approach her." Grenville dabbed his mouth with his handkerchief, sniffed, returned the handkerchief to his coat, and adjusted his hat. "But, my good fellow, do be kind and warn me next time you're about deliver a blow like that."

CHAPTER 12

$\mathcal{B}$y the time we reached Grimpen Lane, I thought Grenville would change his mind about facing Marianne. He was a trifle white about the eyes as he descended from his carriage, though he looked airily around him as though he had no qualms about being in the street outside the rooms of his former lover.

Brewster accompanied us. Matthias and Bartholomew had volunteered to stay behind and continue to search the passage for any other signs we might have missed. Bartholomew was of the mind that those who lived in the houses around the narrow lane might have seen something, though Brewster negated that idea.

"The more goes on, the less they see, if you understand me," Brewster had said in his blunt way. "No harm trying I s'pose, but I wish you lads luck."

Bartholomew had looked annoyed but determined to prove Brewster wrong.

As we climbed the stairs to my rooms, Grenville's face grew tighter, and at the same time his expression became more disdainful. He was slipping on his haughty dandy persona, the one he used to mask his true self. Easier to face her if he made the encounter less personal, I supposed.

There was nothing to say Marianne was even home. She might have gone out, not wanting to be there whenever I returned.

We knew soon enough. As we reached the landing, we heard her laughter behind my front door.

My door handle, in the shape of a woman with long wings, had once been gilded, but the gilt had flaked off years ago, leaving worn brass behind. The handle was cool under my palm as I pushed the door open.

Marianne did indeed occupy my sitting room. This morning she wore a gown of light pink that went with her girl-like prettiness, but no modest young debutante would have worn such a garment. The fabric was thin, hiding little, and the gown's décolletage slid from her shoulders, coming danger-ously close to baring her right breast. Ribbons dripped from her ringlets of golden hair, moving as she laughed.

She reposed in my wing chair, lolling as though she had no cares, the position letting the silken skirt cling to her shapely legs. On the footstool, holding her hands and inciting her laughter, was a gentleman in a black frock coat and riding boots, his hair as artfully tousled as Grenville's.

The gentleman turned abruptly at our entrance, an admon-ishment on his lips. When he saw the two of us standing there, Brewster behind, his irritation vanished, and he leapt to his feet.

He was Lord Percy Saunders, eldest son of the Duke of Waverly. I had met him once, briefly, a year or so ago when he and I had been guests in Donata's box in Covent Garden. I'd thought him coolly rude. He'd tried to persuade Donata to marry him, she'd told me, but she'd turned him down. She'd not found much to object to in him, she'd said, beyond his name — she'd not wanted to be called *Lady Percy* — but not much beyond that either.

He is neither good nor evil, interesting nor dull, hard nor soft, she'd said of him in one of our nightly discussions. *He does everything expected of him, converses on predictable topics, loses at cards without fuss, and expects ladies—if they are pretty—to hang upon his every word. He mistakes petty vindictiveness for wit, and I soon had enough of his company.*

I heard Donata's words hanging in the silence as Lord Percy and Grenville faced each other.

Most Mayfair gentlemen knew one another's mistresses, and often the ladies were handed from one to the next when affairs ended. But to be found in the company of the former mistress of Lucius Grenville, without his knowledge or previous approval, had to be the social blunder of the Season.

Lord Percy cleared his throat. "Grenville." His hands clenched in kid gloves, and he looked as though he hoped a hydra would crash through the window and swallow him whole.

"Saunders." Grenville gave him a minute bow.

They exchanged another long look, ignoring the rest of us in the room. Brewster and I, and even Marianne, might not have existed.

"I have come to speak to Miss Simmons," I announced into their motionless fencing match. "If she can spare a moment."

Marianne, who'd remained stiffly in the chair, straightened up and gave me a cool nod. She alone of the players responded to the situation with the most aplomb. She might be a royal at her levee, quietly acknowledging that more admirers had come to greet her.

I would have assumed she'd staged the tableaux except for two things—she hadn't known we were coming, and the strained look on her face as she turned to me masked a boiling fury.

Saunders continued to eye Grenville. I wanted him gone, or for Marianne to come outside with me so I could speak with her alone, but neither she nor Saunders moved. I feared Brew-

ster would simply walk past me and pluck Lord Percy up by
his collar, but Grenville saved the shaky moment.

"Saunders," he said, his voice as smooth as ever. "Walk out
with me, will you?"

Where Lord Percy might have defied me and certainly
Brewster, he'd never refuse a direct order from Grenville.

"Of course," he said, as though he and Grenville were
deciding to have a private word at White's. "Miss Simmons."
Lord Percy gave Marianne a stiff bow, took up his hat and
greatcoat from where he'd pitched them to the chair at my
writing table, and walked past me to the door.

Grenville had already exited, moving unworriedly around
Brewster. He did not wait for Lord Percy but simply walked
down the stairs as though having no doubt the man would
follow.

Percy did, quickly. He barely remembered to give me a
civil nod, ignored Brewster as Grenville had, and strode down
the stairs.

I knew Marianne would begin shouting as soon as the two
gentlemen were out of sight, but they'd be able to hear until
they were well out onto the street. I took her by the arm and
steered her into the bedchamber, closing the door on Brewster's interested face.

"Devil a bit, Lacey." Marianne's voice rang through the
room as she jerked away from me. "Why did you bring
Grenville here? You knew Lord Percy was meeting me,
didn't you? You are hand in glove with *him*, trying to
ruin me!"

I folded my arms, standing like a pillar at the end of my
bed. "How would I have had any bloody idea Saunders would
be here? I didn't even know you knew the man. I came to
discuss something else entirely. In any case, why the devil were
you using my rooms for your tryst?"

"As though I could take him up *there* where it's barren as an
orphanage." She jabbed her finger at the ceiling. "I thought

you'd be off investigating crime, or holding young Mr. Derwent's hand."

"I *am* investigating. Which is what brought me to talk to you. About Mr. Mackay."

Marianne's diatribe cut off, and she shot me a puzzled look.

"The man who arrived here last night to take me to Leland," I said. "I sent him back to you, to ask you to find Grenville."

"Oh, *him*." Marianne rolled her eyes. "He was a poor specimen. He was sick in the street then tore off as soon as I sent the message."

"That was Mr. Mackay. If you will sit down and speak quietly, perhaps you could tell me about him."

She blinked. "I can't tell you anything about him. I barely said a word to the man."

I began to answer, then broke off, opened the door, and ushered her out into the sitting room again. We could at least be comfortable. Brewster had settled himself on the straight-backed chair, reading one of the few books I kept in my shelves, a small tome on Egypt and Belzoni's discoveries. He was truly reading it, his eyes moving along the lines.

I sat Marianne in the wing chair and remained standing over her. "You can tell me a little about Mr. Mackay," I said. "What did you think of him? Was he middle class? Impoverished but respectable? A clerk? A gentleman's son? Did he mention where he lived?"

"Yes, of course," Marianne said derisively. "He gave me his entire family history and a map to his estate in Norwood while he was blithering and dithering about what you wanted him to do."

I suppressed a sigh of impatience. "He might not have been specific. But you are good at forming impressions, Marianne. I want your opinion."

"Well, apparently I am very bad at forming impressions, or I'd not have made myself a slave to *him* for most of a year."

Brewster snorted a laugh, and Marianne turned a freezing look on him. "I'll thank you not to listen, sir."

"I'm ten feet away from yer, miss." Brewster, who did not consider himself a servant and saw no need to behave like one, returned his attention to the book. "You know, Captain, his nibs can find out all about this Mackay cove for you."

"Possibly," I said. "But he might be an innocent man with no need to be dragged from his house by Mr. Denis."

Brewster shrugged. "He gets the thing done, though, doesn't he?" Having said his piece, he closed his mouth and continued reading.

Marianne's look suggested I was mad to let Brewster into my rooms, but she at least began speaking reasonably.

"I would think your Mr. Mackay is a gentleman's son," she said. "Had the look. Not a rich gentleman, I'd say, but not a destitute one either. Coat was well cut and made of good material. Boots made to fit, but no rings or cravat pin. His manservant, if he has one, ties a sloppy knot, but his cravat linen costs a bob or two."

"You see? You have a knack for knowing what a person is like."

Marianne scowled. "Do not try to flatter me—I am furious with you for bringing *him* here. Good Lord, could you not have left him in a pub somewhere?"

Another laugh from Brewster, which, this time, Marianne ignored.

"He insisted," I said. "I would have given you warning if I'd been able. Did Mackay say anything else to you? Anything that would help?"

Marianne thought a moment. "Not really. What he said was, *You must send for Mr. Grenville. He said you must send for Mr. Grenville.* He repeated this several times, and then had to run downstairs and bend over the pavement to lose whatever he had in his stomach. Once I fetched a boy to run with a message to Mayfair—which I paid for, by the bye—Mr. Mackay had dashed off."

"You did not see which way?"

"I saw him turn left onto Russel Street. He could have been making for a hackney stand, or simply running off into the mists. Who knows?"

"Thank you." I dug into my pocket and pulled out a crown, which would more than cover her expenses, and dropped it into her waiting palm. "It is a help."

"I do not see how, but nonetheless." Marianne heaved a sigh and threw herself back into the wing chair, her hand closed firmly around the coin. "Do go away now, Lacey. I would like to sulk in peace."

In my rooms. I felt sympathy for her, but also exasperation. I had since the day I'd met her.

"Tell me," I said to her as I signaled to Brewster. He rose and set the book aside. "Why Lord Percy?"

Marianne gave me a deprecating look. "Because he has plenty of money and doesn't tell me what to do. No, he has not yet offered me anything, and because of your so timely interruption, I doubt he will." She rose to her feet, deigning to leave. "Now if you will excuse me. Good day, Lacey."

She swept past me, and out the door, as arrogant as ever, but I saw the despair in her eyes. I watched her ascend the stairs, her thin gown floating gracefully, until she disappeared into her rooms above.

"She'll lead that aristo a life of merry hell if he does offer her *carte blanche*," Brewster said. He lifted a book from the table, enclosing it in his beefy hands. "Mind if I borrow this, sir? It's fascinating stuff."

CHAPTER 13

My next idea was to retrace the steps Leland and Travers had taken the previous night. They'd planned to meet at Brooks's, where Leland and his father were members, and to Brooks's I would go.

Percy Saunders had vanished by the time I emerged downstairs. Grenville, tight-lipped when I reached his carriage in Russel Street, said nothing at all about him.

We first returned to Seven Dials to fetch Matthias and Bartholomew, but they asked to stay and keep looking about. Grenville agreed they could meet up with us again at his home, gave them fare for transportation and a spot of luncheon, and he and I departed for St. James's.

Brooks's club was in St. James's Street near Park Place. With its elegant facade, Doric columns, and Greek pediments, it held a quiet dignity amid the bustle of the area. Its members were traditionally Whigs, and Sir Gideon Derwent was prominent here.

I considered myself Whiggish, as my father had been, though I had no true political leanings. My father had chosen to align himself with the Whigs because the Lacey family had done so since Whigs had been invented, and my father was happy for the ruling power to be out of the hands of the monarch and into hands of people like himself. Not because he wanted to better England, but because he hated others telling him what to do.

Grenville was a member of Brooks's, and I was allowed in as his guest. Once upon a time, I had cornered one of the members here, a man called Alandale, and done harm to him. I had thought I'd be banished from these halls forever because of that, but not so. Grenville and others had stood up for me, and while the *ton* had decided I was a bit of a bully, being hot-tempered and quick with fists was a far lesser crime than breaking one's word, not paying one's debts, or worst of all, cheating. Gentlemen of society had learned that I was at my most enraged when the honor of a lady was at stake, and that motive was wholly approved. Not many had liked Alandale anyway—I'd not seen him in London since.

This was one building Brewster could not enter, at least not into the main rooms, and he chose to wait outside with the coach. The club was fairly empty this early in the day, containing only a few gentlemen breakfasting or reading newspapers.

The most logical person to quiz was the doorman, who knew all members on sight, and the most likely person to take note of the comings and goings.

"Yes, Mr. Derwent was here, Mr. Travers as his guest." The elderly gentleman stood ramrod straight and watched us with disdainful dark eyes. "They had mutton and beef in the dining room and sat at a game of whist in the card room. Mr. Derwent plays like a gentleman, if I may say so, sir."

Did I detect a faint hint of emphasis on *Derwent*? As though implying Travers did not?

"Indeed, he does," Grenville said. "What time did the gentlemen depart?"

"Very early, sir. Around eight o'clock. I assumed them on their way to another appointment."

"Oh?" I broke in. "Why did you suppose that?"

The doorman gave me a pained look. He was much more comfortable speaking to Grenville and attempted to pretend I did not exist, but he at least thought about it a moment. "I couldn't say, sir. Perhaps they mentioned a meeting. I did not hear precisely, but I formed that opinion."

"They left quite alone?" I asked. "The two of them together?"

"Several gentlemen were coming and going at the time," the doorman said, looking down his nose. "Many were taking an evening meal."

"It's quite all right, Richards," Grenville said soothingly. "What we mean is, they were not obviously part of a group of gentlemen?"

"Not that I could see, sir," Richards answered. He looked back and forth between us, beginning to wonder at our questions. "Has something happened?"

Grenville looked at me inquiringly, and I nodded. We could not keep it from the world for long.

"Mr. Derwent was hurt last evening," Grenville said. "Set upon and robbed."

Richards's haughty look vanished to be replaced with one of concern. "Good Lord, sir. Is the lad all right?"

"We have hopes of his recovery," Grenville said. "But it is not certain at the moment, I am afraid."

"Why do you wish to know if he left with others, sir?" Richards asked, puzzled. "Surely you do not believe other gentlemen of this club are common robbers."

"No, no, not at all," Grenville said quickly. "We are trying to determine where they might have gone, if they'd met up with unsavory types—through no fault of their own, of course." He added the last as Richards's eyes began to widen again. "But you know the Derwents. Always trying to help the downtrodden. We want to find these villains and see that they come up before a magistrate."

"That's what Bow Street's for, innit?" Richards's speech began to slip into its East London origins.

"Yes, but we wish to assist any way we can. Young Leland is a dear friend."

"Of course, sir. Of course." Richards snapped back into his butler-like tones. "But I do not believe Mr. Derwent left this club with anyone but Mr. Travers. Mr. Travers would know, sir. Thick as thieves those two are."

"Unfortunately, Mr. Travers was hurt as well, and can tell us nothing," Grenville said. "Thank you, Richards. If you hear anything else, you will send word to me, won't you?"

Richards assured him he would, and we moved into the heart of the club.

The games room was quiet this morning. Its heavy chandelier hung dark from the vaulted ceiling, which formed a graceful arch over us. The large round tables were empty except for a few gentlemen who idly drank coffee and read newspapers.

I recognized one as the Honorable Mr. Henry Lawrence, son of a marquis. Mr. Lawrence had the reputation of being a man of many appetites, some of them disreputable, though no one had ever stated this to me outright. There were whispers, however, that did not bear close examination.

In light of what had happened to Leland and Gareth, I wanted to know more about him. If the two lads had been lured away, someone like Lawrence might be able to point to where they'd gone and why.

Mr. Lawrence's red-rimmed eyes, peering over his newspaper as we boldly sat down at his table, told me he'd had a very late night and wished he'd remained in bed this morning. He had thinning dark hair and a face covered with dark bristles. His hazel eyes, though bloodshot, held intelligence, and he twinkled them at me as though he guessed my interest in him.

"Mr. Derwent and Mr. Travers," Lawrence said after he and Grenville had exchanged polite greetings, and Grenville had asked the question. "I did not speak to them much, Captain Lacey," he said to me. "I promise. They are much too innocent for me, though Mr. Derwent has the loveliest hair. Like spun silk it is, do you not think?"

Grenville gazed at him steadily. "May we keep this civilized, Lawrence?"

"Of course, my dear Grenville." Lawrence set down his newspaper and lifted his hands in surrender. "But the captain wanted you to speak to me, because he believes I lust after young Mr. Derwent, and he does not approve. Look at his face. You know it to be true."

I frowned at him, my hands curling in my lap. "We are only interested in where Mr. Derwent and Mr. Travers went after they left here."

"Hmm, well." Lawrence debated, lowering his hands and closing his long fingers around a coffee cup. "You will have to promise me that if I confide in you, Captain, what I say will never come to the ears of your Runner friend."

"You have my word," I answered. As long as Lawrence himself hadn't hurt Leland and Gareth—or any other young man—I'd leave him alone.

He seemed to understand my terms, because he gave me a tight but knowing smile. "In that case, I can tell you they might have gone any number of places for entertainment. You'll find establishments beyond Drury Lane theatre, all the way to Lincoln's Inn. You know of the White Swan? Near Clare Market?"

"I thought that had been raided and closed long ago." I had read tales of the molly house that had been invaded by patrollers some years past. Quite a few men had been arrested, and those tried and convicted had either been hanged or given to the mob at the stocks. The incident had happened when I'd been on the Peninsula, but the story had been in newspapers shipped in from London.

"Indeed," Lawrence said. "Such houses cannot stay closed for long. Gentlemen like Mr. Derwent and his friend Mr. Travers need somewhere they can be themselves, don't they?" He sent me a smile. "Did you know, they take ladies' names in these houses? What do you suppose Mr. Derwent calls himself? Miss Lucinda? Or something more regal? Miss Regina, perhaps?" He was baiting me, goading the captain with the reputation for taking matters into his own hands. Perhaps he wanted to see me explode into violence again, for his entertainment.

"Mr. Lawrence," I said, losing my patience. "Mr. Derwent and Mr. Travers were attacked last night. I am trying to discover by whom. If you know anything, you must tell us."

Lawrence's brows shot upward, his arrogance dying into stunned surprise. "Attacked?" He looked to Grenville for confirmation, and Grenville nodded.

Lawrence lifted his disheveled newspaper from the table and nervously began to fold it. "Good Lord, gentlemen, you ought to have said so at once. The Swan, or something like it, is exactly where you should begin to look for a culprit. The more unenlightened residents of the area could have set upon them—the bastards will lie in wait to beat down a gentleman emerging from one of the houses. Or a jealous rival, which happens. A man can be a molly and of prodigious strength. I knew a blacksmith once with thighs like tree trunks. He could bend an iron bar in half without sweating. He had many admirers."

"They had gone to Seven Dials," Grenville broke in.

"Ah." Lawrence set down the newspaper, his brows drawing together. "There is a tavern in Seven Dials called the Bull and Hen. Not Mr. Derwent's usual sort of haunt, I would have thought. It can be a bit rough. My blacksmith used to go there, though he's rather elderly now, and not prowling the houses any longer. The Bull and Hen is in Little Earl Street. You'll find it easily enough."

The twinkle came back into his eyes, as though daring me and Grenville to rush there on the moment.

"Thank you," I said, meeting his gaze. He could enjoy himself imagining what I'd do all he wanted. If Leland and Gareth had gone there, I would find out and also who'd they'd met.

"I do remember something else," Lawrence said. "If you are interested."

"You know we are, Lawrence," Grenville said, giving him a look of disapproval. "Have done with the japes, please. This is serious."

"Yes, very well, forgive me. Teasing Captain Lacey is too tempting. But believe me, I am concerned about young Leland. He is a good lad. Kindhearted. Not many are these days." He lifted his cup and took a deep sip of coffee. "He and Mr. Travers were here, as I've said. They were arguing with each other. I could not hear everything that passed between them, but I heard them arguing about deep play. Leland admonishing Mr. Travers that he played too recklessly, and Mr. Travers saying there was nothing in this club that was reckless enough for him. I cannot imagine why he'd think so—gentlemen win and lose entire fortunes here. But Mr. Travers said he wanted to know a place where the play was more intense. Leland was annoyed with him, but then, his heart is not in the games. Young Leland only lifts a hand of cards to be polite."

"Did they discover a place of deeper play?" I asked. "One of the hells, perhaps?"

Lawrence chuckled. "Can you see Leland Derwent in a gaming hell? I do not know where they went, and there isn't much card playing at the Bull and Hen. But the two lads were in conversation with Saunders before they departed. Left in a hurry, actually, Mr. Travers looking eager, and Saunders walking out with them."

"Lord Percy Saunders?" I asked, surprised.

"Indeed." Lawrence's amusement returned. "Don't know

whether he'll speak to you, Grenville. He's very carefully trying to avoid you."

Grenville did not change expression at all. He conveyed with every part of himself, including the brush of a gloved finger over his cheek, that he was sublimely indifferent to anything Lord Percy did. "If he has been trying to avoid me, he failed in the attempt," Grenville said in cool tones. "We've just been in the company of Lord Percy."

"And he said damn all about speaking with Mr. Derwent," I said, annoyed.

Lawrence reached for his newspaper, sighing. "I am greatly unhappy I missed *that* meeting. Do have your more interesting conversations in front of us from now on, Grenville, there's a good chap. Relieves my ennui something wonderful."

Grenville quirked his brows, but gave him a nod, as though acknowledging and approving of the joke.

I was less patient. "I suppose we shall have to hunt up Saunders again," I said.

"Indeed." Grenville's mouth tightened, but he gave no more sign of caring. "Good morning to you, Lawrence. That first edition of Gibbon you've had your eye on—it is yours."

"Ah." Lawrence looked genuinely delighted, losing his supercilious expression. "You are a gentleman, Grenville. Thank you."

irst edition?" I asked as we climbed into Grenville's carriage again.

"The Honorable Mr. Lawrence collects books," Grenville answered me distractedly. "We have been rival bidders at auction a time or two. But he gave us good information, and I know he wanted the Gibbon."

Grenville did generously reward those who pleased him. A boy slammed the door, and the carriage moved forward into the rain.

"Lord Percy coveted the book too," Grenville said as he settled himself. "Another reason to sell it to Lawrence." He stopped and gave me a despairing look. "I must nip this thing in the bud, Lacey. Dear God, I will be a laughingstock—I already am."

"Hardly a laughingstock," I answered. "Those who've met Marianne will understand. She is not your usual sort of woman."

"Do not remind me." Grenville's eyes darkened, sadness lurking behind his anger. "I regret I made the thing public. If I had continued in discretion, we might have parted without this foolishness."

"I disagree. If you had tried to keep your affair secret, Marianne would have fled you long ago."

"I suppose that is true." Grenville gazed moodily out the window. "But do not worry. I shall bring my attention to the matter at hand instead of becoming irritable and maudlin. What did you make of Mr. Lawrence's claim that Leland and Travers ended up at the Bull and Hen in Seven Dials?"

"We will have to find out," I said. "I suppose hunting up the proprietor is called for, finding out if any of the denizens of the house saw them."

"I have heard of the place," Grenville said. The carriage was moving purposefully through the streets, but what direction Grenville had given his coachman, I had not heard. "You say *denizens*, but I imagine you'd find many of the same gentlemen there who had spent the early part of the night at Brooks's or at a soiree with the highest of the *ton*. I cannot quite imagine Leland at the Bull and Hen, however. Lawrence is correct in speculating it was not Leland's sort of haunt. Leland is not interested in having it off with gentlemen in general, if you see what I mean. He was fixed on Travers alone."

I moved uncomfortably, remembering that Leland had, briefly, fixed upon *me*. "They were in love, you mean. Not out to satisfy base lusts."

"Exactly. They were devoted to each other—well, you saw them. A molly house in Seven Dials is hardly a place Leland would wish to go."

"What about Travers?"

Grenville closed gloved fingers around his walking stick. "He was another matter, from what I understand. A little more interested in the thing, don't you know. I suppose he could have persuaded Leland there. Perhaps that was what he meant by *deep play*. Innuendo, not a complaint about dull gaming at Brooks's."

"They could have been followed when they departed the

club," I said, picturing it. "They might have been cornered at the Bull and Hen, killed there, perhaps, and carried to the passage. Or chased there. We must find out." My agitation grew with my words. I longed to find the culprit and wrap my hands around his throat.

"Yes, well, if you are feeling the need to dash to Seven Dials and shake the house to its foundations, please think on it a moment," Grenville said. "Unless you plan to lead a force and close the place, you going there will be remarked upon, most viciously. Do not think your nemesis in the Runners, Spendlove, would not use it as an excuse to arrest you."

Indeed, I imagined Spendlove would take great pleasure in arresting me for unnatural behavior. Even if the magistrate released me for lack of evidence, Spendlove would have blackened my name.

If I did lead Pomeroy and his patrollers to close the house down in my zeal to catch Travers's killer, a good many men who had nothing to do with the murder might lose their lives. What had happened with the White Swan was still spoken of. Men arrested there had been put to death, and the mob had gone insane over those locked in the stocks. From what I'd heard and read, the crowd Travers and I had witnessed at Charing Cross had been tame and pleasant in comparison.

As much as I wanted the murderer within my grasp, I wanted to put my hands around the *correct* throat. I could not condemn a dozen gentlemen to death or ruin simply because they enjoyed a night in one another's arms.

We would have to try another approach. I studied Grenville, who sat upright on the carriage seat across from me. He was dressed in a slim-fitting black coat and trousers, a greatcoat that was light for spring, and boots that were never meant to get dirty. His polished, elegant hat rested on the seat beside him, and his kid-leather gloves were as soft as finest silk. He was the picture of a wealthy, privileged, English male.

"You cannot go there either," I observed. "While there

would be disapproval of me entering such a house, London would crumble and fall if it was put about that *you* did. Even if your motives were pure."

"It is a dilemma," Grenville agreed without false modesty. "I could hunt up a few gentlemen I suspect frequent the place, and question them, but no one is supposed to know. Even Lawrence took pains to imply he'd never been there, and no one has any doubt about his proclivities. Ah, well, I will see what I can do."

I'd already had an idea how to make inquiries, but I decided not to share it with Grenville yet. I had to mull it through, in any case.

"Where are we off to now?" I asked him. A glance out the window showed me the tall houses of Piccadilly going by.

"Tattersall's," Grenville said. "Percy Saunders, when he departed from me today, said he was heading there. He might have only been making conversation—he tried desperately not to mention what we truly wished to shout at each other about —but I would like to hear what he has to say about his encounter with Leland and Travers."

"Which he never brought up," I pointed out again. "Damn the man."

"Too distracted by the charms of Marianne, I would specu- late. And perhaps he had no idea of our interest." Grenville let out a breath and relaxed his tense façade. "Do you know, Lacey, that though Marianne could provoke me to despair, when we shut out everything but the two of us, it was wonder- ful. We laughed—oh, she can laugh. She knows the best stories of the theatre, things that would appall you as well as tales that would have you laughing until you couldn't stop. We'd have competitions for the best filthy jokes we heard in a given week —" He broke off and flushed. "I beg your pardon. I do not mean to impart confidences you do not want."

"Not at all," I said warmly. "I am glad to hear you were happy."

"We could be. When we were nobody but Lucius and Marianne, when we shut out the world, it was delightful." Grenville's eyes flickered, and he turned suddenly to look out the window. A light rain had begun to fall, streaking the glass like tears.

"She could forgive you," I said, watching him. "If you were humble enough."

Grenville gave a short laugh and faced me again. "Ah, yes, and she would trample me with her pretty silk slippers. Which I purchased for her, by the way."

"She will grow tired of it."

"Of trampling me, or of the slippers?" Grenville let out another laugh. "Both, I suppose. Never mind, Lacey. I will weather this."

As we pulled to a stop near Hyde Park Corner, I reflected that even getting stabbed nearly to death in one of our adventures had not dampened Grenville's spirits as much as had finding Marianne with Lord Percy this morning.

We emerged from the carriage and went into the enclosure that was Tattersall's, where the Jockey Club met, and prize horseflesh was bought and sold. Several horses paraded around the ring today, those interested in buying standing in clusters with those selling, while trainers and riders put the horses through their paces.

Always interested, I stopped to admire a brown mare with a good arch to her neck, but Grenville had already headed to the club rooms.

Inside, Grenville was greeted with a hearty welcome, and I was politely nodded to. When Grenville asked whether Lord Percy was about somewhere, we were informed that he was in one of the back stables looking over a gelding. The gentlemen present did not hide their amusement that Grenville was hunting Lord Percy, and one or two openly guffawed.

"Your laughter is unwarranted, gentlemen," Grenville said, drawing out his quizzing glass and letting it dangle from his fingers. "At our last meeting, Saunders and I parted as friends."

"He did not use the word *friends*," another gentleman said, and rumbles of laughter followed.

The rumbles died away under Grenville's long, cool stare. "I have no hostility for Saunders," he said, when he had everyone's attention again. "The man has my blessing."

A few gentlemen looked abashed; others remained amused but at least strove to hide it.

One gentleman, slender as a reed and full of himself, made a derisive snort. "I hardly think a blessing for such a tart is in order. You are a wise man to trade her for the Carlotti woman. English whey is no competition for Italian wine."

Grenville's gaze could have cut marble. Even the smallest snickers died away as Grenville directed his gaze to the slender gentleman.

When the room was utterly silent, Grenville spoke. "I would pronounce you a wit, Yardley—however I haven't heard a word you've said as I've been trying to decide whether those brown spots on your very green waistcoat are meant to be there, or whether someone has sprayed you with mustard." He leaned forward and delicately sniffed. "Or a more noxious substance, perhaps."

Yardley went red as Grenville carefully touched the tip of his walking stick to a spot in question. Grenville was a half a head shorter than Yardley, but this hardly mattered as he rubbed the stick's tip on one of the waistcoat's brown fleurs-de-lis.

Yardley stood, stunned, and the other gentlemen waited, hanging on Grenville's words.

Grenville stepped back, drew out his handkerchief, and dabbed his nose. "I suggest you change it, Yardley," he said. "Or burn the thing altogether."

With that, he casually turned on his heel and strolled

toward the exit, slipping his handkerchief back into his pocket as he went.

The room was quiet a moment, then, as Grenville disappeared out into the thin rain, the assembled gentlemen exploded into laughter.

Yardley turned angrily on his heel and made for the opposite door, but I stopped him with a heavy hand on his shoulder. He swung to me. "What do *you* want?"

"Miss Simmons," I said. "The woman you called a tart, and English whey." When Yardley focused angry eyes on me, I tightened my grip on his shoulder. "I consider her a very good friend. I advise you have a care what you say about her."

Yardley was nearly my height, and his cheeks reddened as he looked straight at me. News of the outcome of my duel had certainly got around, I saw, reading the blatant fear in his eyes.

I squeezed his shoulder once more, released him, and departed to find Grenville.

WE FOUND LORD PERCY IN A YARD WITH A GROOM WHO held the reins of a gray gelding. Saunders was running his fingers along the horse's side and down to its rear hock, but he straightened quickly when Grenville approached.

Grenville held up his hand. "Peace, Saunders. We wish only for a conversation."

I looked over the horse, a sound beast, in appreciation. "Are you buying or selling?" I asked.

"Buying." Lord Percy's answer was a grunt. "Possibly."

The horse's mane and tail were jet black, a nice contrast to the light gray coat. I patted the gelding's shoulder and stroked his nose, while he observed me with a soft, but lively eye. "Good choice," I said. "A strong mount. Will give you his all when you need it."

"I will consider that." Saunders nodded at the groom. "Please tell Derby I might as well take him."

The groom led the horse away. The gelding had a sprightly walk, and I wished I could buy him myself.

Once we stood alone in the closed yard, Saunders faced us with arms folded, rain glistening on his hat and the shoulders of his coat.

"This is not about Miss Simmons," I said, before Grenville could speak. Grenville shot a glance at me, but I went on. "It is about Leland Derwent."

Saunders's eyes widened, his breath quickening. "Oh, yes? What about him?"

His arrogant expression could not mask his sudden flash of guilt. "Last evening, you were seen speaking with him and Mr. Travers at Brooks's," I said. "After Mr. Travers was overheard saying he wished to find deeper play."

Saunders tried to maintain his indifference. "Deeper play?"

"Travers wanted something more challenging. And then he and Mr. Derwent left with you, apparently. Did you suggest a place?"

Saunders still pretended not to understand, but the stiffening of his shoulders betrayed that he knew exactly what I was talking about. Grenville rarely looked overtly angry; he simply went ice cold. I was surprised the rain falling past him didn't turn to sleet.

Saunders flushed, guilt rising to break through his hauteur. I half-expected him to confess he'd taken Leland and Gareth to the Bull and Hen and then bludgeoned them himself, when he said, "Yes, yes, very well. I took them around the corner, to the Nines. Is this what the fuss is about?"

Grenville's attention riveted to him. "Good Lord. You took Leland Derwent to the *Nines*?"

I wanted to echo him. The Nines was notorious, even among heavy gamblers. The hell lay in Jermyn Street, its facade innocuous, but once down the stairs into its cellars, every kind of game was played by its prestigious, and not-so-prestigious, clientele for hideously large stakes. The ladies who floated about there were high-priced courtesans who would happily take a gentleman's winnings, smiling silken smiles all around.

I had entered the place once, in my poorer days. The courtesans had shown little interest in me once my circumstances were known, and I'd departed when I'd realized the amount I'd need to place even the smallest bet.

I also remembered the thick-necked men who prowled the gaming rooms looking for any signs of cheating or inability to pay. I'd witnessed them seize a young man who'd gazed in despair at his last cards, and haul him up the stairs to toss him into the street.

If Leland had gone to the Nines, and if he or Travers had gotten on the wrong side of the toughs, they could have come by their injuries there, without ever having to go near a molly house.

"A moment," I said. "Let us be clear. You escorted them to the Nines, and then you accompanied them in? What I mean is, are you certain they went inside? You did not simply leave them at the door?"

"No, no, they went downstairs to the game rooms. With me. Travers seemed perfectly happy to be there. Derwent, as you might predict, was not."

"Did you lead them back out again?" I asked.

Saunders blinked. "Pardon? No—I fell in with other acquaintances and quite lost track of Derwent and Travers. I found I had no head for games that night, and I let these acquaintances persuade me elsewhere. What is this all about? Damn it, Grenville, why are you letting him quiz me like this?"

I was vastly irritated with Lord Percy Saunders. The Nines was no place for an innocent like Leland, and if the ruffians who'd kept order there had decided to take him and Mr. Travers outside ...

"Where was Leland when you left?" I asked. "Joining a game? Or trying to persuade Mr. Travers to leave? Did they meet anyone else there?"

"How the devil should I know?" Saunders answered testily. "I told you, I lost sight of them. There was quite a crowd, and someone was scoring well at hazard. The place was in an uproar."

"I see." I wanted to seize him and shake him, not caring that he was the son of a powerful duke. Leaving two cubs like Leland and Travers in a place like the Nines was vastly irresponsible and could have cost Travers his life.

Saunders raised his hands, as though sensing my need for savagery. "Derwent has plenty of money, and Travers, the card sense. I thought it would suit them. They were well when I left them."

"They were not well," I said. "That is the point. They were set upon and robbed, and Travers is dead."

Saunders's face turned as gray as the gelding's coat. "What? Dead, you say?"

"Decidedly so."

"Good Lord." Saunders blinked, the shock on his face genuine, though I thought I detected something more than surprise behind his expression. What, I was not certain.

Saunders took a disjointed breath and let it out, fogging in the cool rain. "The devil you say. I promise you, gentlemen, they were both well when I departed the Nines. You have no reason to admonish me. I could not have foreseen ..."

"You could have," I said in a hard voice. "I suppose you thought it entertaining to lead Leland into such a place. Only disaster could have come from your step. Good day to you, sir."

Saunders began to speak again, protesting, but Grenville cut him off.

"About Miss Simmons," Grenville said. "I am not finished there, old boy. Do keep yourself away, there's a good fellow."

"But—" Saunders scowled in confusion. "You told me not an hour ago that you did not blame me my attentions. And you have Signora Carlotti."

"The newspapers couple my name with Signora Carlotti's, I know," Grenville said. "I cannot help what newspapermen take it into their heads to write about. But Miss Simmons is to be left alone. Do you understand?"

Saunders recovered from his surprise, his anger returning. "I understand you perfectly."

"When the way is clear, I will tell you." Grenville touched his hat, sending a rivulet of water off its brim. "Good day, Saunders."

Saunders bowed stiffly in return, two gentlemen coolly furious with each other. Grenville turned and strolled out of the yard, back through the enclosure, and out to his waiting carriage.

I gave Saunders a polite bow and followed Grenville out.

Brewster wasn't with the coach when I reached it but came tramping from the direction of Piccadilly as Grenville and I got ourselves inside. Brewster swung up to the top to ride in the rain, while we shut it out inside the sumptuous conveyance.

I was puzzling over what I'd thought I'd seen behind Lord Percy's obvious surprise at the news Travers was dead. Disappointment, I thought. Even annoyance. Odd things to come from the announcement of a death.

The thump of Grenville's walking stick to the seat beside him interrupted my musings. "Dear God, Lacey. What the devil is wrong with me? Now I *will* have to run away to Egypt and let London forget about me."

"What are you on about?" I said, out of temper. "Do you mean that last bit with Saunders?"

Grenville balled his fists, stretching his gloves. "I have no idea why I said such a thing. I was fully prepared to step aside, further my acquaintance with Paola Carlotti, and let Marianne do as she pleased. But when I saw Saunders fumble about trying to excuse himself for leading Leland to the slaughter, I decided I'd be damned before I let him anywhere near Marianne. The man is a fool, and she needs someone better than a fool."

"I agree," I said, my anger at him fading. "Will that man be you?"

"How should I know? I have behaved like a boor and a prig all morning. She is likely better off if we all went to the devil," he finished, his face hardening. "I suppose we are making for the Nines now?"

"I would like to question whoever runs the place, and the ruffians there. But no one would be there at this hour, would they?"

Grenville looked pained. "The Nines is open at all hours. Not quite legal, but the magistrates look the other way."

"Then there we shall go," I said.

Grenville tapped on the roof, still disgruntled at himself, gave his coachman the direction, and we rumbled back into St. James's as the rain increased.

CHAPTER 15

$\mathcal{T}$he Nines was discreetly tucked among more ostentatious buildings on Jermyn Street, its plain face unremarkable. The front door opened to a foyer with ivory-colored paneling and a ceiling of lighter white. A polished table with tapered legs and an ebony inlay top stood modestly against the wall, bearing an unlit candelabra and a vase of flowers fresh from the market.

This entrance showed nothing but quiet respectability, and the hall beyond held tranquil silence.

The incongruity was the bull-like man who'd opened the door. He peered down at us with small, glittering eyes in answer to our knock, then at Brewster, hulking behind us, with no less belligerence.

However, he admitted Grenville without question. The Nines was not a club like White's, Boodle's, and others, where membership was granted by very careful selection. The Nines let in anyone who could put their money down and buy the appropriate number of markers used to place bets in the game. Only those who could not pay were barred.

The bull-like man opened one of the doors in the quiet hall to reveal a staircase leading downward. A musty mixture of smoke and perfume, both ladies' and gentlemen's, wafted upward from the room below.

Grenville did not hide his distaste as he led the way down. I came behind, leaning on my stick and trying to ignore the acrid odors.

Brewster followed directly behind me. I'd tried to order him to wait upstairs when he scrambled down from the carriage to stand at my shoulder at the front door, but he'd have none of it.

"His nibs won't want you going down there alone, Captain, and it's not worth my life to let you." He paused. "Oh, and he wants to see you." To my surprised look, Brewster added, "I nipped off to his home when you were in with the horseflesh. Mr. Denis said for you to come as soon as convenient."

For Denis, *as soon as convenient* meant *immediately*. I did not gasp and hurry away, however. Denis could wait while I saw what was what here.

Gentlemen were already at the tables when we entered the main room. Down here, away from the street, with no windows to let in daylight, the hours of the clock had little meaning.

While the clubs of St. James's could not be breached unless one had the appropriate family connections, the Nines admitted anyone with cash, no matter his background. Here, a trader from Liverpool, who'd grown fat from shipping, could set his bulk next to a duke; an actor born in the gutter could sit next to Lucius Grenville without censure. I recognized a few gentlemen from the circles Grenville and Donata had introduced me to, but most of the men were strangers.

One of the ladies meant to entice gentlemen into immodest play instantly drifted to Grenville, laying a gloved hand on his arm. Grenville, always charming, gave her a smile that promised nothing.

"What games do you play, Captain?" a second butterfly

asked. Her perfume was expensive, her clinging silk gown as much so.

That she knew who I was did not surprise me—everyone knew the captain who had become Grenville's privileged friend. The lady must have been instructed when we'd been seen entering. "I am not the gambler Grenville is," I said truthfully.

The woman betrayed no disappointment in her liquid dark eyes. She was very young for this game, her face unlined and a little bit plump. Her look was practiced, however, and no woman would be allowed to work here without having proven herself an expert at beguilement. "Whist, then?" she suggested in her velvet dark voice. "It is a game of skill, not chance."

"It's a bit of both, actually." I moved away from the gamers to an empty table, exaggerating my limp as I went. "I will rest while Grenville enjoys himself. Perhaps you can keep me company."

The young woman did not want to—no doubt she received a portion of the winnings from those she dragged into games—but she gave me a gracious look as she sat next to me.

"You were here last evening?" I asked. "Perhaps you saw a friend of mine. Mr. Leland Derwent?"

She stilled, her acting so well-done that had I not been watching, I might have missed the uneasiness in her eyes.

I decided to press her. "You must have seen him. Young lad. Very blond hair, as well dressed as Grenville. I imagine he looked a bit out of place."

"I did not notice in particular." The woman's smile returned. "Play was quite exciting last night. I am afraid I was not paying much attention."

She lied smoothly, but it was a lie nonetheless. "I am anxious about him. Mr. Derwent was badly hurt and is near death's door. I would like to find out who did that to him."

My voice hardened as I spoke. Leland was dying, his

family plunged into grief. Here, gamers bent over tables, and ladies like this one washed their hands of another's suffering.

Her gaze lost its softness as she truly looked at me. "What do you mean, near to death's door?"

"Just as I say. Mr. Derwent was hit quite hard, enough to kill him. He is at home now, but we have no idea whether he will recover."

"Oh." The young woman bit her lip. "I had nothing to do with that. I never saw—" She cut off the words and rose swiftly from her chair, gliding off without another word.

The woman moved so elegantly that for a moment, I didn't realize she was running away. By the time she reached a door at the far end of the room, I was on my feet, after her.

Grenville was deep in conversation with a hard-faced man at one of the tables, along with the butterfly who'd attached herself to him. None of them noticed as I moved by.

The door through which the lady exited slammed before I reached it, and when I tried the handle, the door was locked. I rattled the handle in frustration, but the door itself moved under my buffeting, its hinges flimsy.

One hard shove broke the door from the frame, which let me into a narrow hall that ended in a blank wall. The elegance of the rest of the house was gone here—peeling paint and damp floorboards held prominence. I heard staccato, hurried footsteps and followed, keeping a tight hold of my walking stick.

A draft told me a door to the outside had opened. I hastened forward and found a short flight of steps upward to my left. I climbed the stairs and went out another door into a grimy, confined yard.

These yards hidden behind the houses of wealthy neighborhoods could be as rundown as St. Giles slums. Slops left by nightsoil men lent a stench, and rubbish and mud filled the corners.

I spotted the lady making for a narrow gate that led to a

passage behind the houses. I hurried forward, ignoring the strain on my leg, and seized her just as she wrenched the gate open.

She swung to me, fury in her eyes. Gone was the pleasant-voiced butterfly who had cajoled me to game and then condescended to sit with me. Now I faced a harpy, her face blotched with rage, who tried to rake her claws across my face.

"Leave off," she said in East End cant. "They don't pay enough for this. Lemme go!"

We struggled, the young woman strong. She managed to land a single blow across my face. The next moment, a large pair of hands grabbed her wrists and jerked her away, and Brewster slammed her against the wall.

"Stop," I told him, my breath coming fast. "Don't hurt her."

"Nah, don't go soft on her, guv. She's got a knife in her pocket and will slash both of us. Won't you, luv?"

She spat at him. I folded my arms, walking stick dangling. Now that we were in daylight, I could see that the lady's dark hair had a red cast, her true color, I surmised as her eyebrows and lashes were the same. Rain glistened in the ringlets that now straggled across her face and on the silk finery of her dress. The anger in her eyes also showed desperation and hint of true fear.

"If I talk to you, they'll kill me," she said, blinking rapidly until tears wet her eyes.

"Huh," Brewster said, not impressed. "But you don't know what *we'll* do, do ya? Open yon gate, Captain."

I did not know what he had in mind, but I pushed open the gate the young woman had unlatched. Beyond was a passage that ran parallel to Jermyn Street toward St. James's Street, where traffic rumbled by.

The woman didn't fight much as Brewster pulled her down the lane toward the main road. If she expected help to come from the Nines, she did not get it.

When we emerged into St. James's Street, Brewster split

the air with a whistle. Moments later, a coach, one I did not recognize, stopped for us.

"In we go," Brewster said. "You first, Captain, to make sure she don't dash out the other side."

I had no idea who this coach belonged to—if Denis, it would be the least opulent vehicle he owned—and I did not relish climbing into it with my leg now aching from the cold rain and my pursuit of the woman. But curiosity overcame hesitance, and I scrambled up, clenching my teeth against pain.

I settled myself where I could block the lady from hurtling herself out the opposite door, and Brewster lifted her in. He followed her inside the coach so quickly she'd have had no chance of escape. The coach lurched forward and the open door banged shut with the momentum.

Brewster gave no direction to the coachman, but the horses picked up speed and turned us east onto Piccadilly. We were going who-knew-where and moving toward it at a rapid pace.

I at first assumed Brewster was taking us to Denis, but we began heading quite the wrong direction. Any chance of turning north and west to Curzon Street quickly fell behind us.

The lady in the coach had collapsed into the seat, her eyes filled with bright fear. The fight seemed to have gone out of her, but I did not relax my guard, and neither did Brewster.

We rolled through Leicester Square and went north and east, past the roads that led in to Seven Dials, and so on to St. Giles. In a narrow street here, one almost too small to admit the coach, the driver stopped.

Brewster immediately had the door open and was dropping out of the coach, hauling the woman after him. I climbed down, the coach rolling a bit as the horses moved nervously in their traces. I nearly lost my footing and had to slam my stick to the dirty cobbles to keep my balance.

Brewster had already entered one of the crammed houses on the street. I went through the open front door after him, and found myself in a musty hall with a staircase. Brewster was climbing the stairs with the woman, who'd regained her spirit enough to start trying to fight him. Brewster, unbothered by her, pulled her up past the first floor and started toward the second. I followed as quickly as I was able.

The landing at the top of the second flight of stairs had been scrubbed clean. The other two floors were grimy, but not so this one, still damp from whoever had labored to wash it.

Brewster's boots left muddy tracks as he approached the door, which jerked open before he reached it.

"'Ere," a woman's voice rang out. "Watch what you're about, Tommy. I've just done that bit."

"Sorry, love," Brewster answered. "I'm bringing the captain in."

CHAPTER 16

A curse sliced into the hall and then the woman the voice belonged to charged past Brewster as he hauled his hostage inside.

I found myself looking down at a woman of medium height, thin but given to plumpness in arms and hips, her face narrow and lined. Her brown hair, which was peppered with gray, was done up in a loose knot. She gazed up at me with brown eyes that held fire and also strength.

"You should have sent word," she said, not to me, but to Brewster. "I'd have tidied the place." She shook her head. "Never learns, does he? Well, you'd better come in, love."

I was ushered into a sitting room that was low ceilinged and dim but scrupulously clean. The mismatched furniture, some of it cobbled together from scraps, was free of dust, the threadbare upholstery on the old sofa, spotless. A small fire burned in the grate behind gleaming andirons. The sole decorations in the room were pictures cut from ladies' magazines and artfully pinned to the faded wallpaper. The place was worn but homey, clean, and smelled of soap.

Brewster had dragged the courtesan to the sofa to unceremoniously plop her onto it. The woman moved to them and stood over the courtesan, hands on hips. "Who's she, then?" she asked Brewster.

"Ladybird what fleeces at the Nines," Brewster answered. "I thought maybe you'd know her."

The woman leaned down and peered into the young woman's face before pronouncing her verdict. "Nah, never seen her. Who's your mum, girl?"

The young woman gave her a sulky look. "Sally Pryce."

"Ah, Sally." The woman nodded, enlightened. "Old Sal is a mate of mine. You must be the daughter she worries herself to death over."

"Nothing wrong with me," the butterfly said churlishly.

"Can't be right, or my Tommy wouldn't have dragged you home with him."

Brewster leaned against the mantelpiece and tugged off his thick gloves. "She knows something about the murder last night. The captain here starts asking her questions, and off she goes."

The woman questioning the butterfly straightened up and turned to me, where I'd remained, nonplussed, by the front door. "You should sit down, love, and I'll fetch you some coffee. I'm Tommy's missus."

I glanced at Brewster, who shrugged. Mrs. Brewster pointed at the nearest chair as she strode out a door at the far end of the room. Presently we heard the clatter of crockery. I took myself to the chair and eased into it.

I supposed I shouldn't be astonished that Brewster was married. I knew so little about him—the men who worked for Denis remained rather faceless, rarely revealing themselves to be human beings at all, which was likely part of the job. Brewster had grown more talkative with me, but he'd made no mention of his private circumstances. He might have been married several times and had thirteen children tucked away in rooms upstairs for all I knew.

Mrs. Brewster came back in bearing a tray with a coffeepot

and cups on it. She poured, handed me a steaming cup and her husband another. She didn't take one herself and offered nothing to the sullen young woman.

"This here is Bertha Pryce," Mrs. Brewster announced once Brewster and I had our coffee—Brewster's thick with cream and sugar, mine plain and bitter. "Her mum, Sal, was on the game, just like she is, but her mum never tried to help a house cheat money from fancy gentlemen." Mrs. Brewster sent Bertha a disapproving look. "They get a cut there, the butterflies at the Nines, don't they Bertha?"

"Yeah," Bertha said, scowling.

"Is that what happened with Mr. Derwent?" I asked sharply. "Did they try and cheat him?"

"That one was a right fool," Bertha said. "Like a babe in the woods. I tried to stop them ..."

"Don't lie," Mrs. Brewster said without heat. "You helped, like they told you to, for some of the profit. Now, why don't you tell the captain all about it?"

I took a sip of the coffee. It was very good, rich and full. I suspected Denis supplied it, perhaps as part of Brewster's wages.

Bertha picked at the fingers of her gloves, pulling at the stitching. She seemed far more cowed by Mrs. Brewster's admonishments than Brewster's strength. "He was supposed to be easy," Bertha said. "Rich and not knowing a blessed thing. But the bloody lad wouldn't sit down to cards or take up the dice. He kept going on about how he promised his dad and mum he wouldn't wager, not like they do at the Nines, anyway. He'd brought his friend in to prove to him how low the place was, that's what he said."

"And his friend," I broke in. "Was he as reluctant to wager?"

"No, but I could see he wasn't going to do much with the pious blond lad hanging about him." Bertha scowled. "I tried to steer Mr. Derwent to another room, where we could chat by ourselves, but he said he promised his mum not to have anything to do with low women like me either."

"Mr. Derwent would never have said that, not in those words," I protested. Leland never insulted anyone—he saw women like Bertha as downtrodden and deserving of compassion. If anything, he'd have tried to reform her.

"Of course he didn't say that," Bertha went on. "Butter wouldn't melt in his mouth. He was polite as anything, but he wouldn't leave his friend's side. Plastered there, trying to talk him out of tossing down the dice and laying his bets. Mr. Travers won at first, then he lost—a pile of coin, it was. Then Mr. Derwent starts saying how the croupier is cheating, and Mr. Travers shouldn't a' lost all that money. He talks about marching out of there and informing a magistrate he knows. Mr. Travers and some others tried to make him be quiet, but Mr. Derwent was very upset." Bertha drew a breath. "And so the owner, Mr. Forge, says I need to bring him upstairs."

My hand was tight on my cup. "And Leland went to him?"

"Eager to." Bertha looked the slightest bit pleased with herself. "I led him in, with Mr. Travers trying to stop him and urging him to run out the front door. Mr. Forge apologized for the misunderstanding, and offered to return Mr. Travers's money. Very prettily he said it too, I thought. But Mr. Derwent, he'd have none of it. He kept saying how the Nines was a bad place, and he was going to bring his father to it, *and* the magistrates, to shut it down. Well, Mr. Forge couldn't be having that, could he? He told his men to take Mr. Derwent and Mr. Travers out into the yard and teach 'em a lesson. And promise more if they went to a magistrate." Bertha wiped her lips with her fingers, a nervous gesture. "But I swear to you, I never thought they'd hurt 'em bad. They were supposed to scare 'em a little, that's all. Nothing Mr. Forge hasn't done before. Works a charm."

That could explain everything. I pictured the scene, Leland

and Travers struggling, both alarmed, as they were strong-armed into the dirty yard behind the house.

Perhaps the ruffians had enjoyed the beating too much and hadn't stopped in time. Mr. Forge could have instructed them to take the two far away, to someplace like Seven Dials, where crime was rampant, so the murder wouldn't be traced back to the Nines. Perhaps, knowing that the two were lovers, and molly houses were nearby, they'd half undressed them to give the idea they'd been bludgeoned while in the act. Easy to picture street toughs doing that.

But why steal Leland's clothes? Or had that been done by another? And what did Mr. Mackay have to do with any of this?

"Did they have another friend with them?" I asked Bertha. "One with black hair, a little older? Name of Mackay."

Bertha gave me a blank stare. "No. It were the two of them, no one else. They came in with another bloke, an aristo, but he soon left them alone, like he wanted nothing to do with them. He didn't bother helping out when Mr. Forge sent for them."

I believed she told the truth. Lord Percy had likely washed his hands of Leland and Travers as soon as Leland began crusading.

"Where did Mr. Forge's men take them afterward?" I asked.

"I dunno, do I? I didn't go out into the yard with them. But Mr. Forge's men didn't look worried or anything when they came back in, like they'd accidentally killed the two gents. No blood on them, or anything."

I wondered how she could remember so specifically if she hadn't followed them to the yard. "How long were the men outside?"

Bertha blinked, again perplexed by the question. "Quarter of an hour, maybe. Long enough to thrash 'em a little."

Not enough time to trundle two young men across London

and back, although Forge could have assigned other lackeys to
do that.

"If that was all that happened," I said after a casual sip of
coffee, giving Bertha time to grow nervous again. "Why did
you try to run away when I talked to you?"

She wet her lips. "Well, Mr. Forge would have my hide if I
told you there was cheating going on in his rooms, wouldn't
he?"

"But you *have* told me," I pointed out.

"I know. But I'm afraid of *them*." Bertha glanced at Mr.
Brewster and his wife, then gave me a look of appeal. "You
won't tell on me, will ya? You won't tell Mr. Forge nothing? I
need that place, and he don't turn a hair about hitting a
woman."

"Then you should not return there," I began sternly, but
Mrs. Brewster cut off my words.

"You don't need 'im," she said. "Go home, Bertha. You
mum wants to see you."

Bertha gave her a scornful look. "She's got six others. I'd
just be drudging to look after them, wouldn't I?"

I imagined she was correct. I recognized that Bertha was a
liar who would fleece a mark in a trice, but I couldn't condemn
her too much for choosing to work for Mr. Forge. Likely she
got more money from him than she would laboring in a factory,
and would be safer at the Nines than walking the streets. Life
in London was easy only for a few.

Brewster, who'd listened without a word, drained his cup
and pushed himself up from where he leaned on the fireplace.
"Give her tea or something, love, and shove her back out the
door. I've got to take the captain to his nibs."

Mrs. Brewster nodded at her husband, not moving, her
position blocking Bertha's way out. Bertha did not seem
inclined to rush away and escape, however. She sat slumped on
the sofa, her arms folded. Her sultry softness was gone, and
she looked young, sullen, and unhappy.

In contrast, Mrs. Brewster turned to me with a sunny smile on her plain face. "Nice to have met you, Captain. You keep warm now, and watch your game leg. It's turning into a raw sort of day."

———

"SHE'S A GOOD CREATURE, IS MY WIFE," BREWSTER SAID once we were settled in the coach again. Grenville must be wondering wildly where I'd disappeared to, but I'd have to wait to find him again after I discovered what Denis wished to discuss with me.

"I know what you're wanting to know, Captain," Brewster went on. "My Em used to be on the game herself, but didn't mind giving it up for a softer life."

Which she had with Brewster. Mr. Denis paid his employees well. "How did you meet her?" I asked.

Brewster gave a short laugh. "On the game. Where'd ya think? She was in a house, I went in for the night, and we took a fancy to each other. I had to pay the madam to let her go, and then we married. Right and proper, with a parson, and all."

"Congratulations to you," I said sincerely. "Have you been married long?"

"Ten years. We never had no young 'uns, if that's what you'll be asking next, but maybe it's better. My sort of life would be hard on 'em."

Working for Denis was dangerous, and Brewster was part of the danger. The fact that he understood that said much about him. My estimation of Brewster's character had changed today.

I'd assumed Denis would meet me in Curzon Street, as usual, but Brewster took me to the house in which I'd sat with Leland the night before.

By daylight, the place was not as sinister, I saw as we went inside. The undraped windows showed me that the paneled walls were white, the furniture, what little there was of it, whole and well crafted. No holes in upholstery, no nicks on tables.

Brewster led me up the stairs to a front sitting room, where James Denis waited for me.

He stood near a window looking out, but not so close that anyone from the street, or even the nearby houses, would see him. He had one other pugilist in the room with him, but that was all. Denis, who usually surrounded himself with guards, was almost alone.

"I sent word to Mr. Grenville that I had detained you," Denis said without turning around. "I did not need him rushing to the nearest magistrate to report you missing. I wanted to speak to you. *Right away.*" He at last turned his head and looked, not at me, but at Brewster.

Brewster paled slightly. "The captain was questioning one of the ladybirds at the Nines. I thought my Em would loosen her tongue, is all. And she did."

Denis looked him over and gave him a nod. Brewster relaxed again, and Denis turned his attention to me.

"Captain, I brought you here to ask you to assist me." He held up a hand, his old eyes in his young face intent upon me. "Do not worry that it will compromise your principles or break the law. In fact, you might even approve."

CHAPTER 17

*D*enis did not invite me to sit down, but I did anyway. My leg was hurting, and the Greek-style divan looked comfortable. I did not bother to ask Denis what he wanted me to do. His ideas of staying on the correct side of the law and mine were never the same.

"You visited the Nines," he said in his cool way as I rubbed my bad knee. "What did you make of it?"

"I made very little of it, to be honest," I said. I gave the back of my knee a last knead and stretched the leg out in front of me. "Respectable front hall upstairs, den of iniquity below. The ladies entice players to bet recklessly while the blacklegs fleece the marks. Toughs standing by to take anyone out who makes a fuss, which they did with Leland."

Denis gave me nod. While never moving from his spot in the barebones room, he commanded it. "The running of the Nines is inefficient. It is a house with potential to bring in plenty of money, but they squander their opportunities by blatant cheating. They risk not only being shut down but offending their wealthiest clients."

"But wealthy gentlemen still go there," I pointed out, thinking of Lord Percy.

"Yes, but not often twice. Mr. Grenville has made the place unfashionable with his disapproval."

He fell silent. I waited, but he was no more forthcoming.

"Was that all you wanted?" I asked. "My opinion of the Nines? If so, I would like to return to Grosvenor Square and look in on young Mr. Derwent. I put it to you that the Derwents need more help than you do at this moment."

Denis did not change expression. "I sent the best surgeon in London to see to him last night and lent you this house. If necessary, I will provide more care to ensure that Mr. Derwent recovers his health, and that Mr. Travers is given a decent burial."

His tone was firm. I had no reason to argue with him, except that I always had the compulsion to contradict him. "Mr. Travers's family will bury him."

"They are threadbare poor. The second Mrs. Travers presents a picture of respectability, but the truth is that her husband is nearly always drunk, and the family is ever in danger of creditors. I will settle the account for Mr. Travers's funeral myself."

I remembered Mrs. Travers stiffly proclaiming her husband was in bed and would not rise. Had he been too inebriated to come down and receive me? Or perhaps not in the house at all but at a nearby taproom?

"You know much about them," I said.

"I make it my business to know. What I am coming around to telling you, Captain, is that I wish the Nines to close."

I raised my brows. "You do? Why? Because it is a criminal enterprise you do not control?"

Denis gave me a look that was almost amused. "Precisely. I own many interests in the area, but the Nines eludes me. I would like you to shed bad light on the place. Spread the tales to the right people. Mr. Derwent has been badly hurt, Mr. Travers killed. The Nines has played a part in that. This should be enough to gain the attentions of the magistrates and reformers, including Sir Gideon. My voice, in this case, would have little weight, but yours would speak volumes. All are aware of your zeal about disreputable places. Remember the Glass House."

An establishment in the East End I'd had a hand in closing. I felt the need, however, to point out flaws in his plan. "I have not established that Mr. Derwent and Mr. Travers were badly hurt at the Nines," I said. "Bertha—one of the butterflies—says not."

"And you believed her?"

"Not necessarily. She is the sort who would say anything to keep the blame from herself. I am certain Leland and Gareth were roughed up at the Nines, but the mortal wounds came later."

"I am not interested in precision in this matter." Denis made a motion with the flat of his hand, as though wiping away my arguments. "It will be enough that the Nines is implicated. I wish its doors to be closed by the end of the week."

"And then?" I gave him a penetrating look. "You will open them again?"

"Probably." He said nothing more than that. I imagined that when Denis ran the Nines, wealthy gentlemen of Mayfair would still be turning over all their money but this time to him.

I could not yet give in. "If the ruffians at the Nines are arrested and convicted for the murder of Gareth Travers and bodily harm to Leland, the real culprit gets away. I do not want that to happen."

Denis made the slightest shrug. "Whoever did the crime is used to battering his victims. He will no doubt be caught for a similar occurrence."

"The Derwents deserve the truth," I said stubbornly.

Denis gazed at me for a long time. "It is you who seek the truth, Captain. You feel responsible, but that is foolish."

I thought back to my conversation with Gareth the afternoon before the terrible deed had happened. I'd been adamant about extricating myself from the affair and bidding him and Leland to have nothing to do with me. I'd told Gareth to make up his differences with Leland, to be friends again. They'd met up that evening and gone out, perhaps to celebrate being together once more.

If I'd left them alone, hadn't tried to play peacemaker, only for the selfish reason of keeping them far from my person, perhaps they'd be whole and well now.

I did not bother to ask Denis how he knew of my guilt. Brewster had likely reported my meetings with Gareth, and even what Gareth and I had discussed.

"I have regrets," I said. "And I do not wish to disappoint a family who befriended me when I knew few in London."

"They are kind people," Denis surprised me by saying. "I do not know many who act without a selfish motive, but members of the Derwent family are the exception. I can understand your protectiveness toward them. But we cannot protect everyone from the world. It is impossible."

His words were blunt but wise. "That does not mean I sit back and do nothing," I said. "The Derwents shall have the truth."

"As you wish, but you will assist me in closing the Nines. Tell Sir Gideon and his band of reformers that Leland came to grief at that hell, and I will lend you help to find the real villain."

"If I deliver the men from the Nines to the magistrates," I said, "will they listen when I hand them another set of villains who actually did the crime?"

"They will if the evidence is strong enough. If you wish to appease yourself, Forge, who runs the Nines, is not innocent. He rigs his games, he assaults those who threaten to bring him to court, and he more or less runs a bawdy house. Plenty of reasons to shut him down."

I wondered who owned the Nines. Forge himself? Or perhaps it was owned by Denis's competitor, a woman who called herself Lady Jane. She and Denis had a long-standing rivalry.

"What sort of help are you lending me?" I asked. "In return for railing about the Nines?"

Denis indicated Brewster with a nod of his head. "Mr. Brewster can be trusted, and he knows much about the London underworld. He will assist you in anything you need."

Brewster, who'd remained stoically by the door, indicated neither pleasure nor dismay at this announcement.

"I have plenty of connections of my own," I said. I knew a magistrate, Sir Montague Harris, who was always keen to catch villains, plus a man of the River police I trusted. "Mr. Brewster does not need to bother."

"Your 'connections,' as you call them, do not know the people I do, or Mr. Brewster does," Denis said. "Brewster will be assigned to you until you are satisfied that justice has been done. But first, you will make a report about the Nines. I want everyone out of that house by the end of the week."

I took my time considering. I could tell Denis to hell with his offer and continue investigating on my own, but it was true that Denis could discover things I could not, and that Brewster could go among villains and come out unscathed. I doubted any denizen of the East End or rookeries around Seven Dials would like to go up against Brewster. Also, I would be happy to see a place like the Nines close, and Denis knew it.

I'd tried since I'd met him to oppose Denis, and yet, I seemed to end up helping him a great deal. He knew how to play me, how to put his finger directly upon my weaknesses.

"I will tell Sir Gideon and Sir Montague Harris what I believe happened at the Nines," I said at last. "What about the Bull and Hen? Would you like that closed too?"

Denis lifted his brows. "The house where gentlemen go to bed other gentlemen? I have no reason to see it shut down. In fact, if its clientele were arrested, I might feel a pinch. You would be astonished at the names to be found there."

Gentlemen in his pocket, I imagined. Denis owned MPs and magistrates—I wondered whether knowing they went to the Bull and Hen was part of his net around them.

"I would like to find out if Leland and Gareth ended up there last night," I said. "I imagine you have spies there, if you know so much about its clientele."

Denis only watched me. "If I can discover the information without putting those who work for me in jeopardy, you will have it. If there is too much risk of exposure, however, I cannot ask it."

I knew I had no say in the matter. Denis would not do a damn thing he did not want to. "I suppose I must be content with that."

Denis made no sign that he was pleased with my capitulation. He straightened his gloves. "Then I will bid you good day. Brewster has the key to this house, which you may use as you need it."

Without further word, he walked out of the room, lifting his hat from one of the tables as he went. The lackey he'd brought, who'd not said one word since we'd arrived, followed him closely out.

"Well, sir," Brewster said once we were alone. "Best be getting on, hadn't we?"

I picked up my own hat where I'd dropped it to a chair. "Mr. Denis never consulted you in this, Brewster. If you have no wish to assist me, I will not compel you."

Brewster shrugged. "I work for Mr. Denis, don't I? He gives me a job, I do it. I'd like to finish this one soon, though, if you don't mind me saying so. I've promised the wife a trip to the seaside, when Mr. Denis can spare me."

IN SPITE OF BREWSTER WANTING TO RUN UP AND DOWN London to lay my hands on the villains at once, I preferred to return home. It was after noon, I needed to reassure my friends and family that I was well, and I wanted to confer with Grenville.

The plain coach, which Brewster explained did belong to Mr. Denis, used when he wanted no one to realize he was out and about, took us to Mayfair.

My wife's house was one in which Brewster would concede to wait in the kitchens, and I went up to our private parlor alone. Donata was out of bed and dressed, reclining in her favorite place on the divan, and Grenville was with her, seated in an elegant chair.

When I entered, Donata looked up with relief in her eyes, which she quickly masked. Grenville's reaction so closely matched hers that for a moment, I wanted to laugh.

"We feared the rough men of the Nines had spirited you away, old fellow," Grenville said, rising to greet me. "A message from one of Denis's chaps that you were being looked after did not relieve me much."

Donata sank back, the black and white day gown she wore flowing to the cushions beside her, which she patted. "Do sit down, Gabriel. Barnstable, bring the captain a large quantity of coffee and those cakes he likes so well. I doubt he's given a thought to a meal." When Barnstable departed, Donata spread her arm across the back of the divan. "Gabriel, tell us *everything*."

These were the two people in my life I'd learned to keep nothing from. I sat next to Donata, the fold of her skirt now over my leg. I talked, telling them what had happened since I'd followed Bertha from the card room of the Nines.

Donata's gaze rested upon me when I finished. "And will you?" she asked. "Shut down the Nines for Mr. Denis?"

I shrugged. "It is a bad place."

"You have no guarantee he will not make it a worse one," Donata said. "Whatever shall you do, Gabriel?" She was not admonishing me; she was stating a fact.

"My choice is not much of a choice," I admitted. "Do I ignore the place, and have it continue cheating its customers and beating them when they complain? Or let Denis run it?"

Grenville tapped his fingertips together. "You could report to the magistrates that Denis means to have it. Montague Harris might be able to stop the sale."

"Possibly. Possibly not. He might also believe the house is better off under Denis's control."

"Or," Grenville said delicately. "You could report the matter to Mr. Spendlove."

Spendlove yearned to stop Denis and his empire by any means necessary. Of course, he'd be sure to drag me into the matter right alongside Denis. "I dislike being caught between the two men," I said, my temper stirring. "Why they cannot leave me in peace is unfathomable."

"You are a loose cannon, my friend," Grenville said. "When you charge about, there is no telling exactly what will happen."

I did not know whether to be indignant or to laugh. "Denis has called me that before. Is that your opinion as well?"

Grenville raised his hands in surrender. "A mere observation to explain their interest in you. I must admit that there is no telling what will happen around you. It is why I befriended you in the first place."

Grenville had made no bones about telling me in the early days of our friendship that he had sought my acquaintance because he found me refreshingly interesting. I'd also foiled a burglary at his house, which had won me his respect and gratitude.

"This discussion is bringing me no closer to a decision," I said. "But I think it is clear. I will report what I've learned to Sir Gideon and Sir Montague, and no doubt they will make things happen. Sir Gideon will want to know exactly what happened to his son."

"Will you tell him all of it?" Grenville asked.

Donata knew what we meant. I had told her, as we'd lain twined together, how I'd found Leland and Travers.

"I swore to Leland I would keep his secret," I said with a sigh.

"I would not be surprised if Sir Gideon already suspected the lay of the land with his son," Donata said. "But I do not believe knowing exactly how you found them would be of any comfort to him."

"Did you know?" I asked her. "When I was suggesting him as a potential husband for Gabriella, did you know what an idiot I was?"

Donata leaned to fetch a cigarillo from a gilded box on the table beside her. "I had suspected Gareth and Leland of having a passion for each other, as have most of the *ton*. This sometimes happens with young men thrown very close together in their lives. They might grow out of it as they make their way in the world, but even if they do not, their proclivities should not prevent them making a good marriage. An astonishing number of married gentlemen take lovers, male or female, sometimes both. My objections to Leland were purely based on his character, and I have not changed my mind." Donata closed the cigarillo box, rolled the dark stick between her fingers, and gave me a fond look. "I forget that you are unfashionable enough to consider possible infidelity as a bar to marriage."

"And we like you for it," Grenville said quickly. "But it makes you rather singular in our set."

The discussion discomfited me. "I am sorry to hear I am so unique. Marriage vows should mean something." Especially those involving my daughter, I added silently.

"Again, we like you for it," Grenville said. "My own father forgot his vows ten minutes after the ceremony. He could not keep his trousers buttoned for half a day, as I heard it. When I meet a lady I fancy, I have to quiz her about her antecedents before I consider any sort of liaison, for fear my father sired her."

Donata chuckled appreciatively. Her own husband had been unfaithful to the point of parading his mistresses through the house under Donata's nose.

"I believe I will keep my silence about Leland to his father," I said. "For now. What about you, Grenville? Were you able to pry any more information from those at the Nines? And what about this man, Mackay? Has anyone heard of him?"

$\mathcal{N}$ot a thing about Mackay," Grenville said, shaking his head. He lifted a delicate teacup that was nearly lost in his hand, but he held it with the carefulness of a gentleman used to handing fragile things. "As for Percy Saunders, when Leland started making a fuss in the Nines, Saunders took himself to the far corner of the room, not wanting anyone to remember they'd come in together."

"Bloody coward," I muttered.

"Quite," Donata said crisply. "Percy Saunders never had much to recommend him. Too fond of pushing the blame for things onto others."

Barnstable broke our discussion at that moment by bringing in steaming coffee for me and a large platter nearly covered with teacakes. I thanked him politely, though I wasn't hungry, and the coffee Brewster's wife had given me had been excellent. Barnstable liked to coddle me, and I'd learned that he grew hurt if I objected. He presented me with the tray and then bowed and took his leave.

"We are not much further forward," I said, lifting a currant-laden cake onto a plate with silver tongs. I knew the staff would not be happy if I didn't eat some of the spread. "We must account for what happened after Leland and Travers left the Nines. So far, Leland remembers nothing, and there is no way to know whether he will regain the memories or not."

"Denis has a man inside the Bull and Hen, you say?" Grenville also took a cake, handling the tongs with an air of long practice. "What tales that fellow must tell."

I had no doubt that Denis used the information to tighten his hold upon many a man of power. "Denis indicated that he will not have his contact asking questions if he feels it will be too great a risk to him. We might have to discover what happened ourselves, after all."

"As we discussed, it is a bad idea if either of us go inside," Grenville began. "However, I—"

"I could go," Donata said.

Grenville broke off, his mouth still open. Both of us stared at her as she took a pull of her cigarillo, its end crackling quietly as it glowed orange-red.

"I could dress as a young man." Smoke weaved around Donata as she spoke. "Go in, play cards, drop Leland's name, listen to the response."

"No!" Grenville and I said at the same time.

Grenville recovered first. "Dear lady, it would be far too dangerous, no matter how good your disguise. They will not know you and consider you fresh blood. You would never be left in peace."

Grenville articulated better than I did when I was in a fury, but now I let my words fly. "It is a damn fool idea, Donata. They would take you aside and have at you, without bothering to discover whether you were male first. In the dark, drunk, they might not realize their mistake until too late. I forbid it."

Anger flared in Donata's eyes at the word *forbid*. "If you would let me continue, gentlemen, I said it in jest." She flicked ashes into a porcelain bowl with an irritated jerk of her fingers. "I did such a thing not long after I was first married—a dear friend and I dressed up as men and went to a hell. It was one of the most entertaining nights of my life. Not one gentleman there suspected us—they were far too engrossed in play and the sort of women who did float about there. We emerged unscathed."

The story did nothing to calm me, and I was not convinced Donata had spoken in jest at first. She'd looked a bit too eager. My wife had a lively curiosity and a bold courage that made my blood run cold.

"Very brave of you," Grenville said, his neutral voice what we needed to smooth over the moment. "I have a better idea for infiltration—as I said, I will search among my acquaintances I know to be of Leland's mind, and try to find one who knows a bit about the place. One might have been there that night, or knows someone who was."

"Questioning someone who works at the Bull and Hen would be preferable," I said. "A barman, the man who admits the clientele … someone of that nature."

"Same problem, my dear Lacey," Grenville broke in. "Who do we send to question them? Or do we waylay the workers on their way home?"

"Which I will quickly point out would be as dangerous for you," Donata said, anger sharp. "I am happy Mr. Denis sends someone about after you. Make use of Mr. Brewster and send him."

"Denis might not let him," I said. "If he doesn't want anyone poking around there. I was thinking of another resource we have at our disposal. Marianne."

Grenville froze in the act of lifting a teacake to his mouth, his cheeks staining red. "If you mean sending her in, I will not let you. Now *I* forbid it."

"Of course not," I said impatiently. "But through the theatre, she is acquainted with many people in all walks of life. Perhaps one who knows their way around molly houses will agree to help us. If we have to pay them, so be it."

Grenville looked slightly appeased, but still angry. "If she will help. It is not a bad idea, I will grant."

The discussion had left the three of us uncomfortable, Donata going coldly silent as she continued to smoke. Grenville, the master of social niceties rose and bid us a graceful farewell, saying he had many appointments to take up the rest of his day.

I walked with him to the door of the sitting room, but he insisted on going downstairs himself. I closed the door behind him and turned to face my wife's silence.

Donata was furious with me. I had never before this day asserted my husbandly authority over her, but she had goaded me into fear, which I had let emerge as anger.

When I had done so with my first wife, Carlotta, she'd cringed and fled me. Donata only watched me with flint-hard eyes.

"I had thought to call upon the Derwents," she said in her cool voice. "To see if they need anything and offer what comfort I can. Shall you accompany me?"

"Donata," I began.

She stabbed out the cigarillo in the porcelain bowl. "Please, do not try to be appeasing, Gabriel. It does not suit you. Let us forget, and continue."

Her stiff manner told me she would not forget for a very long time. "I can apologize for my abruptness, and my rudeness," I said, "but not my choice. It was a foolish thing to suggest. There is a difference between being brave and being bloody reckless."

"A difference I have not noticed *you* mastering." Donata unfolded herself from the divan, every inch an elegant lady. "Excuse me, but I must ready myself for our call. Unless you have an objection?"

She glided toward the door that led to her dressing room even as she spoke. She glanced back at me, and I made her a formal bow. "By all means," I said. "I will await you below."

"Excellent." Donata returned my bow with a nod and continued into her dressing room.

We were icy and polite. *Everything a gentleman wishes in a marriage*, I thought, as the dressing room door closed with a decided *click*.

"LADY DERWENT IS VERY ILL TODAY," THE DERWENT footman told us as he let us inside. The young man's face was wan, and his eyes held worry. "They are not at home to anybody, but Sir Gideon said *you* should be admitted, sir and your ladyship. He would like to speak to you, Captain, if you will follow me."

Donata broke away from us, saying she'd go up to Lady Derwent. She'd been cool as frost as we'd ridden the short way up South Audley Street to Grosvenor Square, but not one word of admonition had left her lips. I remained out of temper, and we'd traveled in silence.

I followed the footman to a study on the second floor, where Sir Gideon waited. The lad ushered me in and left us, Sir Gideon struggling up from his desk as I walked inside.

The man looked wretched. His eyes were puffy and red-rimmed, his white hair a mess, as though he'd been repeatedly tearing at it. His clothes were rumpled, his face too pale, unshaven bristles on his jaw.

"Captain Lacey," Sir Gideon said sorrowfully, reaching a shaking hand for mine. "I am so glad to see you. What on earth will become of me if I lose my wife and son in the space of a day?"

"Lose them?" I asked in alarm. "Is it that certain?"

Sir Gideon waved his hands in front of his face. "No, no, forgive me. I am … not myself."

I grasped his elbow, steadying him. "Has Leland taken a turn?"

"No, no. He is resting, thank God. But he is so sorely hurt, Captain—he lapses in and out of a stupor, and he is in such pain when he wakes. The doctor feeds him laudanum, which Leland doesn't want to take. He wakes up asking for Mr. Travers, not remembering, and I have to tell him, over and over again ..."

"Sit down."

I guided the distraught man to the room's one sofa and settled him onto it. Sir Gideon professed to abstain from spirits, but I set the flask of brandy I carried with me to his lips and poured the liquid into his mouth.

Sir Gideon coughed and protested, but finally he swallowed and collapsed against the cushions. "Oh, my dear fellow, what must you think of me? I have missed every appointment today, but I fear I will never have the wherewithal to leave this house again."

He wanted to weep, I could see, but no tears came. He must not have much left to cry. I lifted the flask and made him swallow another sip.

Sir Gideon coughed as it went down, and he brought out his handkerchief. "I remember now why I gave up spirits," he said, attempting a weak laugh.

"I will tell Grenville you made a face at his best brandy. He will tease you something awful when next he sees you."

Sir Gideon coughed again, handkerchief at his lips. "I apologize, Captain. I am not the best company today, I am afraid. My wife ..."

"I know. Donata has gone to her. She is, believe it or not, a rather good nurse. She brooks no nonsense."

Sir Gideon gave me a watery smile. "And I am a terrible one. My own dear wife sent me out of the room."

"There, you see? She is stronger than you think."

"I would like to believe you." Sir Gideon laid a shaking hand on my arm. "But I am not a fool. I've known for years now that I must prepare for the worst, but I am finding the worst bloody difficult."

I had never known Sir Gideon to use strong language, which only told me how upset he was. I tried to reassure him. "Donata will look after Lady Derwent, and Leland is amazingly resilient. He will be well, a sturdy prop for you for years to come."

I spoke with confidence, but I knew that head wounds were tricky things. Leland might spring up in the morning, restored, or lapse into unconsciousness until he died.

"I must ask you about Mr. Travers," I said, sitting beside Sir Gideon and restoring the top to the flask. "What have you done regarding him?"

Turning to practical matters seemed to pull Sir Gideon from his stupor. "I sent him to his family this morning. They will hold the funeral tomorrow. The second Mrs. Travers wrote me of it." He shook his head. "She is a troubled woman."

I let out a short laugh. "I've met her, sir. If she has trouble, she will weather it, and possibly beat it to death for bothering her."

Sir Gideon allowed himself a look of quiet amusement. "She is not the warmest of women, no. I never discovered exactly why she agreed to marry Gareth's father. Gareth was not fond of her. Nor she of us."

Indeed, she'd been the first person I'd ever met who did not speak admiringly of the Derwents. Even those who thought them a pack of fools had at least grudging respect for the good Sir Gideon had done for the poor of the nation. James Denis himself pronounced them incorruptible.

"She did seem very angry at you," I said.

Sir Gideon shrugged. "She has always resented the fact that Gareth found more of a home here with us than with his own father. But his father, unfortunately, is too fond of the bottle. I have tried to amend that, many times, but with no success."

"It is not an easy thing to make a man give up drink," I said. My father had been a dedicated drinker, and while I did not linger in my cups as he had, I could not fathom going a day without a glass of wine, ale, or brandy.

"Quite so. I have made it clear, since the day Leland begged me to let Gareth spend his holidays with us when they were first at school, that Gareth would always be welcome in my home. Leland had never had a friend before—he was a shy boy, and I worried very much for him when we sent him off to school. I was happy he'd found a kindred spirit. It became a habit—Gareth staying here in London or in the country with us during the holidays. Kept on all through school and university, and even when they became young men out in the world. Gareth had planned to take a profession in the law, but Leland convinced him to work for me instead of training to be a solic- itor or barrister. I even paid Mr. Travers a small salary, since he could expect nothing from his father. We never spoke of it." Sir Gideon gave me a soft smile. "A gentleman does not openly work for pay, does he? But Gareth needed something to live on. It was our little secret."

A salary would explain how Gareth could live well without apparent means, although I continued to suspect that Leland out and out paid for Gareth's wardrobe. Such tailoring was costly, as I was well aware.

"What exactly did Gareth do for you?" I asked, curious.

"Oh, various things." Sir Gideon scrunched up his brow as though striving to remember. "He would write reports for committees on situations that needed attention. He believed himself better at speaking to certain people, such as abbesses of the low houses, than I was. And he was right. He had a knack for soothing tempers and understanding the fallen as I never could. Perhaps it was his upbringing—clergymen see so many of the lowest, who are looking for forgiveness, or at least a hot meal, bless them."

I had not known any of this. Gareth had never spoken of

helping the downtrodden with Sir Gideon, and neither Sir Gideon nor Leland had mentioned it either. But some men were embarrassed by philanthropy, or perhaps Gareth had wanted to be seen as a man of leisure, keeping his charitable works anonymous.

"What had he been looking into of late?" I asked.

"I ..." Sir Gideon again frowned and broke off. "I will have to examine my notes. I'm afraid I do not remember, and it scarce matters at the moment."

"It might matter," I said. "If Gareth had been threatening to tell you about a house of ill-repute or a gaming hell, perhaps that person did not want him to complete his report."

Sir Gideon's eyes widened. "No, no. Gareth and Leland were the victims of robbers, struck down by them. Mr. Grenville told me so."

"So it would appear," I said.

I wanted to tell him that I was unhappy with the simple explanation, which left too many questions unanswered, but I stilled my tongue. If I proved that Gareth had been killed while investigating something for Sir Gideon, Sir Gideon would never forgive himself. The man had enough to worry about with his son and his wife that I could not pour more troubles upon him at the moment. Time enough to prepare him if this speculation proved true.

"Do you think I could look in on Leland?" I asked.

Sir Gideon wiped his eyes, which had at last grown wet, and gave me a nod. "I warn you that he might not wake. Or know you if he does."

I did not like the sound of that. "What does your physician say?"

"He tells us that we must wait and see. Change the dressing on Leland's wound, give him laudanum to take away the pain —that is all we can do."

I did not trust doctors one whit, and had no reason to trust this one, though Sir Gideon could afford the most prestigious in London. Doctors refused to get their hands dirty by touching a patient, and often gave their diagnoses from across the room. Grenville's opinion about the tragic death of Princess Charlotte this past November was that her physicians had killed her, and I shared it.

I rose. "Do you mind if I ask a fellow to come in? A surgeon, not a doctor. The one who treated Leland last night, in fact."

Sir Gideon looked bewildered, but he climbed to his feet with me. "Certainly, if you think it will help."

"I do." I thought of the emotionless man who'd competently dressed Leland's head wound in Denis's empty house. I hadn't made friends with him, but he was likely the reason Leland was alive at all. "And do you mind if I look at any notes Gareth had given you? It might help me understand his last movements—perhaps to learn why he and Leland were near Seven Dials at all."

Sir Gideon did not look as though he shared my optimism, but he said, "Of course."

"You ought to take a sip of laudanum yourself," I advised. "You will not help your wife and son if you faint from exhaustion."

Sir Gideon nodded, but in a vague way. "I will hunt up the notes," he said, turning to his desk. "If Leland wakes, please give him my love."

His voice broke. I did the best thing I could for him—left him alone so he could weep in private.

SINCE BREWSTER HAD BEEN MADE AVAILABLE FOR MY USE, I sent him for the surgeon who'd attended Leland. Brewster did not want to leave me, but he put on his hat and trudged out into the rain, though not before he let me know what he thought.

"I'm no errand boy," he growled.

"Send a message to Denis, then," I said, uncaring. "I want the surgeon here to make sure Leland is healing as he should."

Brewster gave me a disparaging look but left the house.

I remembered how Brewster had, when he'd helped demolish my house in Norfolk, encouraged me to sell obviously stolen goods we'd found, and had thought me a fool when I refused. Not a man easily tamed. I wondered how Denis had done it.

CHAPTER 19

I returned to Leland's bedchamber, knocked softly, and walked inside when I heard a woman's voice telling me to enter.

Leland's bed was piled high with blankets. His head was turned on the pillow, the bandages all but obscuring his face, and he was asleep, his breathing labored.

Mrs. Danbury sat in a chair next to the bed. Her cheeks burned red when she saw it was me. "He is not well," she said, almost churlishly. "As you can see."

I bowed and close the door behind me. "I beg your pardon. I came only to give him my good wishes, even if he can't hear me."

"He needs to rest," she said, her tones still abrupt.

I pulled an armless chair near the bed, and seated myself, uninvited. Mrs. Danbury watched me, her gray eyes, once full of good humor, now hard with anger and sorrow.

"Will you tell me why you are so unhappy with me?" I asked. "Please."

Mrs. Danbury watched me for a time, as though debating whether to grant my request. She leaned toward me, the fabric of her gown rustling, and spoke in a near-whisper that held fury. "You hurt him, Captain. You pushed him away. He told me. I am the only one in this house he can speak to of such matters. He was crushed."

I regarded her in surprise. "I do regret that he was hurt by my response," I said, speaking quietly. "But what would you have had me do, madam? Seduce him? I knew his true feelings lay with Mr. Travers. And, I am married, with no interest in taking another to my bed, of either sex."

"Of course I did not expect you to become his lover," Mrs. Danbury snapped, sotto voce. "But you might have treated him more gently. He told me you looked upon him in vast disgust."

"Shock, more like. I had no idea of his feelings."

"No?"

"No."

We faced each other, close, our voices softer than Leland's breathing.

"All I know," Catherine said after a time, "is that he was quite devastated, and of course embarrassed. Convinced you would cut him entirely."

"He was wrong." I glanced at the bed, where Leland looked too thin and pale against the dark covers. The blue of his veins threaded through his hand and cheek. "It was not aversion, but complete astonishment. I hardly consider myself the stuff of romance to other gentlemen."

Her eyes glinted. "I have heard otherwise from one or two. I will not worry you with their names. Gentlemen tend to speak too frankly in my presence."

I had no wish to know, in any case. "I would have prevented what happened to him and Gareth, had I been able. Please know this." I studied Leland again. "How is he?"

Catherine let out her breath, her anger leaving her. "Not well. He is grieving for Mr. Travers—I fear he will not mend because of it. Mr. Travers was his anchor."

"The love of his life," I said, understanding.

"Indeed." Her voice lost its harsh note. "It is unfair that

they did not have more time together. We never know how long we will have with others, do we?"

Mrs. Danbury had been married twice already, and she was no older than Donata. "I am sorry for your losses," I said.

"Mickey Danbury swept me off my feet." Catherine smiled, a dimple appearing in her cheek. "More fool I. But my first husband, Mr. Grey ..." She fingered a locket at her throat. "I could have wished more time with him." The catch in her voice, the sadness in her eyes told me all.

I reached over and took her hand, and she did not pull away. "You are right," I said. "We must treasure every moment. Thank you for reminding me."

I'd lost my daughter long ago. I'd been most fortunate—I'd found her again, and I'd found Donata. I intended to savor every second I had with them.

Catherine pressed my hand, no longer looking at me in anger. Then she sighed. "Now to help Leland. Poor lad."

We subsided, studying Leland. If we could have healed him with our hopes alone, I believe he would have sprung from the bed, fully recovered.

We were still there when the surgeon arrived, and with him, Donata.

I RODE HOME WITH DONATA, ARMED WITH SIR GIDEON'S notes. She was subdued after her visit with Lady Derwent but put forth her opinion that Lady Derwent would recover from this spell.

"I believe she needed someone from outside that morose household to cheer her," Donata said. She sat next to me during the short ride home, but there was space between us. Her bonnet, a tall creation with an entire bird's worth of feathers, prevented me from leaning to her. "She did not want anyone to fuss over her when Leland was far worse off, she said. I told her that was nonsense." She gave a decided nod, the feathers dancing. "And how delicious for me," Donata continued, an acerbic note suffusing her voice, "to enter Leland's sickroom and find you holding Mrs. Danbury's hand."

"I was not holding her hand," I said indignantly. I'd released it well before Donata had come in.

"Perhaps not at the moment." Donata looked out the window, ensuring that all I saw was the brown, gray, and blue tips of the bonnet's feathers. "I recognize that she is very pretty, in a helpless sort of way."

"I confess to believing so when I first met her," I said, always wanting to be truthful. "But this was, of course, before I entered a sunny billiards room and saw your eyes."

My remark was meant to begin a reconciliation, and Donata did turn to look at me, but she remained distant. She had not yet decided, I saw, how to take my high-handedness.

"You hated me on sight," she said without belligerence. "I admit that I was furious with my husband at that house party and wanted to punish him for his beastly ways, or at least indicate how much I did not care what he did. I thought I could use you to make my point, and then you ignored me utterly. So galling."

"You ought to have told me. If I had understood your scheme, I might have gone along with it."

Donata raked me with a skeptical look. "Doubtful. Your highly developed sense of honor would have forbidden it. Not long after that, I encountered you again, pursuing Mrs. Danbury."

"Not pursuing her," I corrected. "I happened to arrive at a house she was in. You were there too."

"Yes, indeed. I remember. Do not rewrite the past, Gabriel; you were besotted with the creature."

"And yet," I said, making my voice light. "Here I am married to you. How do you think that came about?"

The carriage halted before the house, a footman dashing forward to open the carriage door for us.

"I am, unfortunately, a jealous harridan," Donata said as she made her way past me. "I always will be. Especially of soft, pretty young women with whom you danced, never mind your bad leg. I make no apology."

She bent to descend from the carriage, careful of her hat, and I steadied her from behind. The rain was coming down fairly hard now, and two footmen stretched a canopy over Donata so her ladyship would not get wet.

Once inside, Donata removed the enormous bonnet and handed it safely to her maid, and stripped off coat and gloves to give to the footman—a ritual dance she performed every time she came home. Before she could head for the stairs, I turned her around and kissed her on the mouth in front of the entire household.

When I let her go, she stepped back, the quiet anger she'd regarded me with since Grenville's visit softening. "I am afraid that will not cure me of being a harridan," she said.

"No matter." I handed my own things to the delighted footman. "I like you a termagant. Barnstable, will you send coffee to the study? Thank you."

———

BREWSTER HAD REMAINED AT THE DERWENTS WITH THE surgeon, saying he needed to pay the man and get him safely home. I told Barnstable to send Brewster up to me the moment he arrived here.

The hard-faced surgeon had cleaned Leland's wound again, checked the lad over, added another stitch to his head, and rebandaged him. The man had said little except that Leland needed to be well looked after and his wound washed every day. He left a clear liquid, which smelled strongly of spirits, to be rubbed on the gash. Must be done, the surgeon said, even if

Leland complained of the pain. Donata and I had stayed at the Derwents' long enough to hear this before we'd departed.

I did not have to wait much time before Brewster came into the study, ushered by Barnstable, who expressed his disapproval by being coldly haughty. Brewster was a ruffian, hired for his fighting prowess, hardly fitting to be upstairs in the house of young Lord Breckenridge.

"The surgeon is quite competent," I said once Barnstable had served coffee with the minimum necessary politeness and left us. "I met another like him in the army, very good at saving his patients. My man was chatty, though, immensely cheerful. I suppose good surgeons come from all temperaments."

"If you're coming around to asking who he is, I can't tell ya," Brewster said with his characteristic frankness. He took a noisy slurp of coffee. "Let's just say he and His Majesty's government came to a bit of a disagreement over his skills. As in, he's good at healing, but knows exactly where to stick the knife if he has to. He shouldn't even be in the country, if you take my meaning."

"Ah." The man had been transported. A transported person returning to England before his sentence was up would be condemned to death.

"So, Mr. Denis would be pleased if you didn't mention him," Brewster finished.

"He must owe Mr. Denis an enormous favor for hiding him," I observed.

"Or t'other way around," Brewster said. "Now, why am I here, or was it just to put your butler's nose out of joint?"

"his." I laid Sir Gideon's notebooks and papers across the desk. Brewster had pulled up a chair to the end, and I pushed a stack toward him. "Since you can read, I'd like you to help me go through these. You might know some of the people in Mr. Travers's reports."

Brewster set down his coffee after another loud sip and put his thick fingers on the top page. "Right. I'll have a go."

Sir Gideon had given me not only Travers's reports but his own for everything he'd been working on in the past six-month. He couldn't think straight, Sir Gideon had said, thrusting the bundle at me before I'd gone. He'd hoped that perhaps I could make some sense of it all.

True to my word to Denis, I'd told Sir Gideon about Leland being at the Nines and what he'd seen happening there. Sir Gideon had given me his sorrowful look, said Leland was a good boy, and hobbled back to his desk, taking out paper and pen. I had no doubt he'd pass the information on to his cronies, who would set wheels in motion.

Travers's notes were well written and thoughtful. He'd visited slums and rookeries, reporting on how many people lived in a house and how many to a room, and visited factories where children worked all hours and were black with filth. He'd investigated the dangers of the cotton spinning factories that could ignite and roast all inside within minutes, painting the lives of the workers in grim detail.

He wrote with compassion, describing very young mothers taking care of far too many children, fathers who were drunks or couldn't find work and were on the edge of despair. He wrote of tiny children taking care of babies while their parents labored all day just to feed them. Travers had opined that the vast factories operating to churn out goods everyone now wanted in quantity meant that the English middle-class lived well on the backs of the factory workers, who saw little for what they did.

Travers also reported on how the desperate often turned to crime. Game girls, rent boys, pickpockets, robbers, and house-breakers — they preyed upon the genteel, and they preyed upon one another. Game girls and boys were sent out by gang leaders to "work," then the leaders took all their money and gave them bare subsistence in return.

Travers was especially indignant about the plight of the game girls and rent boys. *These children*, he'd written, *know nothing but selling their bodies for another's use, often being beaten or even tortured to fulfill a man's unclean pleasure. They receive very little for their humiliation, and what they do receive must be delivered to their overlords or they risk more beating. The overlords are not always the madams or fleecers in their houses, but often the parents of the children themselves.*

"He ain't wrong," Brewster said when we'd read these passages. "My Emily, she was turned out to make good when she were twelve years old. Started working in the house when she were sixteen. She liked it, she told me, because she knew she'd get a bed to lie in and food the next morning. On the street it's catch as catch can."

"The houses are not much better, in Mr. Travers's opinion," I said, paging through the notebooks. "He mentions many brothels by name. He has addresses, names of the madams and men who work there, and names of the girls and boys too."

"I can't imagine the madams being happy with that. The young 'uns neither. How else are they going to make a living? Go to all those nasty factories?"

"I agree, the problems seem insurmountable," I said. "But reformers like Sir Gideon are trying to help."

Brewster snorted. "Some lads and lasses have a hard time of it, that's true. But some prefer letting a bloke dip his wick to starving. Starve sometime, Captain. See how you like it."

When I'd been set upon by French soldiers in Spain, who'd beaten me, hung me from a tree, and left me for dead, I'd gone about five days without food. I'd been in so much pain I hadn't given it much mind, but I remembered when the Spanish woman had rescued me. She'd put a piece of bread in my hand, and I'd devoured it, animal-like, not caring that my hands were so filthy I must have eaten plenty of mud with it.

I'd lain outside her farm, where I'd dragged myself, for days, watching while a French soldier, a deserter, ordered her about and took his pleasure with her. She'd found me when she'd gone out to the well for water. I'd been hidden in tall grass, whispering to her in Spanish, begging for a drink. She managed to give me the water without the Frenchman seeing me, and I'd promised her my help. At the time, I thought I might die before I could, but finally, she'd brought the man close enough to me. I'd risen from hiding, taking his gun from him, and shot him through the head. Then I'd collapsed into a raving fever.

"I've been hungry," I said. "And thirsty."

"*Starving,* I said." Brewster's eyes held no sympathy. "Where you can't think of nothing but the horrible pain in your insides. Weeks since you've had a meal. Where a bite of bread is a feast. Where you'll do anything for anyone who'll relieve that pain in you."

I sat back. "You speak from experience."

"Oh, you saw through me little story, did you? Yeah, I was tossed out by me mum when I was a small chap because I was too hungry for her to keep. She had six others, and my da' was gone, probably dead. I learned how to steal to keep fed. I and a few other lads banded together, pooled the takings, and started to live a damn sight better than we had at home. The reformers, now, they want to round up poor things like I'd been and take them back to their mums—the women what slung them out in the first place. Me mum could swill the gin, I can tell you."

"They're seeking to remedy such things." My voice did not carry a great deal of conviction, because I agreed with Brewster. The world's wrongs were too complicated for an easy solution. Mothers did abandon their children, and workhouses and orphanages were places of misery.

"Mr. Travers doesn't like some of the reformers either," Brewster said, going back to the papers. "He takes these two, who run a workhouse, to task. Good lad."

Indeed, Mr. Travers had reported that one workhouse pocketed much money from the parish and philanthropists and kept the children in straits. Had we found motive for someone to silence Mr. Travers?

"I know 'em," Brewster said, almost proudly. "Mother Mary and Sir Baxter. Pious as angels. Virtuously brings the young 'uns in the front door, sells 'em out the back."

I put my finger on Gareth's words. "Those aren't the names I have here."

"Wouldn't be, would it? They were banged up, their orphanage closed. Opened up a new one under new names as soon as they were free."

"Gareth exposed them again," I said. "Would they kill him for that?"

Brewster shrugged. "Could do. Wouldn't need to, though. The law starts looking their way, they slip town and turn up somewhere new with different names, and start all over again."

"They couldn't if they were convicted and transported," I said. "Perhaps Gareth and Sir Gideon were trying to close them permanently."

Brewster did not look convinced. "What reason would they have to try to kill the Derwent lad, then? They'd wait in the dark for Gareth to come walking alone and gut him. Why lurk about until he's doing the deed with his lover?"

"To humiliate Sir Gideon, Gareth, Leland, and their reforming zeal," I suggested. "How can Sir Gideon be so upright, they would be saying, when his own son and Mr. Travers are unnaturals themselves?"

"Maybe," Brewster said. "But Mother Mary ain't so devious. She and her man are very straightforward. Clout you if you get in their way, yes, but they wouldn't have the cunning to set up the two lads as they were found. Some other person did that."

"How can you be so certain?" I, for one, wanted to get my hands on this Mother Mary and shake a confession out of her.

"The criminal classes ain't like what's in novels," Brewster said comfortably. "They ain't madmen coming up with strange ways to kill a young woman in an old house somewhere. Your basic criminal is a straightforward bloke. Smash and grab. Even Mr. Denis ain't hard to understand. He sees something he wants; he puts out his hand and takes it. He's good at the game, but he ain't complicated."

"You have a point, but regardless, someone did kill them and set them up to be found as they were. I want to see this Mother Mary and her cohort. Can you arrange it?"

"Mr. Denis can. If they see *me* coming, they'll duck out the back and be long gone. Mr. Denis is more subtle-like."

Indeed, Mr. Denis could be very subtle. "Any other names jump out at you?" I asked.

"A few. Gimme some paper, and I'll write 'em down for you."

I obliged with paper and pen, and watched Brewster

painstakingly scrawl out a short list of names. I took it, wondering if any laid before me in black and white would prove to be Travers's killer.

After another half hour's perusal of the reports, Brewster announced he'd return to Denis and request, from me, that he put his hands on a few of these people for questioning. "Better than Bow Street, is Mr. Denis," he said proudly.

I'd seen enough of Denis's methods to believe that.

The day had darkened while Brewster and I had conferred. I returned to my rooms upstairs after he left to find Donata preparing herself to go out for the evening.

My wife went out every night, when she wasn't hostessing a do here. It was the height of the Season, and the dowager Lady Breckenridge was invited everywhere. Hers was a world of soirees with champagne and ices, balls that lasted well into the morning, and visits to the opera and theatre in between. A far cry from the world Brewster and I had been reading about where children had to give in to the sordid appetites of the gentlemen who might well turn up at the society balls Donata loved. The reports had angered me. No wonder Sir Gideon had turned reformer.

I entered Donata's dressing room after a knock to find her at her dressing table, her abigail fussing with her hair. Jewelry glinted in velvet-lined trays, waiting to adorn her neck.

The abigail, who was devoted to Donata, glanced at me, pushed one final pin into Donata's complex knot of hair, laid down the brush, and discreetly retreated.

Donata paid no attention to me. She smoothed one curl then lifted a heavy diamond necklace. It was a piece her mother had given her, one that had been in her family for years. Donata refused to wear the Breckenridge jewels or any gift her first husband had bought her.

As she started to clasp the strand of diamonds in the back, I took them from her, closed the clasp myself, then leaned down and pressed a kiss to her neck.

"I grow frightened for you," I whispered when she did not move. I traced a curl above her ear. "Any thought of you being hurt, or lost to me, makes me ... brusque."

Donata's gaze sought mine in the mirror. "You are used to giving commands."

"I am. But I never give a foolish one."

We studied each other, her smooth face and sleek hair a contrast to my hard, rather weather-beaten countenance. "You are unpolished," Donata said. "I question whether I married you to remedy that or to remind myself that the world is not a tame place."

"I'm certain Breckenridge reminded you of the latter quite a lot."

Her eyes flickered. "*Breckenridge* is now my beautiful son, and my husband is an army captain uncomfortable in my house."

"I would not say uncomfortable." I laid my hand over her slender one. "The furniture and carpets are quite soft. Unused to it is closer to the mark."

"Will you ever grow used to it?"

"You would not like me if I did. I would simply stretch out on the divan and snore all of the time."

Donata twined my thick fingers with her slim ones, and for a time, we only looked at each other in the glass.

"It is Lady Darymple's musicale this evening," Donata said presently. "Signora Carlotti has consented to perform. I sent word that you were unwell and unlikely to attend."

Kind of her. I was worn out with worry, tired of death and the evil people who dealt it.

"I will attend," I said. "Perhaps a night of music would do me good. As an old, married man, I can nod off in the back row with the gray heads."

"You will do no such thing," Donata said, her brisk self once more. "No need for you to bestir yourself, Gabriel. Lady Darymple will be a success tonight only because of her guest.

There will be nothing else to recommend the evening, I can assure you."

"Yes, there will," I gave her neck another soft kiss, tasting diamonds. "You will be there."

I smiled at Donata's sudden, pleased look and left her to garb myself in suitable attire.

"YOU ARE CRUEL," DONATA SAID AS WE DESCENDED IN AN hour's time before a townhouse, this one in Upper Brook Street. We hadn't spoken much during the short, rainy journey, except for Donata explaining who would be at the gathering and whom I should ignore.

I stood in the wet while I helped her from the carriage and to the door. "Cruel?" I asked. "I thought I was a gentleman of honor."

"You respond to my anger and jealousy by flattering me shamelessly and melting my heart. Quite ruthless of you."

Before I could answer, we were surrounded by the other guests. Donata became the lady she was born to be—witty, popular, and in turns charming or biting, depending on her audience or the subject.

Chairs had been set in the ballroom for us to sit in comfort while we listened to the soprano. A pianoforte waited, with a male pianist running through scales to loosen his fingers.

Donata brushed past me as guests began to fill up the room, the feathers of her headdress tickling my nose. "Notice who is *not* here," she said in a low voice. "And if you stare at me and ask *who*? I shall snub you."

I glanced over the entering guests in what I thought was a nonchalant way, and saw what she meant. Signora Carlotti sang tonight, and the one guest who ought to have been there —her lover, Lucius Grenville—was strikingly absent.

CHAPTER 21

I settled in with the rest of Mayfair to enjoy the soprano, wondering as much as any of them why Grenville had not come. He'd confided in me no reason for staying away, but I'd learned long ago that Grenville was his own man. Though I might be curious, he'd tell me when he wished and not sooner.

Signora Carlotti, a woman with a lush bosom and a quantity of silky curls, stood gracefully, one hand on the pianoforte. She looked in no way distressed about Grenville's absence and smiled warmly as we applauded her entrance, taking her due.

When she sang, she filled the room with joy. Those are the only words I have with which to describe the sensation. Her voice erased every emptiness, every angry and troubled thought, and replaced it with beauty. I sat, entranced, feeling myself be cleansed.

She finished the first piece with her voice almost a whisper, but a whisper of such strength it was palpable. As she at last dropped her head and closed her mouth, the audience went wild with applause. I clapped until my hands stung through my gloves. Donata, sitting a row ahead of me with friends, wiped tears from her eyes.

Signora Carlotti sang three more pieces, and then a fourth when the room begged her for more. At last, Lady Darymple, a sallow and small woman who looked vastly pleased with herself, told us we must spare Signora Carlotti's voice.

Signora Carlotti bowed humbly as we praised her, then straightened to greet her admirers.

I had met the soprano once before, very briefly, with Grenville, who remained blatantly absent. When Donata managed to push us through the crush to Signora Carlotti's side, I saw no anxiousness in her eyes. If she noted that Grenville had not come, it did not worry her.

Signora Carlotti greeted me smoothly when Donata and I reached her, graciously acknowledging our previous introduction. She'd met Donata more than once, and the two began to speak in the rapid, flowing way of women who loved to talk.

I turned to leave them to it, and had my arm caught by a woman I had not seen much of this spring — Louisa Brandon.

"Gabriel, how wonderful to find you here." Louisa gave me a kiss on the cheek then stepped back, holding my hands as she liked to, to study me. "You look well," she said, pleased. "Happy."

We stood in a relative bubble of privacy, the other guests either departing for the next entertainment or waiting to speak to Signora Carlotti. I did not see my former commander, Colonel Brandon, in the crowd, and concluded that Louisa must be here with friends. Brandon did not have much patience with musicales.

"Married life agrees with me," I told Louisa. "And Gabriella returns tomorrow." The thought lightened my heart.

"We look forward to her come-out. I would not miss it for the world." Louisa's eyes crinkled with her smile. "I believe Aloysius will pry himself from the house and attend as well. He was on hand when Gabriella was born, remember?"

So long ago. And yet, the time had passed with disheartening rapidity.

"Gabriella is quite excited about the ball," I said. "I have … trepidation."

Louisa's smile deepened. "Of course you do. You are her father. I remember my father's apprehension at *my* come-out. I was so innocent, and surrounded by young men, many of them soldiers. He nearly fainted when I said I wished to marry Aloysius, a dashing cavalry captain."

I sympathized with her father. "I will no doubt be swooning all night," I said.

Louisa gave me another warm look, appreciating my humor, then her amusement faded. "I heard about the Derwents, Gabriel, and the death of young Mr. Travers. How awful. I went to Grosvenor Square earlier today, and I'm off to see them again. Mrs. Danbury does her best, but even she is not free of the Derwent delicacy of mind. I will relieve her and look after Lady Derwent and Leland as I can."

"It is good of you," I said. "They need true friends at the moment."

I half-expected Louisa to ask me to accompany her, but she touched my cheek. "I will give them your best wishes."

"Thank you," I said. "Tell them I will call tomorrow to pay my respects."

We said our good-nights. I pressed Louisa's hand, and she went off, signaling to a footman to run for her carriage.

I turned to find Donata near the open double doors of the ballroom. I knew she'd seen my tête-à-tête with Louisa, but as I moved to my wife, she walked away as though ignoring me.

She was not alone. It was a fashion of the time, one I loathed, for gentlemen to devote themselves to a married woman. Ladies and gentlemen who were married to each other did not sit next to each other at suppers, or dance together at balls, or circulate anywhere near each other at events such as this one. To do so would make them laughingstocks, so I had been informed. We would be accused of being tiresome lovebirds and living in each other's pockets. A husband did not dance attendance on his wife without being mocked.

Bloody nonsense to me. Why the devil should I marry a woman if I never wished to be in the same room with her?

Donata's two swains were Terrence Berwick, an untitled, but well-connected gentleman, and, to my surprise, Henry Lawrence, the gentleman Grenville and I had questioned at Brooks's.

Lawrence saw me, but appeared unabashed. I might know where his proclivities lay, but he was enjoying himself playing at being besotted with my wife. He knew the rules, his amusement told me, and no matter what sort of liaisons he enjoyed in secret, here I was the one out of place.

Mr. Berwick stuck fast to Donata's other side, tucking her hand firmly under his arm. The two men were languidly arguing about who would get Donata an ice and in whose carriage she would travel to a supper ball in Berkeley Square.

I was not to notice, to bury myself with my cronies in conversation or in the card room. If I wanted to go home, I should send Donata a message by one of the footmen, or simply leave. When next I saw her, perhaps a few days hence, I might ask her how she enjoyed the musicale—to make conversation. I should not care what amusements ladies got up to, and instead find a mistress to devote myself to.

I would never be a fashionable gentleman. I intercepted Donata when the two men both turned to procure her an ice, and cut them out.

"Gabriel," Donata said, smiling. "Did you enjoy the performance?" The arch of her brows told me she spoke of more than Signora Carlotti's singing.

"I did," I said, "but I grow weary. Time for me to retire. Enjoy the rest of your evening." I leaned down, and in full view of the gathering, deigned to kiss my wife on the cheek.

"You will not accompany Mrs. Brandon to the Derwents'?"

Donata asked in surprise. "I assume that was what you and she so fervently spoke of."

"No." I hesitated. "I mean, yes, that is where she has gone, but ..." I knew I ought to go as well, to continue to lend the Derwents my strength. I should say my good-nights and look in on them, helping as much as I could. They needed friends, as I'd told Louisa.

But I thought of the hushed and changed atmosphere of the Grosvenor Square mansion, Sir Gideon weeping in his study, the brittle smile of Mrs. Danbury, the wisp that was Melissa silently moving from her mother's bedroom to her brother's. I could not go back there. Not yet.

"They are friends who have been kind to me," I said, trying to understand myself. "Why do I not wish to rush to their side?"

"Because it is unnerving to watch those you care for suffer," Donata said, her frankness cutting through the fog of my thoughts. "And the Derwents, unfortunately, are very good at suffering. Go home, Gabriel. Mrs. Brandon knows how to take care of them. She will send word if anything happens."

"You are saying guilt is a bad master." I had her hand between mine, holding on, finding a lifeline in her.

"Indeed it is," she said. "I know you regret that you were not on hand to keep Leland and Gareth from being hurt, but the hard truth is, it is likely you could have done nothing to prevent it. Hovering over Leland's bedside while you beat your breast will do you no good, nor Leland either. You know Mrs. Brandon well, and you trust her, do you not?"

Donata knew quite well my connection to Louisa and our long history. "Yes," I replied.

"Then I will say good night." Donata rose on her tiptoes and kissed my cheek in return. "There, now we have shocked the entire *ton* by demonstrating affection. I must put in an appearance at Mrs. Gardiner's supper ball, or all will say I cannot tear myself away from you, but I will return after that.

At Mrs. Gardiner's we will chatter about Lady Darymple's coup at persuading Signora Carlotti here, and Grenville's notable absence."

She smiled, and I knew I had married the woman best for me. Whenever I fell into the haze of self-pity and doubt, her brutal clarity would pull me back, like a rope stopping a fall from a cliff.

"Thank you," I said, pressing down on her hands.

The look in her eyes warmed me to the bone. She at last extricated herself from me and moved off to wave dismissively at the ice Mr. Berwick presented to her, and I went home.

I let Barnstable put me to bed. Bartholomew was not there, and I knew I should wonder about his absence, but I was too tired. He might be with Grenville and his brother, and would come bounding in and proudly present some new snippet of information for me, which I would deal with in the morning.

I was still awake a few hours later when Donata returned, the scent of perfume, smoke, and the night following her. The hour was early for her, but I did not question as she entered my room alone, let her dressing gown fall, and slid into bed next to me.

I became thoroughly unfashionable with my wife then, because I was of course not to take delight in her. She took equal delight in me, and then we drowsed together under the blankets on this chilly spring night.

———

I WAS STILL HALF ASLEEP AND QUITE COMFORTABLE WHEN Bartholomew did come home, right into the bedroom, bringing a draft of cold air with him.

Bartholomew and Donata's abigail were the only ones allowed past our doors after we retired, and they never entered without good reason. Now Bartholomew halted just outside the curtains of my heavy tester bed and said, "Sir," in agitation.

I reached for a dressing gown and got out of bed, not liking the note in his voice. I twisted my bad leg in the process of standing up, and Bartholomew ended up having to help me.

"What is it?" I whispered.

"Mrs. Brandon. She says for you to come at once."

My heart squeezed with dread. "Leland?"

Bartholomew shook his head. "Mrs. Brandon said nothing about Mr. Derwent. She said to tell you that Bow Street is there. Someone got into Sir Gideon's house, and now he's dead."

"Who is dead?" I asked in alarm. "Sir Gideon?"

"*No*, sir. I'm telling this all wrong. The man who came into the house is dead. Mrs. Brandon sent the message, but she didn't write nothing down, and their footman was blithering like a fool. But Mrs. Brandon says *can you come*?"

"Yes, yes. Help me find some clothes."

Bartholomew got me to my dressing room, and I sat down to put on my trousers while he bustled around shaking out a shirt and waistcoat. "Were you at the Derwents?" I asked as he snatched a frock coat from the wardrobe, his movements shaky.

"No, indeed, with Mr. Grenville," Bartholomew answered. "When the Derwents' footman ran to his house. Sorry, sir."

"I am not unhappy, Bartholomew, just worried. We left you in Seven Dials."

"You did, sir, but Matthias and me returned to Mr. Grenville's as ordered. We had to wait for him there a long time."

"He's there now?"

"No, sir. He went out again, a bit ago. It was so late, I thought to sleep there and return this morning, knowing this house would already be shut. But then the Derwents' footman came, and I hurried here and banged on the door until they let me in."

"I am glad you did." I pulled on my boots and opened the

dressing room door to see Donata climbing out of the bed, her abigail at her side.

"Stay there," I told Donata sternly.

"No, indeed." Donata's lithe body flashed as she took her dressing gown the abigail had retrieved and competently closed herself into it. "If you are rushing into the arms of Bow Street, I am coming with you. Someone must keep you from being arrested again."

WE WERE ADMITTED TO THE GROSVENOR SQUARE HOUSE BY the Derwents' very agitated footman. The entire ground floor was alight, servants swarmed up and down the stairs, and foot patrollers from Bow Street walked into and out of the rooms as though they had a right to.

I caught sight of Mrs. Danbury, fully dressed, looking over the railing from a landing near the top of the house. She watched me and Donata come in, but she remained where she was and did not call out. I saw nothing of Lady Derwent and her daughter—I also did not see Louisa, and assumed her with the Derwent ladies.

Bow Street Runners had arrived in the form of both Pomeroy and Spendlove. Pomeroy came at me as I started to enter the drawing room, where I spied Sir Gideon, but it was Donata muffled in her large coat that he focused on.

"Best not, your ladyship," Pomeroy said. "It's a right mess."

"Nonsense," Donata replied briskly. "Sir Gideon is about to fall down. Let me go to him." She walked past a frowning Pomeroy and strode to Sir Gideon's side, catching him as he swayed.

The drawing room's tranquility had been much disturbed. The room looked forlorn enough without the family in it, the pianoforte shut and quiet, the harp covered, sewing baskets closed. Now books lay everywhere, having been pulled off shelves and scattered about. An urn of flowers on a pedestal had been overturned, spreading broken blossoms and water across the patterns of the ivory and blue oriental carpet. The ivory of the carpet was marred, near the fireplace, with a large pool of blood.

A man lay in the middle of the blood, full length, on his back. Someone had closed his eyes, but his face was frozen in a twist of rage and fear. This gentleman was fully clothed, in an evening suit, and he'd been beaten again and again until he'd died.

CHAPTER 22

I looked down at the man and drew a quick breath. "That's Mackay."

He was battered, but I recognized the dark hair, the soft face. A fireplace poker, coated with blood, lay next to him.

Spendlove came to stand next to me as Donata led Sir Gideon into the adjoining chamber, a smaller sitting room. She did not close the door, and I saw her bend over him as he collapsed onto a chair.

"Now why am I not surprised you know the deceased, Captain?" Spendlove asked, both of us peering down at Mackay's lifeless body.

"I don't *know* him," I said. "I met him only once."

"Did you?" Spendlove switched his gaze to me. "And who is he?"

I looked straight into his eyes, Spendlove ever ready to be suspicious. "I have no idea," I said. "All I know is his name. Nelson Mackay."

"Draws a blank with me," Spendlove said. "Pomeroy?"

Pomeroy, still watching Donata and Sir Gideon, shook his head. "He's a stranger to me, guv."

"Tell me how you met him, Captain," Spendlove said. "Every detail."

Spendlove liked to gaze upon a man as though he knew all his thoughts and waited for him to blunder. His light blue eyes fixed on me, his red lashes fading into his freckled face.

I decided not to lie ... very much. Mackay might have been a witness to the attack on Leland and Gareth—and now he was dead.

"He discovered Mr. Derwent and Mr. Travers in the passage in Seven Dials," I said. "And he came to find me. Leland asked him to. Mackay arriving at my door in Grimpen Lane was the first time I'd even seen him."

"Ah," Spendlove said. "So this Mackay was a great friend of young Mr. Derwent?"

I shook my head. "Leland says no. He is not sure where Mackay came from, though he does not remember much about the night."

"A well-dressed, soft-handed gent just happened to be wandering about Seven Dials?" Spendlove gave me a long look of disbelief. "How convenient for Mr. Derwent."

"Not really," I said, my voice cold. "He is sore hurt and may not recover, and his closest friend is dead. Whether Mr. Mackay was part of that or not, I suppose we'll never know." I folded my arms. "Question the ruffians at the Nines, where Leland objected to their fleecing."

"Bow Street at the Nines?" Pomeroy boomed with a grin. "Off-limits for us. Mr. Forge sees to that, if you know what I mean."

Spendlove looked pained. "We have been warned off, yes, but if a murder occurred there, Mr. Forge can whistle."

I directed my next words at Pomeroy. "If you do find that Mr. Forge is responsible, please direct him a good kick with your large boot."

Pomeroy laughed again. The room seemed to flinch at his boisterousness while a man lay dead not ten feet from him. "I'll be sure to, sir. But what about who did for this bloke?" He jerked a thumb at Mackay. "The toughs at the Nines had nothing to do with *this*."

"Servants say the doors and windows were closed and locked for the night," Spendlove said. "No sign of anyone breaking in. What do you make of that, Captain?"

I studied Mackay on the floor, forlorn, so alone. "Had he come to see Sir Gideon? Or ask about Leland?"

Spendlove shrugged. "Seems to be a mystery. Footman says he never admitted the man. Sir Gideon claims he didn't know him. So, if no one broke in, but no one came to visit, however did he come to be here?"

The spark in his eyes told me he believed someone in the house was lying. He suspected Sir Gideon, I was certain, who'd found the body and was the only one downstairs.

I did not think Sir Gideon had it in him to commit murder, especially not to so young and fit a man like Mackay. But then, if Mackay had angered him, or Sir Gideon had thought he was defending ones he loved ...

I needed to divert Spendlove's attention from him, but I had no plausible suggestions, wouldn't until I asked questions of the household myself. They'd be less likely to close ranks against me, a friend of the family, than two hearty Bow Street Runners who made their living on rewards for convictions. I praised the foresight of the Fielding brothers for not paying their Runners per arrest. Half of London would be in the Bow Street nick by now.

Pomeroy rendered his opinion. "Could be this Mr. Mackay slipped in with someone else who was admitted, maybe when the footman's back was turned. Mrs. Brandon came here tonight. Maybe while the footman was taking Mrs. Brandon's wraps, Mr. Mackay dashed inside."

Spendlove did not look convinced. "Damned unobservant footman then. Why should Mrs. Brandon call so late, Captain? Surely she has a husband to go home to."

His words and knowing look made me bristle. "Mrs. Brandon is a good friend to the family. She called to minister to Lady Derwent and Leland."

Spendlove's eyes glinted, seeing he'd found a weak spot in me. "Seems the only ones in the house while Mr. Mackay was being killed were the Derwent family, Mrs. Danbury, and Mrs. Brandon. No break-ins, and most of the servants in their beds. An interesting puzzle."

"There is nothing to say when Mackay arrived, is there?" I asked, irritated. "He could have come in at any time during the day and hidden somewhere. This is a large house."

"So I'd noticed. Sir Gideon is a very wealthy man." Spendlove ran a practiced eye around the room, noting the multitude of books, the silver vases, porcelain figurines, and gilded candelabra, stopping his gaze at the dead man. "Why would he bother to hide in here? So he could rob the place? He doesn't look the sort. A City clerk or some such. And he brought no large bag to carry off the swag."

Pomeroy chuckled. "*He'd* never carry off all the silver. Soft gent like that? I'd wager he never lifts anything heavier than his pocket watch. Unless he planned to pass it to a confederate."

A rustling of skirts and a firm step announced that Donata had returned to the room. "Gentlemen, your loudness and laughter are upsetting Sir Gideon. Please cease it." She fixed Spendlove with her dark blue gaze, her head at its most haughty angle. "I and his valet are taking him upstairs. Do finish and go as soon as you can. And take Mr. Mackay somewhere, *not* in this house."

Delivering her commands in a tone that didn't expect to be disobeyed, her ladyship swept back into the smaller sitting room.

"That is a point," Pomeroy said to Spendlove. "These people ain't the criminal classes. Depend upon it, this bloke sneaked in here when someone else was admitted, maybe followed by an accomplice, who crashed him over the head and ran off. Maybe they disputed about what to steal and how to split it up."

"A neat and simple explanation," Spendlove said, his skepticism apparent. "Not the right one, but simple enough. Depend upon it, Pomeroy, this household had something to do with it."

"Maybe so," Pomeroy said. He tapped the side of his nose. "But Sir Gideon has friends in very high places."

Spendlove did not like Pomeroy's insinuation one bit, but he shrugged. I could almost read his thoughts—Spendlove would continue needling everyone in the house until he convinced himself he had enough evidence to arrest Sir Gideon.

"As a point of fact," Spendlove said, turning to me, "where were *you* tonight, Captain?"

"At a musicale in Upper Brook Street," I answered readily. "Then to bed." I let him decide what I'd been doing there.

"Upper Brook Street is just around the corner from here," Spendlove said. "So is South Audley Street. And where is that tame pugilist who follows you about?"

"At home, I imagine," I said. "He cannot stay awake all the time."

But I wondered. Whether culprit or witness, Mackay had known something about the attack on Gareth and Leland. Brewster *could* have followed Mackay here to question him, perhaps threaten him, perhaps started to rough him up if he wouldn't answer questions. Brewster was a strong man and a bully. He could easily have killed a weaker man like Mackay.

But Brewster was also a professional, I'd come to understand. I doubted he would have left Mackay lying in a pool of blood in the Derwents' drawing room. He'd have gotten the body out of the house and disposed of and the room cleaned up, erasing all trace that anything had occurred there, and he wouldn't have let the man bleed all over the rug. Or Brewster

would have taken him out of the house altogether before beginning violence. If Brewster had killed Mackay, it would likely
have been a long time before anyone discovered he'd died.

Spendlove watched me. "Do you have a witness to being
home in bed, Captain? Your lady wife, perhaps?"

"My lady wife went on to a supper ball while I retired," I
said. "You may, of course, question my entire household, from
her ladyship's butler all the way to the scullery maid. I went to
bed directly after returning from the musicale, and everyone in
the house knows it. The beds are soft at South Audley Street. I
stay in them as much as possible."

Spendlove gave me a wintry smile. "I have no doubt her
ladyship's servants would say anything her ladyship ordered
them to. You would have had plenty of time to leave your *musicale*, as you call it, tramp up here, smack this man over the
head, and go about your merry way. You'd be snug in your bed
by the time your wife returned home."

"That is possible, of course," I said. "But I had no reason to
kill Mr. Mackay. In fact, I very much wanted to question him
about the night Mr. Travers died. And even if I took it into my
head to murder him, I would never have killed him in the home
of dear friends."

"Perhaps not, unless you had no choice." Spendlove stared
at me a moment longer, a hard light in his eyes. "As much as I
would enjoy arresting you, Captain, I will not tonight. I'll do as
her ladyship directs, and let them all go to bed, but tomorrow I
will question the household again. These people know more
than they're saying. I will want to question Mrs. Brandon as
well." He waited, certain I would object.

"Mrs. Brandon will be happy to help in any way she can," I
said coolly. And I'd make bloody certain I was with her when
Spendlove spoke to her.

Pomeroy, who'd been listening, gave a nod—everything
settled—and said he'd have the foot patrollers trundle
Mackay off.

I left the sitting room for the house's grand hall, its staircase winding upward into shadows. Mrs. Danbury had vanished, and someone had extinguished all the lights in the upper reaches.

Spendlove followed me. "I'd like it if you departed, Captain. I see Sir Gideon for this crime, and I don't want you here to cover things up for him or spirit him away in the night."

I had known he'd return to blaming Sir Gideon. "He had nothing to do with this," I said quickly.

Spendlove's eyes were flinty. "This is his house, and the man was found in his drawing room. I imagine Mr. Mackay came here on purpose to see Sir Gideon and said or did something Sir Gideon didn't like. Suppose Mr. Mackay told Sir Gideon he'd killed Mr. Travers, or that he knew young Mr. Derwent and his friend were unnaturals? Do not look surprised—it is no secret to me. Sir Gideon, enraged, takes up the poker and strikes him down."

I listened in growing uneasiness, not liking that such a scenario was possible. But I could not let Spendlove make such an accusation. "First," I said, "I cannot imagine Sir Gideon, the most harmless of men, growing angry enough to kill, even if he did not mean the blows to be fatal."

Spendlove only watched me. "I've been chasing criminals a long time, Captain. You would be amazed at what the mildest men can get up to when provoked. That is your first objection. What is the next?"

"That anyone who struck Mr. Mackay would be bloody. Sir Gideon's clothes are quite clean."

"Plenty of time to change them and dispose of the soiled ones," Spendlove said.

"Which you can always check."

"Oh, no doubt he or his loyal valet got rid of the damning clothes." Spendlove shrugged. "You might be right and he didn't do it, but that remains to be seen. You can be assured I won't arrest him now. The Bow Street lockup is a nasty place. He can stay here until morning, and then we'll escort him to the magistrate where he can tell his story. I will sleep in his dressing room, in case he decides to bolt during the night." He spoke with finality, convinced he had the right of it.

"It's nonsense," I said. "You cannot believe that of him."

"I can," Spendlove said. "If no one broke in, and yet, this gentleman was dead on the floor, then either Sir Gideon or another member of this house struck him down. Sir Gideon will go to the gallows, or he'll give up the real culprit to save his neck. Murder is a crime, Captain, and no one is above the law."

Anger had replaced his amusement. He pinned me with a flat stare, and I knew I would have to work hard to prove that none of the Derwents had anything to do with this.

He obviously wanted me to leave right away, but I turned my back on him and walked into the dining room, asked the butler to provide me pen and paper, and wrote a letter to Sir Montague Harris, magistrate of Whitechapel.

I INSTRUCTED ONE OF THE FOOTMEN TO DELIVER THE LETTER —Spendlove let him with poor grace, but he seemed to decide he couldn't stop me writing to a magistrate—and then Spendlove told Pomeroy to throw me out. My former sergeant pointedly opened the door for me, grinning widely. I knew he truly would assist me from the house if I did not go, so I departed, but I would be back.

Brewster was lying in wait for me as soon as I stepped outside. "He wants to see you," he informed me.

"By all means," I said, my energy returning. "Let us not keep Mr. Denis waiting."

CHAPTER 23

I started to walk toward South Audley Street, which would take me along to Curzon Street. The rain had ceased, but the air was brisk. After the closeness of the Derwents' house, huge as it was, I found the night refreshing.

Brewster gave me an irritated look, then whistled to a carriage that came along the square and pulled up beside us. "In you go, Captain."

We rode without speaking to Denis's understated but elegant house. I lowered the carriage's window, letting the air flow over me, knowing I'd be shut up in another stifling interior soon.

I did not mean that Denis kept his house roasting hot. When I entered, the air was a pleasant temperature, not too harsh a change from the outside. I meant the atmosphere—at the Derwents', there was bewilderment. The harsh world had been thrust at them, breaking their sanctuary, and they had no idea how to combat it.

Denis's house was hushed, even serene, but it was overlaid with a breath of tension. This was the heart of Denis's empire, and those brought here, at his sufferance, did not always know if they'd be able to leave again.

Not long ago, a man had tried to kill Denis in his own study. Denis was alive because I'd detected a whiff of gunpowder and known what was afoot. As I climbed the stairs this night, I saw that most of the damage the explosion caused had been repaired. The painting I'd admired in the past, of a young woman standing in a sunlit room, pouring water from a gleaming jug, was again hanging in its place.

Even in the middle of the night, Denis's house ran efficiently. One of his footmen took my coat, hat, and gloves, and the stiff butler led me up the stairs. The butler reminded me of the surgeon who had looked after Leland—cold-faced, with nothing behind his eyes.

Denis was sitting at his desk when I entered. The repaired and repainted walls were a different shade of pale green, but other than that, nothing had changed. The incident with the incendiary device might never have occurred.

I'd wondered from time to time what had become of the man, Ridgley, who'd made the devices. Denis had been furious with him, but Denis was not a man to throw away a resource. Whether Ridgley lived or not, I had no idea.

"Good evening, Captain," Denis said. "Mr. Mackay is truly dead?"

I remained on my feet, though the butler had indicated my usual chair with a glass of brandy set on the table beside it. "Yes, he is," I answered. "Did you know him?"

Denis inclined his head. "Mr. Mackay was one of mine. He worked for me."

I stopped. "Good Lord." I swung on Brewster, who had followed me in. "Why the devil did you not tell me so?"

Brewster met my gaze, unrepentant. "I didn't know, did I? Not until I reported what had happened in the Derwents' drawing room tonight. *Then* he tells me who Mackay was."

Brewster sounded vastly annoyed, but Denis did not admonish him. "Not everyone who works for me knows everyone else," Denis told me. "I see no reason to post a list. If you had come to me and told me everything right away, Captain, I might have been able to clear this up." His tone was terse, irritated, the closest he came to emotion.

I was not as prone to hiding my temper. "Am I to assume that everyone I meet in London is in your employ?"

Denis gave me a curt nod. "It would be wise to do so. Things happen to you. Fewer things would if you confided in me from the start."

I made a noise of disbelief. "I see. The first time we met, I told you I'd not be under your thumb, and I repeat the statement. I refuse to run to you every time I stub my toe."

"Your feet would be less sore if you did," Denis said. "I am not in the mood for your rages, Captain. I have lost a valuable resource tonight. I would be more pleased if you told me all that has happened, from the beginning."

"Brewster has not kept you informed?"

"He has, but I would like to hear the tale from you. I know you well enough to realize you can keep things from even my best informants. *Sit down.*"

Denis's voice sharpened as he spoke, and the final two words were like ice. I had only seen Denis fully enraged once, and the consequences had been dire.

Brewster had moved behind me, and I knew that any moment, he'd shove me down into the chair with his big hands on my shoulders. I gave Denis a conceding gesture and sank into the chair myself, pretending it was not a relief to take the weight off my sore leg.

"Nelson Mackay worked in the City and was an expert on art," Denis said as I propped my walking stick before me, resting my hand on it. "I employed him to watch for artwork for me, for my own pleasure, as well as to sell on. He had an eye for it, and I will be sorry to lose it. Now, tell me what *you* know about him."

"Very little," I said, still out of temper. But I told him the events that had occurred from the time Mackay knocked on my door to finding him lying dead in the Derwents' drawing room.

"I have been trying to discover who Mackay is," I said, "and what he had to do with Travers's death, if anything. So far I've found him to be elusive."

"Because he kept himself to himself." Denis laid his hands flat on the desk. "I too know little of his origins. He claimed to come from somewhere in Kent, but no inquiry there can find his family. He has rooms near Lincoln's Inn, and frequents a public house two doors down for his food and drink. He was excellent at discovering things for me—who had paintings they wished to sell and what art objects had come on the market, both legitimately and not so legitimately."

"He'd keep you informed about stolen art?" I asked, too tired to be diplomatic.

Denis made an untroubled gesture. "Housebreakers steal things and do not know what they have. I know you admire the painting in my stairwell, the Dutch picture of the woman with the jug—Mackay found that for me, in Holland, on a market stall full of useless junk. He paid the equivalent of two pounds for it, and the vendor was delighted. Mackay had a talent for recognizing worth."

I heard the regret in Denis's voice, and I wondered, uncharitably, if it were only regret for the loss of that talent.

"What was he doing in Seven Dials?" I asked. "I cannot conceive he'd find much art there."

"I have no idea," Denis said, his tone again turning chilly. "He did not work only for me. He made his living selling knowledge. That of artwork to me, and I assume knowledge of other things to others."

"Knowledge?" My hand tightened on my walking stick. "Was he a blackmailer?"

"It is a possibility. I never delved into any other aspect of his life, though he did offer me information on people from time to time. I purchased what I thought would be useful."

I fell silent, my anger easing as my thoughts turned over. If Mackay had made a living finding out secrets, perhaps he'd discovered Leland's and Gareth's. Perhaps he'd threatened to expose them.

But what motive would Mackay have for killing them? If he had convinced Gareth or Leland to pay him or otherwise compensate him, why should he rid himself of them? Mackay would have been the more likely victim, killed by a man tired of paying blackmail. But the question remained—why had Mackay been near enough to find Leland and Gareth? Or was it only coincidence that he'd been on that street at that time? Had he witnessed the attack and then been killed because of it?

"Had he been to the Bull and Hen?" I asked Denis. "In his quest for knowledge?"

Denis shook his head. "My informant there told me he did not see Mackay on the night in question. My informant is quite good, so if he says Mackay was not there, then he was not. He did, however, see Mr. Travers and Mr. Derwent. Brewster was to report this to you in the morning, but then he brought word about Mackay's murder. It is perplexing."

Perplexing indeed. But my excitement stirred at the thought of finding more missing pieces of the puzzle. "Did your informant notice Mr. Derwent and Mr. Travers meet anyone?"

Denis grew calmer as he spoke, a counterpart to my rising interest. "My man was not watching Mr. Derwent and Mr. Travers particularly, but he is fairly certain they met no one. The two came in, entered a private parlor for a time, and then went out again. My man had no need to go into the parlor, and as I had no reason to keep watch on the two young men that night, he did not pay attention to them. But he swears they left the tavern whole and well."

"Alone?" I asked. "No one else with them? None following?"

"He says they went out together, but cannot swear they were alone. As I said, he was not watching them, and he can only give me information it was not dangerous for him to obtain. I will not risk losing him for Mr. Derwent, Captain."

"Here is where you and I disagree," I said. "I am interested in bringing a killer to justice by any means necessary. You would let a villain walk free in order to keep secret a source who helps you control others."

Denis's lips tightened. "If you believe I am pleased that young men are coshed for no reason, you are wrong. But exposing my informant is as dangerous to him as walking about Seven Dials proved to be for Mr. Travers. There are other ways to uncover the killer. For instance, you must find out why Mackay visited Sir Gideon tonight. I want to know what enemy killed him, and I want him brought to me."

"If I find the culprit out, I will send him to a magistrate," I said firmly.

Denis gave me a cold look. "And as always, we will disagree on *that* point. If one of my enemies did this, I must know at once. No one else should."

He meant that he did not want it known that a murderer could kill a man who worked for him. Part of Denis's power depended on the belief that no one could touch him or anyone close to him.

"Mackay served many, you said," I pointed out. "He was not necessarily under your protection all the time."

"Oh, but he was," Denis said, his eyes narrowing. "I take care of those who perform tasks for me, well you know. I do not send my best man after you out of curiosity about what you get up to every day. I send Brewster, because you tend to land yourself in more troubles than most, and I want him there to lend his fists. I usually had someone assigned to Mr. Mackay as well, but even I am sometimes stretched thin."

"Then let me speak to whoever was assigned to him," I

said. "He might at least know what Mackay was up to last night."

"Unfortunately, my man had not been much on Mackay lately. I'd needed him for something else."

I studied Denis, who gazed blandly back at me. The other task was obviously nothing he wanted me to know about, and had been more important to him than keeping Mackay safe.

"If Mackay traded information," I said, "he might have been gathering it on the Derwents to sell you."

"I doubt it. The peccadilloes of a reformer and his son are of no interest to me. Yes, I have long known that young Mr. Derwent and his friend Mr. Travers were lovers, but as this information does not benefit me, I care nothing for it."

"Others might pay handsomely for proof that all was not sunshine and innocence in the Derwent household," I pointed out. "Or perhaps Leland knew something about *Mackay*, and Mackay followed them to Seven Dials to silence him."

Denis looked almost amused. "You are casting Mackay as the murderer now?"

My hand tightened on my walking stick, while the brandy, warming in the room, wafted its pungently sweet odor to me. "Here is a possible sequence of events. Mackay kills Travers, and believes he has killed Leland. Even if he agreed to the dying Leland's request that I be summoned, Mackay might have assumed Leland would not recover. He could not anticipate that Brewster and I would know what to do to save him, or that your surgeon would be so skilled. Once he discovers that Leland might live, he slips into the Derwents' house to finish the deed. He is thwarted by one of Sir Gideon's stronger servants. Or, perhaps a confederate who went with him killed him for a personal reason."

Denis listened skeptically. "There are many flaws in your theory."

"I know," I said impatiently. "I am running through them until I believe one." I braced myself on my walking stick and got to my feet. "It would still help me to speak to the man you assigned to watch Mackay. He likely knows more about Mackay than any of us."

"He is on the Continent at the moment," Denis said without changing expression. "When he returns, I will of course place him at your disposal."

And Denis could, of course, keep him on the Continent indefinitely. I would not win that battle.

"What was the last thing Mackay did for you?" I asked. "It might have some bearing."

The look Denis gave me could have chilled the fires of Mount Vesuvius. "I will tell you if I believe it is important. Know that I never sent him to the Derwents to take a measure of Sir Gideon's artwork. Sir Gideon has only indifferent pieces, nothing worth much."

I'd always found the artwork on the walls of the Derwents' pleasant and pretty to look at. But I knew what Denis meant— great art reaches out and grabs one by the throat, not always a comfortable experience.

"As usual, you ask for my help and then curtail me at the same time," I said. "But very well. I will do my best to get to the heart of it all."

"Which is why I value your assistance," Denis replied. "I know that you will."

LEAVING DENIS'S HOME WAS ALWAYS AN ABRUPT experience. Once Denis indicated he'd finished, his lackeys escorted me down the stairs without hesitation. No cordial good-byes, no lingering to pass the time of day or night. No pleasantries. I was handed my coat and hat at the bottom of the stairs and chivvied out the door.

Brewster accompanied me. I saw that neither of us would sleep tonight.

The most logical place to continue my investigation was back at the Derwents. I needed to speak to Sir Gideon as soon as he was able. I doubted Spendlove would want me to talk with him, but I planned to insist.

As I descended from Denis's coach in Grosvenor Square, a young man in a thick wool coat bumped into me.

"Watch it, guvnor," came a snarl from under the hat.

I would have continued into the house, shaking my head at the lad's rudeness, but Brewster would have none of it. He was out of temper—not only had Denis kept information from him but I imagined he'd prefer to be home with his agreeable wife. He reached out and seized the young man by the shoulder, jerking him around to face us.

Brewster's large fist balled up as he drew it back, ready to crash it into the young man's face. The lad's blue eyes widened, he gasped, and his voice transformed into one I knew very well.

"Devil take it, Lacey, help me!"

I grabbed Brewster's elbow just in time. He glared at me and wrenched himself away, at the same time I reached out and twitched off the young man's hat.

Golden hair pinned flat to a woman's head gleamed in the lamplight. "Marianne?" I said in absolute astonishment.

"Fooled you, didn't I?" Marianne asked, then she flashed a scowl at Brewster. "Until this lummox grabbed me."

"Marianne, what the *devil* are you doing?"

I could not believe her transformation. The curves of Marianne's full bosom and hips were well hidden under a shapeless greatcoat, her legs concealed by high boots. The cap had shielded most of her face, and her chin and jaw were dark with stubble—or what looked like stubble.

She had not only put on the clothes of a man—she stood like a man, walked like one, turned her head like one, and had a growl in her voice I'd never heard. She'd metamorphosed herself, using the clothes, the darkness, and the ideas I'd formed in my head about the wearer of such garments, to make herself into the portrait of a young man of the working class.

"Doing underhanded spying for you as *he* asked me to," she answered. "Would you like to hear what I've found out?"

Marianne's voice coming from the rough, male-looking creature was incongruous and a bit disturbing. I glanced at the open door of the Derwents' house, the footman hovering to let us in. Spendlove and Pomeroy were in there—I could not take Marianne inside without either of them wanting to know all about it.

I took her by the arm and steered her up into Denis's coach. I followed her in—Brewster, of course, came along—and shut the door.

CHAPTER 24

I remember," I said as I faced Marianne across the expanse of coach, "distinctly telling Grenville that I did not want you to go to the Bull and Hen yourself, only to find someone who would." I looked her up and down. "But going there is exactly what you have done, isn't it?"

"Of course." Marianne said. "It is an extraordinary enjoyment for a woman to play a breeches part. I never resist a challenge."

"The point is, it was dangerous." As irritated as Marianne could be, I'd grown fond of her. She'd been forced to do much that would have broken a lesser woman, as she eked out survival for herself and her son. I did not want harm to come to her any more than I'd want it to come to Donata or Louisa.

"My dear Lacey, I have been fending off the groping attentions of gentlemen since I was seven years old," Marianne said, sounding more cheerful than she had in a long while. "I am happy to say I am a much taller and rather stronger woman now. Besides, I did not go alone. I took Freddie."

"Freddie?"

"Frederick Hilliard, brilliant comic actor of the company at

Drury Lane. He plays a wonderful Falstaff, though he has to pad himself out for the part."

Brewster had recovered his temper and regarded Marianne with sudden respect. "I've seen Freddie Hilliard play. He dresses in frocks in plays and pantomimes and does all sorts of japes. Me and the missus don't half laugh."

"Indeed," Marianne said. "I had to ask him *not* to go in a gown for our little adventure, because he'd be sure to be recognized. Not that it would bother Freddie. I imagine he's made friends with the whole lot in there by now."

"He is still at the Bull and Hen?" I asked in surprise.

"He is. He thought I should fetch you so he could tell you what he's found. I called in at your house, but your butler told me you'd dashed up here." Marianne shrugged, and even the shrug was mannish. "I think Freddie simply wants a ride home in a soft coach. He deserves it. He does not like such places."

Brewster rumbled with laughter. "We'll rescue him, missus. Wait 'til I tell my Em I met the famous Freddie-Fredericka Hilliard."

Brewster gave the coachman directions, and to his laughter, we rode back through the dark to Seven Dials.

———

THE BULL AND HEN LAY SQUEEZED BETWEEN HOUSES ON Little Earl Street, an artery that led to the open area where seven streets met, so named Seven Dials. While the original street planners had begun with grand intentions, even erecting a pillar of sundials in the center of the meeting roads, the area had become one of the most dangerous rookeries in London. The pillar was long gone, but the rookery remained.

I would have thought a molly house in this area would be more discreet, with a back way in through noisome passages, but that was not the case. Men strode into and out of the Bull and Hen as though it were a common tavern, and they linked arms or had arms about each other's waists without apology.

It was not unusual to see gentlemen of Grenville's set — gentlemen who had no intention of bedding anyone but ladies — linking arms to walk through clubs or crowds at soirees. To have so close a male friend was considered no bad thing among the *haut ton*.

Here, on the other hand, tall women walked alongside the men, laughing when they were pinched or otherwise prodded. These ladies wore headdresses of ostentation to rival Donata's, and gowns of the latest fashion. And of course, they were not women at all.

Denis's coachman had halted a little way down the street from the Bull and Hen, stopping just shy of the junction of Seven Dials. There, we waited. Brewster sat forward in his seat, gazing out the window, watching every passer-by.

I was aware of what a target we made — only the wealthy could afford a coach like this, even Denis's discreet one, with no markings on the doors. The denizens of the area would assume that inside, a rich toff waited for his fancy man to come out and join him. How surprised a robber would be to open the door and find an actress dressed as a boy, an impatient army captain with a sword, and a ruffian used to solving problems with his fists.

We sat for half an hour. Marianne was unworried — she and Freddie, she said, had agreed on a time for him to come out, and he was only a few minutes late.

Ten minutes after that, a tall man whose physique told me he took regular exercise strolled down the street to us. He was arm-in-arm with two other gentlemen who were obviously drunk, the three of them laughing uproariously.

The taller man paused outside our carriage, extracted himself from the others, and lifted his hat. "I must dash, my friends. I am charmed to have met you."

The other two men surrounded him and tried to kiss him.

The tall man let them sandwich him between them while they pressed noisy kisses to his cheeks. Then he pried himself away.

"Really, I must be off. Performances you know. Say my farewells for me."

He'd opened the carriage door and put one foot on the step. The drunken men, still laughing, reached for him, but the taller man easily pushed them off, swung into the carriage, and dropped into the seat next to Marianne and across from Brewster.

The coachman started, snarling foul words at the tall man's admirers. The drunken men alternately laughed and wailed, waving as Brewster reached out and pulled the door shut.

The gentleman who'd joined us took out a large linen handkerchief and wiped his cheeks.

"Bloody mollies," the newcomer said. "All over one, if one is not firm." He tucked the handkerchief away and reached out a strong hand in a tight glove to me. "Captain Lacey, I believe? I am Freddie Hilliard, at your service."

I shook his hand. His grip was firm, powerful. Like Brewster, I had seen Freddie Hilliard perform as women in comic operas, plays, and the *commedia dell'arte*. *Travesti*, such players were called. He was as famous for his portrayal of women as Joseph Grimaldi was for clowns. Freddie would have the audience in riotous laughter with his acting and enthralled by his extraordinary acrobatics.

He was quite fit, his muscular body filling out a well-tailored suit and half boots. He wore his dark hair close-cropped over a hard face, and his brown eyes held intelligence.

"Very good of you to help me," I said as we released hands.

Freddie sank back into his seat and sent me a grin. "Not what you were expecting, was it? Let me guess, you pictured a prancing, mincing dandy with a lace hanky." He held up his thumb and forefinger as though he waved the handkerchief in question. "My father was such a person, back when gentlemen regularly powdered and rouged their faces and shaved their heads to wear wigs trimmed with ribbons. No one could mince about in high heels like my father could. And he shagged half the women in London."

Not certain how to respond to this speech, I sat back and let him talk. My father had lived in the age of powdered wigs as well, until a tax on powder in the 1790s had effectively ended the fashion. My father had worn colorful silk coats, rouged his cheeks, squandered his money on his mistresses, beaten me regularly, and bullied my mother until she'd tried to run away with another man.

Brewster said nothing at all. He was staring at Freddie in something like awe, far more respectful with him that I'd ever see him be of any other gentleman.

"Marianne told me about your problem," Freddie said. He sat back comfortably, giving the coach's luxurious interior an admiring once-over. Then he sighed in genuine sorrow. "Those poor lads. I was happy to nose around the Bull to discover if anyone there did for them. I intended to cosh them myself if I found them. Leland Derwent is a gentle soul."

"You've met him?" I asked.

"Only briefly. At a gathering, introduced by a mutual acquaintance. Mr. Derwent did not like the little soiree, I can tell you. He is a shy young man, not much liking how bois- terous gentlemen can be. He prefers to be private — Mr. Travers was a bit more adventurous. But Mr. Derwent, no matter how upset he becomes, never loses his ability to be compassionate. It is a rare gentleman who is concerned for others regardless of how he feels himself."

"I agree," I said. "I take it from your words that you did not find anyone to cosh at the Bull and Hen?"

Freddie's grin returned. "No, indeed. Once I convinced Marianne to leave the place — trust me when I say, Captain, that I did my best to dissuade her coming at all, but she is severely stubborn — I was able to get others to talk to me. Mr. Derwent and Mr. Travers did indeed arrive at the Bull last night. They were arguing as they came in, so my new friends told me. Mr. Derwent did *not* want to be there, and Mr. Travers was trying to reassure him. *We'll just meet with him and have it done with*, Mr. Travers apparently said, or something like it."

"Meet him?" I pounced on the word. "Meet who?"

"They did not say, unfortunately. Though I see by the glint in your eye that you have an idea who he was."

Mackay. But why was still a mystery.

"Go on," I said, warming to the man.

"Mr. Derwent was so unhappy in the common rooms that Mr. Travers asked for a private parlor. Mr. Derwent had the blunt to pay for it, I know. No one went into the parlor with them; and I was given much wild speculation about what they got up to in there. But this speculation was given to me by drunken and randy men, so I took no notice of it."

"Did the gentleman they'd made the appointment with turn up?" I asked.

"Apparently not. After about an hour or so, the two young men left the room. *I knew he would not come*, Mr. Derwent said, or so the barman told me. Mr. Travers looked angry; Mr. Derwent, gleeful. Smug, the barman said, as though he'd won a point over Mr. Travers. Mr. Travers was scowling as he put on his hat and departed the house with Mr. Derwent. I put a bit more credit into what the barman said, because he was the least drunken fellow in the place. Careful about sampling the wares. Likes to keep himself alert, so he told me."

I took a moment to digest the information. Freddie's report tallied with Denis's man's—that Leland and Gareth entered the Bull, went into a private room, then departed.

"Did anyone follow them out?" I asked. "Did they leave alone, or in a crowd?"

Freddie shrugged his broad shoulders. "There's much coming and going in that place. Even in the short few hours I sat there, men came in and out, either pairing up with those they met inside, or having an ale, going out, and coming back in again later. Made me rather dizzy to watch. It is unusual for a gentleman to simply sit and enjoy his brandy, I gathered. I had many requests for my person and several proposals of marriage before I departed."

"I see you emerged unscathed," Marianne said.

Freddie turned a serious face to her. "Not without difficulty. I am happy I persuaded you to leave. If I had been less robust, I'd have been dragged off and gone at."

I broke in. "But nothing of that sort happened to Leland?"

"No, indeed. Mr. Travers was protective of him, bless him. Didn't let the rough boys near him. When the two departed, they did so without impediment. But as I say, many go in and out the door at the same time. They could have been followed."

"Or someone lay in wait for them outside," I said.

Why had Mackay missed the appointment? I wondered. Had he simply been late? Or had *he* arranged to have Leland and Gareth waylaid? And what the devil for?

"Did anyone overhear what the meeting might have been about?" I asked, without much hope.

"Not that I could discern," Freddie replied. "Speculation ran from them waiting for a so-called vicar to marry them to waiting for someone to return a book."

"Book?" I asked.

"Yes, an odd thing to go on about there. A French book they said, which, I imagine, means one full of enticing pictures and stories. Of the bawdy sort, if I am not being plain enough for you, Captain."

"I have read French books," I said. I had been in the army, fighting Frenchmen, and I'd lived in France during the Peace of Amiens. Plenty of books of drawings and erotic stories had circulated among the officers. I remembered one story in particular, about a gentleman at a gathering in Paris where ladies and gentlemen of society masked themselves and chose partners at random. The gentleman described himself and the robust lady he'd paired up with disporting themselves on a sofa with such exuberance that they'd bounced off the cushions six feet into the air. The exaggeration had made me laugh. I'd tried to share the silly story with my first wife, and shocked her senseless. She hadn't spoken to me for days and regarded me in trepidation, as though fearing I wished to recreate the tale with her. If I told Donata that story, she'd laugh with me and then say something disparaging about French imagination.

"Not books like these, I'd wager," Freddie said, a wicked sparkle in his eyes. "But as I say, I could only get anything clear from the barman, and he heard very little. I find that when gentlemen reach a place where the forbidden is no longer forbidden, they rather lose their self-control. Why they feel themselves safe, I have no idea. I would hate to be in that place when the Runners closed in. The owner, apparently, has an agreement with the magistrates, but such arrangements are fickle."

"Thank you," I said. "It was good of you to go. You did not know me—you had no reason to put yourself in danger at my request."

"Not at all." Freddie waved my thanks away. "Like any actor, I enjoy a chance to perform. And Mr. Derwent is a good lad. I was very upset when Marianne told me what happened to him. He did not deserve that, and neither did Mr. Travers."

"You do not know a man called Nelson Mackay, by chance?" I asked.

Freddie leaned back and studied the ceiling. "Mackay ... No, I cannot recall such a gentleman."

"Curly black hair, blue eyes, soft face. A City man."

Freddie's brows drew together as he thought, but he shook his head. "I am sorry, but no."

"Never mind," I said quickly. "You have done me a good turn. Thank you."

"Again, it was entirely my choice. I hope it has been of some help."

I assured him it had. Though he had not jerked the killer from the shadows and presented him to me, I had more to think about, and who knew where that would lead?

Freddie asked to be let out in Great Wild Street, where he had lodgings. He shook my hand when the carriage stopped, and held out his hand to Brewster as well.

"I am always pleased to meet a patron of comedy," Freddie told Brewster. "I have a gift for it, yes, but alas, the public only takes seriously the tragedians. Delighted to have met you, Captain. Please give my kind regards to Mr. Grenville, if I can make so bold. He is a fine figure of a man, but I know he only has eyes for our Miss Simmons. Good night, dear Marianne. Thank you for the adventure."

So speaking, he pressed a kiss to Marianne's cheek, climbed nimbly out of the carriage, shut the door himself, and lifted his hand in farewell. The coach rolled forward, and Freddie was lost into the night and rising mist.

"Well," Marianne said, as she sat back, crossing her booted ankles. "You have met the famous Frederick Hilliard. What do you think?"

"Quite the gentleman," Brewster said at once. "In spite of him being an unnatural."

"He seems personable enough," I said.

"He is one of the most kind-hearted gentlemen I know," Marianne said. "A lovely man. Unless you step on his lines, and then he will destroy you. With his rapier wit, of course. More than one actor has found this out, to his detriment."

CHAPTER 25

*M*arianne declared she was exhausted and went home to her rooms in Grimpen Lane—more likely mine, but I made no objection. Brewster remained with me after we dropped her at the corner of Grimpen Lane and Russel Street, and we returned to Grosvenor Square. I knew Spendlove would not want me back, but I intended to be there when he questioned Sir Gideon and the others.

Another carriage waited in the square near the Derwent mansion. I did not recognize it, but discovered quickly, once the footman had admitted us, that Sir Montague Harris had arrived.

I had not expected him until morning, but I was very pleased he'd come. The imminent arrest of so well-known a gentleman as Sir Gideon must have spurred him to race here from Whitechapel.

"Lacey, my boy," Sir Montague said, puffing his way from the drawing room as I entered the house. "A pretty problem you've brought to my attention." He bent an eye on the two Runners who followed him. "Mr. Spendlove and Mr. Pomeroy are going over the details of the murder with me. I am lucky to have two of the best investigators in London on the spot, and I look forward to them impressing me."

Pomeroy barked a laugh, but Spendlove scowled. He and Sir Montague had tangled in the past, with Spendlove emerging the loser.

Under the watchful eye of Sir Montague, Pomeroy and Spendlove questioned every member of staff, none of whom had gone to bed this night, again. I followed Spendlove and asked questions of my own, much to his annoyance. He tolerated me hanging at his elbow, but only just.

The trouble was, though the servants below stairs responded with truth in their eyes, it became clear that a determined person could have gotten past them into the house. No break-in would be necessary. Every night, before the house was shut up, a stream of the poor and hungry flowed down the outside stairs to receive the scraps the kitchen threw away. They never lingered, lest the neighbors complain, only took their food and left. The kitchen staff knew most of them by sight, but strangers came from time to time as well.

Leftovers had amassed since dear Mr. Derwent's injury, the cook told us, because the family wasn't eating much, so more of the hungry had been coming. The cook had continued producing the abundant meals she usually did, not being instructed to cease, and she liked the family's practice of giving the unused portions to those who could use them.

"I grew up hungry," the cook told us. She was an ample woman now, with plenty of flesh on her bones. "I understand what it is not to have enough in the belly, and many of those who queue up have hungry mouths to feed at home. We'd just throw away the lot or let it spoil, so why not give to those as need it?"

Spendlove listened without sympathy. "Well, one of those as need it got in here and did a murder, didn't they?"

"Could they have?" I asked her in more friendly tones. "Slipped past you, I mean?" The cook liked me—I often came down here or sent Bartholomew with compliments for her meals. Now that I had a few more coins to rub together, I'd begun giving her substantial tips as well.

The cook directed her answer to me. "I'm sorry to say, they could have, sir. We've been at sixes and sevens below stairs — you can't know the chaos before and after meals. And while we have our own supper in the hall, none of us are minding the back door."

"You make it easy for the criminally minded then," Spendlove growled. "A horde of burglars could come in that door and clean out your master and mistress, and you'd be none the wiser."

"No, sir," the cook said firmly. "There's nothing much to steal and everyone knows it. The family gives away everything they have, poor lambs. They send it out as fast as the master rakes it in. The only thing of value is the silver, and Mr. Bridges has charge of that. No one gets past Mr. Bridges."

Mr. Bridges was the butler, who did keep a sharp eye on the silver plate, locked up after it was cleaned every night in the butler's pantry. The plate came from Mrs. Derwent's family, handed down to her through her mother's line, and Mr. Bridges kept it jealously guarded. No silver had ever gone missing, he said proudly, and none was missing now. I thought about the lesser pieces in the drawing room, and the porcelain figurines, but none of that was missing either. Denis had said the Derwent artwork was not worth much, and his judgment was expert.

We asked the staff to think about which persons they hadn't seen before last night and give a description. They did their best, and we came away with the particulars on three men and two women, who had lingered after they'd taken their handouts. They'd gone by the time the house was shut up, but as the cook emphasized, in the chaos of clearing up and settling in for the night, anyone could have been missed.

"He'd have been able to walk right out the front door,"

Spendlove said as we returned above stairs. "The lad in the foyer isn't there all the time."

True, the footman was called upon by members of the family and other servants to run errands, plus he would have to relieve himself once in a while.

"Surprised the lot of them aren't murdered in their beds," Spendlove said sourly. "Thanks to you, Captain, I don't have a suspect to bring to Sir Nathaniel in the morning. And it was bad of you to bring in Sir Montague Harris. He has no business this far from Whitechapel."

"You were going to arrest an innocent man," I said. "I won't have it."

"Don't tell me what you will and won't have, sir. I'll have *you* in irons for something, along with Mr. Denis, see if I don't. You'll hang right beside him."

"As long as I've truly done the deed," I said coolly, "you're welcome to me."

I DON'T KNOW WHEN I FELL ASLEEP. I MUST HAVE BEEN SO relieved that I'd turned Spendlove's attentions from Sir Gideon and the Derwent family that I finally succumbed to exhaustion and sank into a chair somewhere.

The next thing I knew, Bartholomew and Brewster were stuffing me into a carriage under the strident tones of my wife. I fell against the seat, then my senses were bathed in the warmth and scent of Donata beside me.

I slept on her shoulder, vaguely aware she was speaking to me, but I have no idea what about. At the South Audley Street house, Bartholomew was joined by Barnstable to help me upstairs and to bed.

The sun was already rising, the streets filling with servants from the great houses, rushing to fulfill their masters' wishes.

The master of this house, such as he was, fell into a stupor and began to snore.

Donata woke me by sitting up on my bed, her legs folded under her. She clutched a lit cigarillo between her fingers, filling the bed with fragrant smoke. I coughed.

"Ah, you are awake at last," she said. "This is a pretty pickle. What are you going to do?"

"Lie in bed." I laced my hands behind my head, every limb heavy. "And enjoy looking at my wife. She is quite beautiful."

"Flattery will not solve things," Donata said, though she looked pleased. "I must admit, I was never fond of the Derwents before I met you. Too unworldly, holding themselves to higher morals than anyone else. At least, that is how they seemed to me, and to many others, I might add. Now I feel terribly sorry for them. They have no idea how to deal with what has been thrust upon them. Their predicament is very *Vicar of Wakefield*, is it not?"

The vicar's family in that novel—good, upstanding, and kind but naïve people—suffered trouble after trouble that poured upon them. But like Job, the Vicar of Wakefield stood steadfast and patient, and eventually, he and his family were restored to some happiness.

"I hope the ending of the Derwents' story is as satisfactory," I said.

"At least no one has kidnapped Melissa into a bawdy house." Donata shuddered. "But it could so easily be done. The Derwents believe that because they are good people, the rest of the world is good as well. How awful that they have discovered otherwise."

I laid my hand on hers. "And we, the cynical, worldly, and embittered must help them back to the path of righteousness."

My wife gave me the disparaging look the statement deserved. "Do not take the metaphor too far, Gabriel. But yes, I want to help them. While they once drove me to distraction, the Derwents now move me to pity."

I had not had a chance to tell her about my adventures the previous night, so I related what Denis had revealed about Mackay and then my meeting with Marianne and Freddie Hilliard. "So I know Gareth and Leland were alive and well when they left the Bull and Hen," I finished. "But not who they met between leaving there and finishing up in the passage."

Donata lifted one shoulder in a shrug, holding the cigarillo negligently between her fingers. "You are a step further. Closer to the place they died."

"True, but I am still not certain what to make of it. Did they meet with Mr. Mackay at all? Or were they waylaid by others before they could? Mr. Hilliard made mention of a book." I remembered Gareth's last conversation with me, when he'd explained that he'd found the means to ease himself from being dependent on Leland. *A windfall,* he'd said. *A fine one.* "Books of forbidden erotica, especially well-bound French tomes, can be quite costly," I went on. Grenville collected first editions and historic books, which fetched large prices. "Perhaps Gareth came into possession of such a book — somehow — and wanted to sell it to Mackay, or have Mackay sell it for him. This could explain Leland's anger at Gareth's method of obtaining money. Leland is not the sort who would approve of naughty books."

"No, indeed," Donata agreed. "He engages in what Mr. Spendlove would call unnatural behavior because he loved Gareth, not because he enjoys lewdness. He is a very proper lad."

"Mr. Hilliard was disapproving of the clientele of the Bull and Hen as well," I observed.

"I have made the acquaintance of Mr. Hilliard," Donata said. "At racing meets and other country events. He is very sporting. Quite a gentleman, and not what one expects from a man happy to dress up in a frock."

"Perhaps he disapproves of those in the Bull and Hen

because he does not want to be arrested and hanged. The men I saw at the tavern were not at all discreet."

"Hmm." Donata's eyes narrowed. "And we have no idea why Mr. Mackay went to the Derwents' last night."

"Not yet, no." I let my hand rest on her silk-clad thigh. "Did he come to inquire after Leland's health? Had he paid Gareth for the book already and assumed it was at the Derwents'? Or had he decided to help himself to it, whether money had exchanged hands or not? Books were scattered all over the drawing room, as though someone had rifled the bookshelves, so perhaps Mackay, or his killer, was looking for it." I'd seen none that appeared to be very costly when I'd scanned them—all books were expensive, but I had not noted any that were extraordinary. The Derwents' books, like their artwork, were acquired for the pleasure they gave, not their value as objects.

I moved on to another possibility. "Or did Mackay seek Sir Gideon to blackmail him about Leland's proclivities? If so, Sir Gideon might very well have taken up the poker and struck him down. Though I do not like to think it."

Donata considered. "You said yourself that Sir Gideon had no blood on him. And he did not. I would have seen it."

"I know. But Spendlove is right that he could have rid himself of the clothes long before we arrived." I absently stroked Donata's leg, savoring the warmth beneath the silk. "The explanation I like more is that the killer gained the house through the kitchens, perhaps after seeing Mackay entering and noting the hungry lining the stairs to the scullery door. He waits until Mackay is alone and strikes him dead. Then our murderer exits through the busy kitchen or out the front door when the footman isn't watching." I let out a sigh, resting my gaze on the brocade hangings above me. "I have no idea what truly happened. I feel as ineffectual as ever."

Donata gave me a wise nod and dropped the end of her

cigarillo into a bowl on the bedside table. "You always do. And then a solution presents itself to you. The correct one."

"I do hope it presents itself quickly. I would like to return to being a lazy, married man."

I traced the curve of her leg through the fabric and turned my head to look at her. Donata regarded me calmly.

"Gareth's funeral is today," she said. "Lady Derwent told me. She also told me that they'd received a polite note from Mrs. Travers indicating that they should not bother to come. Far too difficult for Lady Derwent in her poor health, and Leland still not recovered. A pointed request for them to stay away."

I drew my finger along the crease between thigh and calf of her folded leg. "Mrs. Travers is the only person I've ever encountered with severe dislike for the Derwent family," I said. "Sir Gideon speculates it is because Gareth found more of a home there than his own house." I let my hand slide away. "I will go and pay my respects. Gareth deserves that."

"But I will not," Donata said. "A dowager viscountess coming upon them suddenly would throw a vicarage in Bermondsey into disarray. Kinder if I stay home. The funeral should be for Gareth and his family, not a grand reception for me." Donata unfolded herself and stretched out beside me, propping herself on her elbow. "Besides, your daughter arrives this evening, and I want to be certain all is ready."

My heart rejoiced once more at the thought of seeing Gabriella again, with her sunny smiles and sensible forthrightness. Gabriella was still coming to terms with the fact that I had sired her, rather than the French major she'd grown up with, but she was making a great effort, and I loved her for it.

I wanted to thank Donata for accepting Gabriella and helping her, but words would not come. I ensnared my wife with one hand, pulled her down to me, and thanked her without words.

Passion might have come of our embrace, but Bartholomew entered just then with a tray heaped with breakfast.

Donata showed no shame about lounging about in bed with her husband, only pulled her dressing gown closed and sat up, reaching eagerly for coffee.

I pried myself up as well, my loose nightshirt falling from one shoulder. "What time is it?" I asked as Bartholomew set a tray heaped with enough breakfast for two across my lap.

"Eleven of the clock, sir. I shall lay out your black suit in the dressing room."

Eleven. I had prided myself, since my marriage, on rising early, keeping at bay my fear of becoming a pampered, useless fool. But events this week had put paid to my usual habits.

"Thought you'd like to know, sir," Bartholomew said. "My brother and I, and Mr. Grenville, we found Mr. Derwent's clothes."

I lifted my brows, nearly dropping the slice of toast I had picked up. "You did? Where? Why did you not tell me?"

"Didn't have a chance until now," Bartholomew answered reasonably. "What with Mr. Mackay getting himself killed, and Mr. Denis pulling you about, and you dropping over on your feet in weariness."

Donata poured herself a cup of coffee and daintily lifted a square of toast. "Grenville might have sent word."

"Don't know about that, madam," Bartholomew answered. "He went out again, as I said, sir, last night, and we've not seen him since. He didn't leave any notes with us to deliver."

"Doesn't matter." I waved my hand, scattering crumbs. "Where did you find the clothes?"

"Bloke had them." Bartholomew stood easily next to the bed, unembarrassed about speaking to his master and mistress while they were en dishabille. "A man local to Seven Dials. I spied him walking around after you and Mr. Grenville left us there. I thought, good Lord, there's a shabby man in a coat far too fine for the likes of him. Matthias and I gave chase, and we ran him down. He was terrified of us, two large lads as we are. We asked him where he'd gotten the clothes. He tried to put us off with a tale of finding them in the river—he thought at first we were the Watch or foot patrol with the Runners. When we got him calmed down, he admitted he found them on the ground in a street one away from where Mr. Travers got himself killed. Nothing in them, no watch or money, but he could have been lying and already sold them."

Very quickly, I had no doubt. "Had he seen who discarded them?" I asked hopefully.

"No, sir. But I'm not surprised. He was terrified of his shadow. A poor specimen, shivering and gaunt." Bartholomew hesitated. "I let him keep the clothes. I hope I did right."

Donata answered for me. "Leland would have done such a thing. Reasoned he had many others. I trust you took his name so that the captain may quiz him again if necessary."

"I did, your ladyship." Bartholomew took a scrap of paper from his pocket. "Wrote it out plain."

He handed me the paper. On it Bartholomew had written in block capitals, *Mr. John Olmstead, Number 17, Shorts Gardens*.

"He lives with half a dozen other blokes there," Bartholomew went on, "He says you'll mostly find him at home."

CHAPTER 26

I went to the funeral of Gareth Travers with only Brewster to accompany me. We took a hackney from Mayfair, leaving Donata's carriage free for her use.

Gareth was to be buried in the churchyard at Bermondsey, beside the small church his father presided over. The Reverend Travers did not perform the service—another vicar, whose jowls nearly obscured his dog collar, did so. I'd never met Gareth's father, and when I saw him, sagging against his wife's shoulder, I knew he'd never have been able to say the words over his son's coffin.

Whether Reverend Travers was drunk or simply bowed with grief I could not tell. His young wife stood straight next to him, her lips pursed in disapproval. The rest of the small turnout consisted of men and women from the parish, plus a few straight-backed ladies who appeared to be friends of Mrs. Travers.

Rolling up at the last minute, his carriage stark black against the gray buildings and gray skies, was Grenville.

His arrival caused a stir. I could not tell if anyone there knew who he was, or simply wondered why a toff had turned up for the funeral of an impoverished vicar's son. Grenville came to stand next to Brewster and me at the edge of the gathering as the second vicar began to read the burial service.

I had heard the words far too often, and I never liked them. The phrases about how man is born to misery and suffering did not match the Gareth Travers I'd known. He'd been happy with his life, not worrying about much beyond his pride, embraced by a kind family who'd treated him as one of their own.

The part about man having only a short time to live and being cut down like a flower was true, however. Someone had cut off Gareth's life far too soon. Though he'd not lived an entirely blameless existence, he had not deserved that.

Once the casket had been lowered into the muddy hole, I moved forward and tossed in a clump of earth as well as the flower I'd purchased. Leland could not be here to send off the man he'd loved best in life, and so I said his good-byes for him.

"Sleep well, my friend," I whispered, and then the damp soil hit the wooden coffin with a melancholy sound.

GRENVILLE WAITED FOR ME, AND WE WALKED TOGETHER TO the Traverses, who lingered in the circle of their friends. Mrs. Travers gave me an unfriendly look, but the Reverend Travers took my offered hand.

His bloodshot eyes confirmed he was both grieving and far gone in drink, using one to relieve the pain of the other. "You knew my son well?" he asked. He was about ten years my senior, but already stooped and gray, his hands trembling.

"Not as well as I would have liked," I said. "I am a friend of Leland Derwent."

Mrs. Travers snorted in derision, but Reverend Travers paid no attention to her. "Young Leland is a good lad. Gareth's letters were always filled with him and the Derwents. Kind people." He squeezed my hand. "A point of fact, sir, if you are such friends with them ..."

"Yes?" I asked as he trailed off.

Reverend Travers tugged me closer, as though wanting to whisper to me, out of his wife's hearing. Grenville took the cue and became his most charming, turning Mrs. Travers away and gesturing to the church, asking about its history.

Reverend Travers put his lips to my ear. "Could you ask young Mr. Derwent to return the book? I will need it."

"Book?" I whispered. Surely not the French erotica ... but my interest piqued.

"A prayer book. About so big." Mr. Travers released my hand to frame the air approximately five inches high by a few across. "It was mine, has been in my family for years. I gave it to him at New Year's, but now that Gareth is gone, it belongs at home."

Ah. I drew back, disappointed. A family Book of Common Prayer would not be as costly as a valuable French tome filled with drawings, even risqué ones.

"Certainly," I said. "When I next visit the Derwents I will inquire."

"Thank you, sir. You are a gentleman."

Mrs. Travers looked daggers at both me and her husband. I was not certain whether she had heard or was angry because she hadn't.

Grenville expressed his condolences to the reverend once again, and we both took our leave.

"Good Lord," Grenville said in a quiet voice as we made our way to his carriage, Brewster following. "Mrs. Travers must have been a comely woman once, but she has thoroughly ruined her looks. And so young too. Tragic."

I tried to be charitable. "She cannot have an easy time, married to an elderly man who lives in his cups."

"She has my sympathy, of course, but only so far," Grenville said. "I've met ladies with difficult husbands who manage to remain both lovely and agreeable. She has decided what she will be."

"Some women are born shrews," Brewster said unapologetically. "They'd be that way no matter who they married." With that, he climbed up onto the seat with the coachman, and Grenville's footman helped us into the carriage.

As we went, I told Grenville that Bartholomew had informed me of finding Leland's clothes, which he confirmed.

"I thought it kindest to let the man have them," Grenville said. "The chap was terrified. I gave him some coin as well. I do not think he had anything to do with the attack, before you ask. If he did see what happened, he was far too afraid to tell me."

"Well, if you could not persuade him to tell you all, I doubt I could. But Sir Gideon might."

"True." Grenville subsided. "We would have to take Sir Gideon to the man, however. I doubt Mr. Olmstead will travel to Mayfair."

So be it. I, in turn, told Grenville about Freddie Hilliard's visit to the Bull and Hen, and my speculation about their intended meeting with Mackay, who was now dead. Grenville knew about the death—Matthias and Bartholomew had dutifully reported it to him—and he looked interested at what Freddie had observed.

As we rumbled over Blackfriars Bridge and headed toward Mayfair, Grenville said, "Why don't you take dinner with me, Lacey? We'll have a long natter over this case and sift through everything we've learned."

I shook my head. "Gabriella comes home today. I want to be there when she arrives."

"Ah, yes, that is so. In that case, I will descend at my club. Jackson will be happy to deliver you to South Audley Street." He idly lifted the blind and looked out at the Strand as we passed along it. "By the way," he said in a casual tone, "I have ceased to be on intimate terms with Signora Carlotti. I decided

I could hardly warn Percy Saunders off Marianne and then pursue my own *inamorata*. Signora Carlotti is a shrewd woman, and we parted amicably." He dropped the blind and gave me a wry smile. "I am certain Paola has someone waiting in the wings, so to speak. I went to Marianne and used the excuse of explaining your scheme of her finding someone to send to the Bull and Hen to tell her what I'd done."

Thus explaining his absence at the musicale, and Marianne's better spirits on our adventure the night before.

"As you can imagine, she was very angry with me over Saunders," Grenville said with a slight smile. "I do understand her predicament—she has had to grub her way for so long, she thought to continue grubbing with Saunders. I have set up a trust for her, to pay her and her son an annuity for the rest of their lives, even if she marries and hands over every penny of her share to her husband. Least I could do for her putting up with me."

"That was uncommonly generous of you," I said, impressed.

Grenville's hand on his walking stick stiffened. "I know you think me a fool. But I won't see her starve because we could not get on. She shall not prostitute herself to selfishly cruel fellows like Saunders. Or marry a brute to keep herself and young David fed. I have only ever wanted to help her."

He glanced out the window again, but I saw the depth of emotion in his eyes. I realized in that moment that Grenville loved her.

The revelation surprised me, but it should not have. Grenville had always been different with Marianne, both kind and bad-tempered at the same time. He'd never quite taken to any other woman since he'd made her acquaintance.

I waited to let him regain his composure, before I asked, "And how did Marianne take this news?"

Grenville flashed me a sudden grin. "Once I made her

understand, I am pleased to say that, for the first time since meeting her, I rendered her speechless."

I RETURNED TO A HOME THAT WAS LIVELY AND CHAOTIC, which was just what I needed. Gareth's funeral had stirred my melancholia, but in a house preparing for my daughter's return, I had no opportunity to indulge in it.

Donata saw me from the first floor landing and started down to me. I met her partway up, took her by the elbows, pushed her against the wall, and kissed her, hard, on the lips. Her protests silenced as soon as her back touched the paneling, and her eyes sparkled with interest.

I would not have embarrassed her so in other circumstances. But the sound of earth hitting the coffin still echoed in my ears, and I needed life to chase away the clinging odor of death.

Donata was life. She looked upon it, seized it with both hands, and wrested it to her will. She was warm and welcoming, and had enough spice to chase away dullness.

She gave me a calculating look when I released her. The glimmer in her blue eyes told me she was not displeased with what I'd done, no matter that all her servants busily rushed about us.

She touched my cheek, her fingers gentle. "Sir Gideon sent word that Leland is awake again and asking for you. Why don't you run along, Gabriel? Your daughter isn't due for another few hours, and you'll only be in the way here."

I leaned my fist to the wall near her head. All the responses I could make flitted through my mind, and I decided on one.

"God bless you." I kissed her lips again, and took myself away.

LELAND DID NOT LOOK MUCH BETTER. HE LAY FLAT ON HIS back, his face too white, his hair in lank and unwashed wisps. His eyes were hollow, with a sunken look that disquieted me.

I sat down beside him in the chair that had become fixed in that position. The seat was flattened now from Catherine Danbury, Melissa, Lady Derwent, Louisa, and Sir Gideon hunkering there, waiting for what would come.

Leland studied me a long while, his lashes damp, while his labored breathing filled the silence. A clock on the bureau *tick, tick, ticked*, contrasting the rumble of wheels on the pavement below. Outside, the world moved on. In here, death hovered patiently.

When the clock struck four, small, polite chimes in the quiet, Leland asked in a hoarse whisper, "He's buried, then?"

"Yes." My hands hung between my knees, limp. "It was a dignified service. I said good-bye for you."

Leland groped for me, and I clasped his cold, shaking hand. "Thank you," he said. "I loved him. I'd have done anything for him. I'd have gladly gone in his place."

"I am sorry," I said sincerely. I was sorry for a lot of things, including hurting this very young, vulnerable boy.

"Not your fault." Leland wet his cracked lips. "I was a fool. So was Gareth. We'd been quarreling over so many things. But underneath it all, we still loved. Do you understand?"

I gave him a nod. I'd known married couples less devoted than Leland and Gareth.

"Not your fault you didn't know," Leland went on. "About us, I mean. Not many did."

"What about Gareth's parents?" I asked. "Did they ever discover your secret?"

"They never said. Mrs. Travers hates me and my family. She told me so. Blames us for taking Gareth away from his father. Which is true—we did."

I released his hand and leaned my elbows on my knees. "Leland, Gareth ran to you willingly. I had an unhappy home myself; I too found refuge in other boys' houses. You and your father and mother gave Gareth the family he needed."

"But I never gave a thought to *his* father," Leland said, determined to be guilty. "I was selfish, and wanted Gareth around me all the time."

I made an impatient noise. "Please, do not browbeat yourself. Gareth could have reconciled with his family at any time. Not doing so was his choice."

"They did reconcile a little this year," Leland said, his haunted look easing. "Gareth took me home with him at New Year's, and we spoke with his father. My father sent along some pamphlets about how to wrest oneself from the evils of drink—not the horrible kind of pamphlets about driving oneself to hell, but ones that address the real struggles of the drunkard. My father writes them himself, with the help of other men who have had to do battle with the vice."

I imagined the pamphlets did not go over well with the Reverend and Mrs. Travers, even if given in the best of intentions.

"Mr. Travers and Gareth talked together, alone, for a time, I was happy to see. I was too shy to say much to Mrs. Travers." Leland gave me a faint smile. "Not that she wanted to speak to me at all. She made herself scarce."

I wondered. Mrs. Travers was a shrewd woman and must have concluded at some point that Leland and Gareth shared a bed. Had she told her husband? Would either of them have become so ashamed and enraged that they sent someone after them to kill them?

The meeting Leland described had been at New Year's— the same time I had been in Oxfordshire getting married. It was March now. Would Mrs. Travers have waited that long to assuage her anger? And I could not see Gareth's broken father having either the will or the strength to send an assassin after his own son.

"Have you remembered anything more?" I asked Leland. "I

know you went to the Nines, I know you kicked up a fuss. Not very tactful, my friend. If you threaten someone, make sure you're at a safe distance before you do so."

"Did I?" Leland rubbed his bandaged head. "I don't remember."

"Unfortunately, those at the Nines do."

"Well, if I did, then they must have deserved it," Leland said with conviction. "I have heard of the Nines—a terrible place, my father says. It ought to be closed."

"I believe it will be soon," I said. "The man who runs the place, Forge, had his bullies take you out into a yard and rough you up a little. Do you remember that?"

"No." He sounded mournful. "There are vast blanks about the night. I do remember arguing with Gareth in a carriage. About ..." Leland scrubbed at the side of his head and let out a moan when he touched something sensitive. "I don't know."

"You were in a carriage?" I asked. "Your father's? Your father's coachman did not mention picking you up at the Nines."

Leland looked puzzled. "No, not ours. I do not know. Gareth never owned a coach, that is for certain. It must have been a hackney—I remember a particularly long tear in the upholstery, and my father's coachman would never stand for that. Gareth must have hired it, to take us to the man Gareth said he had an appointment to meet."

"What man?" I asked, sitting up straight. "Do you mean Mackay?"

Leland blinked. "I do not know. Gareth and I were heading to meet a man about business, somewhere near Covent Garden." He looked at me in perplexity. "Why did I suddenly I remember that? When everything else is gone?" He furrowed his brow, pain entering his eyes as he thought. He sighed. "No, nothing more. Forgive me, Captain."

CHAPTER 27

$\mathcal{T}$he point is, you are starting to remember," I said, trying to sound reassuring and hide my growing convictions at the same time. "I know for a fact that you went to a tavern called the Bull and Hen in Seven Dials, in Little Earl Street, near where you were found. Do you recall that?"

Leland frowned and shook his head. "I do not remember a tavern. As I said, it is only flashes."

"Tell me about the flashes," I said. "Perhaps we can piece together what happened between your snippets of memory and what I've managed to discover."

Leland sent me a grateful look. "Very well, I will try. As I say, I remember now that Gareth had an appointment that evening. I did not want him to go, and no, I do not recall why. I know nothing of what happened at Brooks's or the Nines, but I know Gareth was very excited. I'd never seen him like that. Both enraged and happy. The next thing I remember, we were in a coach, and he …"

Leland closed his mouth, flushing a dark red. It was not a healthy color, but Leland's fair face was not one that could hide embarrassment.

"You mean you became intimate," I said. "In the coach."

"Yes, Gareth, he liked … unusual places … when we found ourselves private. I was quite happy we had made things up between us, so I did not stop him. I let my appetite overrule my common sense." His hand balled to a weak fist. "I should not give into such things. A man ought to always be in control of his appetites."

His self-chastisement made me want to laugh. "Leland, my friend, every man on earth has let his appetites rule him from time to time. Common sense does not come into it."

Leland regarded me in surprise. "Even *you*, Captain?"

Now I did laugh. "Good Lord, especially me. I've never been one to retain my sense when tempted by a beautiful lady. And I find so many ladies beautiful."

His puzzlement was very Leland-like. "But you are married."

"Lady Breckenridge tempted me most of all, and she continues to do so, even though we are now staid and married. But enough of the hair shirt, lad. What happened?"

His flush did not ease. "It is unclear after that. You say we went to the tavern? But I do not know. I only remember being … with Gareth … and then… Nothing. I woke up and …"

Leland's voice broke. I placed a hand on his shoulder, my laughter gone. "Do not think on that that. Remember Gareth as he was." I waited, letting his regain his composure. "Was your intimacy with Gareth before or after the meeting?"

Leland shook his head. "I have no idea. Before, I should think. Gareth was saying this would solve everything. I was trying to stop him going. If I hadn't, if everything had gone as it was supposed to, then perhaps …"

"Leland," I said severely. "Whatever did happen is not your fault. You must believe that. It is the fault of whoever waylaid you and struck you down. What you have told me clarifies one thing—that you were positioned to be found half-undressed. You say Gareth liked unusual places, but Gareth was fastidious, took such care of his clothing. A coach is one thing, the dirty cobbles of a passageway is something else. You were led there or taken there, coshed, and arranged as you were." The killers might have meant the tableaux to be even more explicit, but Mackay had come upon the scene. Though I hadn't yet ruled out that he might have directed it.

"You've already told me how you awakened," I said. "Did you see Mackay right away? Was he hovering over you? Or did he run in?"

"I was on the ground," Leland said in a faint voice. "I couldn't move. The next thing I knew, this man was bending over us. He looked respectable enough, and I begged him to run and find you."

"Which was a wise thing to do," I said. "I'm glad you summoned me."

"You saved my life," Leland said, his gratitude reviving my guilt.

"I wish I'd been in time to save Gareth's." I let out my breath. "I am sorry to keep asking you questions, but if I'm to find out the truth I need to be ruthless. I am convinced Gareth meant to meet Mackay, who was a dealer, of sorts, but of mostly stolen goods. And he was a blackmailer."

Leland's confusion was genuine. "A *blackmailer*? Why would Gareth want to have truck with a blackmailer? Gareth wouldn't blackmail anyone."

"I was rather thinking Mackay blackmailed *him*. Perhaps about you."

Leland weakly shook his head. "I doubt Gareth would have been so happy if we were on our way to pay a blackmailer. No, he was quite anticipating something."

"Then I believe Gareth went to see Mackay in Mackay's other capacity. The man bought and sold artwork for others. I have heard mention of a book. Think back. Before this all happened, did Gareth talk about a book he either wanted to buy or sell?"

Leland frowned. "He never mentioned a book. But I would

not be surprised if he wanted to sell something to make money. Gareth was ever trying schemes like that, and they never came off. He was very conscious about taking money from me and my father. It is one of the things we'd quarreled about—in the past and recently. Always, in fact. He wanted a way to be independent from me, he said. I told him he never had to worry about an income whether we stayed together forever or parted, but Gareth was always proud."

Like Marianne. She depended on others to live, but she hated to be kept.

"He'd told me he'd found a way," Leland went on. "But he never explained what he meant. I doubt the sale of a book would set him up for life, though."

I felt a warmth run through me, which I'd come to know was a sign my brain had stumbled upon something important. "Perhaps it was not a book itself," I suggested. "I might be too fixated on such a thing. Perhaps he found something *inside* the book. Something valuable, and he knew Mackay would know exactly how valuable."

"If he did, he never told me what it was." Leland deflated. "He ought to have told me."

I understood why he hadn't. Gareth had wanted to be certain he'd come into the money before he announced it to Leland. He'd set the appointment at the Bull and Hen, a place so notorious that anyone who saw them enter would assume Leland and Gareth had gone in for the usual reasons a man did. A private parlor, a meeting with a third man—the clientele of the Bull and Hen would likely not realize Gareth meant for a wholly business transaction to occur.

Gareth had either planned to collect the money from Mackay for whatever he'd brought to sell, or fix another appointment for the transaction. If a robber had got wind that Gareth or Mackay was walking around with a valuable object, they'd have motive to follow them and strike.

I was not certain a straightforward robber would then half

undress the lads and leave them in a passage, but perhaps he'd known they were mollies and had a sense of humor. Or, perhaps he'd realized that them being found thus would hint that it was a crime by someone disgusted at them, steering us away from the true reason they were set upon.

If my speculations were correct, then we were looking for a killer or killers who had been wandering near the Bull and Hen—or actually inside it—and happened to hear Gareth talk about this valuable object he possessed. Or, we needed to find someone else who knew about Gareth's prize and followed them to Seven Dials that night.

I also wanted very much to know what Gareth had been selling and where it was now.

"I'd like to go through Gareth's things," I said. "Would you mind?"

"Not at all." Leland's expression turned sad. "I will have to sort through them myself, sooner or later."

"I can make a start for you. Where did he have rooms?" The Albany housed many an upper-class bachelor gentleman, and if Leland liked to provide Gareth with the best, the Albany was a good possibility.

Leland looked confused. "He had rooms here. He was living with us."

I hadn't realized that. Another reason Gareth must have chafed. This house was luxurious in the extreme, but I remembered Gareth telling me he felt his confinement and wanted to be his own man.

"Bridges will unlock the door for you," Leland said. "My mother ordered it shut, but no one will mind if *you* enter his chamber."

"Then I will do so directly." I rose, more animated than I'd been in a while. I could not turn back time and prevent Gareth's murder, but I would see whoever had done it cowering at my feet before I handed him over to the Runners.

Leland subsided, his breathing still labored. "What does it

all mean, Captain?" he asked me, tears in his eyes. "Why did Gareth die?"

"That is what I will find out," I said. I reached down for his hand and squeezed it again. "I promise you."

———

GARETH'S CHAMBER WAS ON THE NEXT FLOOR UP, IN THE front of the house, overlooking the street. Mrs. Danbury, I learned when I reached the landing, had the chamber in the rear, with a view of the garden. She came out of that bedroom as Bridges led me toward Gareth's.

"Captain?" Mrs. Danbury quickly closed the door of her room, flushing, as though a look at her furniture would compromise her modesty. "What are you doing up here?"

I briefly explained. Catherine's startled expression changed to one of understanding and curiosity. "I will help you," she announced. "Bridges, do unlock the door. And have tea brought."

I entered a chamber that was as elegant as any other in this house. The bed had delicate posts and a brocade canopy to keep out drafts, the drapes on the window matching those on the bed. The room was cold, the fire out, and Catherine ordered one built so we would not catch a chill.

Bridges hurried off to obey, and I stood in the center of the chamber and looked around me. While expensive and comfort-able pieces furnished it—chairs, writing table, low sofa under the window—matching the décor of the rest of the house, Gareth had left his own mark here. Books and papers were piled on the writing table, a few markers from a gaming hell had been left on the nightstand, along with a programme from an opera, and a pamphlet on the latest political dilemma in Parliament. The armoire was filled with a fashionable young man's suits, the small dressing room holding his boots, a dressing table with brushes, razor, teeth cleaners, scissors for precisely trimming side whiskers, a rack of neatly folded cravats, boxes of gloves. Everything was neat, because the Derwent servants tidied up after him, but this was a bachelor's room through and through.

"What are we looking for precisely?" Catherine asked me, already opening and going through the night table.

"Precisely, I do not know. Anything valuable, or a book worth selling. Or something inside the book."

Catherine turned at once to the low bookshelf near the window. I intercepted her. "The book in question might be ... indelicate," I said.

She flashed me a smile, sunlight dancing on her fair hair, reminding me why I'd been enchanted when I'd first met her. Donata had firmly supplanted her charms, but I could not pretend that Mrs. Danbury was not a beautiful woman.

"My second husband had all sorts of indelicate books," she said. "Mickey enjoyed everything about the act, unfortunately with a good number of people other than me." Her smile dimmed. "He liked to read about it, and showed me the books. So, do not worry. I cannot be shocked."

Catherine turned quickly to the shelves. She'd laughed, but I'd seen the pain in her eyes. Her wretch of a second husband had much hurt her.

She and I looked over those books, and then everything on the writing table. I doggedly went through the armoire, the night table, then slid under the bed and checked the mattress. A maid carried in a tray of tea, uttering a small cry when she saw only my boots sticking out from under the bed.

I heard Catherine soothe her, and the delicate rattle of porcelain as the tray was set down. I scrambled out, let Catherine pour me tea, then I searched the dressing room.

I finished as the tea ran out, and sank glumly to the sofa. Catherine perched on the chair next to the writing table, nibbling a tea cake.

"Nothing," I said. "Whatever Gareth had, it is not here."

The only books had been ordinary ones that could be purchased in any London bookshop—novels, travel books, and tomes on philosophy and natural history. They were finely bound editions, bought new, as opposed to the secondhand ones I'd collected, but nothing that would make a man rich for life. We'd found no exquisite volume of French erotica or even the prayer book Gareth's father had given him. We'd rifled the pages of all the books and found nothing but a dried flower and a lace handkerchief, used as bookmarks. I felt behind the end papers and found nothing there either.

Catherine was more cheerful about the failure than I was. "He must have kept it somewhere else, or given it to someone. I'll continue looking, Captain. We'll turn it up. If this book does prove to be a gilded pictorial of people doing unmentionable things to each other, what would you like me to do with it?"

"Hide it," I said. "And for God's sake, show it to none in this household."

Catherine laughed. "I think you are wise, Captain."

She and I were friends again, at least. I departed the house, ready to leave the rest of the search to her. My daughter was due any minute, and I wanted to be nowhere but home when she arrived.

BREWSTER MET ME OUTSIDE AS I EMERGED. "DID THE LAD tell ya who done it?" he asked as he fell into step beside me. I'd walked the short distance, to the dismay of Donata's servants, but the day had turned fine.

"He does not know," I said. "But I'm ever more certain that Mr. Forge and his men had nothing to do with it."

"His nibs don't care," Brewster said reasonably. "He only cares that the Nines will close and be ripe for the plucking."

I lengthened my stride, my knee protesting, but I ignored it. "I want to ask his nibs more about Mackay."

Brewster shrugged as he kept stride with me. "You can ask."

"Do you know if Mackay had been hired to procure anything of late for him?"

"No." Brewster's blank expression told me nothing. "I don't ask what Mr. Denis gets up to. It's his business, innit?"

"You simply do what you're told?" I asked, impatient.

"It's what I'm paid for. I work for Mr. Denis because it's a good job, and what other work was I going to get when me fighting days were behind me? If you do what he asks and leave him be, he looks after you. Nothing more. I didn't have nothing to do with this Mackay bloke, and I don't know nothing about him. If I'd been asked to watch him, maybe I'd have something to tell you. But I wasn't, so I don't."

Brewster looked untroubled—he simply stated facts. It must be restful to possess a mind that held neither curiosity nor obsession.

"All right then, please send Mr. Denis word that I wish to speak with him again about Mackay. Is it your job to do that?"

Brewster gave me a grin, unoffended. "In this case, it is. I'll trot down there now while you say good day to your daughter, shall I?"

BY THE TIME MY FRONT DOOR IN SOUTH AUDLEY STREET came into view, a carriage had halted before it. I quickened my pace as much as I could on the drying cobbles and reached the house as the cloaked bulk of the white-haired Lady Aline Carrington disappeared inside.

I followed closely after her to find Gabriella in the ground floor hall, shedding her wraps into the footman's hands.

Gabriella looked around at me as I charged in, and she gave me a wide smile.

"Good afternoon, Father."

I could not stop myself from catching her around the waist and pulling her into a firm embrace. Very un-English of me, but I'd learned, spending a large part of my life *out*side England, to treasure those dear to me while I could.

Gabriella, raised in France, warmly returned the hug and then kissed me on both cheeks. "I had a fine time with Lady Aline, Father, but I am glad to return to you."

Gabriella was still a bit formal with me, but she relaxed more in my presence every time I saw her.

"She is a well-bred young lady," Aline said, holding out her hand for a mannish handshake. "How are you, Lacey? You look flushed. Been running across London again?"

"As ever."

"I hope you tell me all about it, my boy," she boomed, her grip strong. "If you do not, Donata will. Ah, there you are, Donata. Take me to a soft chair and give me large quantities of sherry and cakes, there's a good gel."

Donata, who'd run lightly down the stairs, her blue-gray morning frock just the thing to set off her eyes, began to lead Lady Aline off. She opened her mouth to tell Gabriella to join them, then she caught my gaze, gave me an understanding look, and continued upstairs with Aline, leaving me with Gabriella.

I led my daughter into the ground-floor drawing room, where a fire was crackling. "Have you learned to love the English countryside?" I asked. "And English society?"

"The countryside was fine, but truth to tell, I found society a bit wearing." Gabriella plopped down on a gilt-armed sofa and let out a sigh. "How nice to sit on something soft, that is not moving." She looked up at me and flushed. "I am sorry. I sound ungrateful."

"Because coaches, after a long day, are uncomfortable?" I

seated myself next to her. "And that remembering how to address a bishop or a baronet can grow tiring? Simple truths. Not ungrateful at all. Although I would not confide the latter to Lady Aline or Lady Breckenridge."

Gabriella sent me a grin. "Only to you, sir. I must admit it is all a bit exciting, although I am worried about the debut ball. I've been learning to dance — Lady Aline hired an instructor in Bath, which she called a *hop-merchant*. That made me laugh so. I've also taken instruction on the harp and singing and how to walk in a ball dress and beaded slippers. Even so, I live in fear that I'll trip and sprawl, or drop my champagne, or break a harp string, or something equally horrifying. I'd be mortified."

She would be, and the *haut ton* was not always forgiving. The only reason they were tolerating her at all, though both Carlotta and Major Auberge came from good families, was because of the patronage of Lady Breckenridge and Lady Aline, and a good word from Grenville.

"I'll speak to Donata," I said. "There is no reason for you to parade about if you do not wish to."

"Oh, but I do," Gabriella said, with the changeability of the young. "Deep down inside, I do want to be an elegant lady at a ball. Really. And they are being so kind to me." She laughed, unself-consciously. "It does not matter, though, does it? I will dress up and dance and let my fingers be kissed, and then I will return to France and be Gabriella again."

I knew Donata would not let things stay that simple, but I said nothing. I took Gabriella's hand and squeezed it. "I am glad, no matter what happens, that you will be here in London until summer."

"As am I." Gabriella gave me a shy smile, then lost it as she studied me in concern. "What is it, Father? You look most unhappy."

"Not unhappy," I said. "Weary. Tired of death and all it means. I need a touch of joy, Gabriella."

"It is all around you," my daughter said, with a sweep of

her hand. "You have Lady Breckenridge, and young Peter, and me. Bartholomew and Barnstable. And all your dear friends."

Had I ever been as young and eager as she? Yes, once upon a time. I'd been filled with that hope the day this wonderful child had been born. The midwife had laid Gabriella into my arms, as I'd stared in astonishment, and I'd had to turn my back so no one would see my tears.

"Will you tell me more about your adventures?" Gabriella was saying. "I mean your life here, since you returned from the army. Lady Aline gives me snippets about you running about to apprehend criminals, and Bartholomew has told me plenty, but I want to hear the stories from you."

I can say honestly that at that moment, I cared about nothing else in the world. Not Gareth Travers's death, or what he'd wanted to sell to Mackay, or James Denis, or even Donata and Lady Aline, nattering upstairs as they planned Gabriella's future.

For now, I basked in delight, holding the hand of my daughter, knowing she wanted to be here with me. I would see to it that though I'd missed fifteen years of her life, I would miss no more, and be with her for many years to come.

I FINALLY RELEASED GABRIELLA SO SHE COULD ASCEND TO her bedchamber and rest from her journey. I heard Donata and Aline speaking animatedly in Donata's sitting room, and knew they could go on for hours, so I left them to it.

As I made my way toward my study to await Denis's response to my request for an appointment, Matthias came bursting through the front door below, followed by an agitated Grenville.

Grenville would never be so gauche as to charge into another's house without good reason. There was an etiquette to visiting, and Grenville never disobeyed it.

"Lacey," he called up to me. "For God's sake, come."

I made my way down the stairs as quickly as I was able. "What is it?"

"Marianne." Grenville's dark eyes were wide with fear, his pupils mere specks. "He has her. He wants the book, and says for you to bring it, or they won't let her live."

CHAPTER 28

read poured over me in an icy blast. Gareth's killers, in my rooms, Marianne trapped with them. There was nothing to say they wouldn't simply kill her when they grew tired of waiting.

"Damnation," I said.

Grenville opened his mouth to continue, but I took him by the shoulder, pushed him into reception room where I'd sat with Gabriella, and shut the door.

I faced him squarely, our feet exactly placed on the black-and-white marble tiles. "Tell me what has happened. Quietly — Gabriella is home."

Grenville's fear and fury poured out of him, the unflappable man terrified. "Three bullies forced their way into your rooms in Covent Garden. Marianne was there, and me with her. I was in no position to fight them off, if you understand what I mean. They told us they'd come for the book. Marianne said she didn't know what book, so they started tearing up the place. When they couldn't find it, they sent me to you to fetch it."

"You did not run straight to Bow Street?" I asked.

"They sent one of them with me — he's outside. I could not

go anywhere near Bow Street, and anyway I couldn't risk they wouldn't kill her when they saw Runners and foot patrollers clumping down the lane toward them. They have big knives and skill at using them." Grenville's hands shook as he rubbed his face. "God, Lacey, they might just kill her anyway."

"We won't let them," I said with energy. "I do not have the book, Grenville."

Grenville's hands came down, fists clenched. "Bloody hell —they said you did—"

"I have no idea where the blasted thing is. No, do not answer ... let me think."

I laid out the events in my head and pictured them from beginning to end. Gareth and Leland traveling to the Bull and Hen to meet Mackay. Leaving when he did not make the appointment—I still did not know why he did not.

Ruffians followed Leland and Gareth from the tavern. Perhaps the two had been on their way to hire another hackney to take them home. The ruffians had followed them and waylaid them. Whether Mackay had been part of that plot or not, I did not know. Leland and Gareth had been felled. If Gareth had been carrying the book these men in my rooms now wanted, Mackay would have had ample time to take it from Gareth's body.

Perhaps that was what Mackay had been doing when Leland had seen the man stooping over them. Leland had asked for help. Mackay had given assistance in the form of coming for me and leading me back there, so he must have had some compassion. A dealer of stolen goods perhaps; a killer, no.

Why should the villains now believe *I* had the book? I closed my eyes. Mackay had been in my rooms twice. First, when he'd fetched me; second, when I'd sent him back to Marianne. He could easily have tucked the book there for safe-keeping, either while I was snatching up my wraps to follow him, or while Marianne was busy writing a note to Grenville.

Mackay might have feared that whoever had set the ruffians on Leland and Gareth would try to steal it from him, and so left it in a place they would not think of looking. His own rooms must not have been safe. He could return at his leisure for it—I did not live there anymore, and Marianne was often out.

Obviously, the book was no longer in my rooms. Had Mackay succeeded in fetching it?

More images ran through my mind. Of Mackay, getting himself into the Derwents' house. Mackay lying in a drawing room, where books abounded. Had he returned to my rooms, found the book gone, and assumed I'd found it and taken it to Leland? That would explain why he was at the Derwents' house, and also his death—someone had followed him and killed him. To take the book for themselves? Or because Mackay had seen them murder Gareth?

In any case, I had *not* taken the book to the Derwents. I hadn't known of its existence until I'd spoken to Freddie last night. So how had it disappeared from my rooms?

A few more images … and I knew.

"Bloody hell," I whispered.

"Lacey." Grenville broke through my churning thoughts, and I opened my eyes. "I cannot leave her there much longer."

"We will not." I started for the stairs again. "Donata has any number of books here—we'll find *something* to take to them."

"But good God, man," Grenville said as he followed me out. "What happens when they find out we've given them a decoy?"

"By that time, we'll have Marianne out and safe. I doubt a thief who sent men to search my rooms was very specific about what book it was—wouldn't trust them not to simply take it themselves. We can even follow them back to whoever hired them, and catch the man."

"You had better be right," Grenville said darkly. "It is a great risk."

I entered the library, a small room lined floor-to-ceiling with books. "What do you suggest?"

Grenville strode swiftly past me and cast his practiced eye over the collection. I had no intention of actually giving one of Donata's books to the villains; I only needed something to show them in exchange for Marianne.

While Grenville searched, I sat down, wrote a short note, and sealed it.

"This," Grenville said. He handed me a small, fat book, leather-bound with gilding on the cover. It was in French, dated from the middle of the last century. No pictures, but Grenville assured me it was valuable, a first edition of Voltaire.

I trusted his judgment. Grenville had a fine collection himself, including hand-lettered manuscripts from medieval times, with exquisite gold leafing and bright drawings in the margins.

I pocketed the book, and we went out and down the stairs. I did not summon my wife, because she would want to accompany us. I preferred she stayed here and safe, no matter how angry she grew with me later.

As we went down the stairs and out the door, I gave the note I'd written to Bartholomew. "Have that delivered when we are well gone," I said.

Bartholomew looked troubled—Matthias would have told him everything. I knew the brothers would want to come with us, but I did not want to endanger Marianne. Jackson the coachman would have to suffice for our protection across town.

Bartholomew glanced at the direction on the letter and nodded. "Yes, sir."

"As for Lady Breckenridge," I said. "I want her here until I return. Do not let her convince you or any of the staff to let her go out. Understand?"

Bartholomew drew a breath, but squared his shoulders. I

was leaving him to guard her, and he appreciated that. "Yes, sir," he said, this time with more conviction, and I departed.

THE MAN WHO'D COME WITH GRENVILLE WAITED FOR US outside, leaning on the wheel of his carriage. He was a fighter, much like the men Denis employed, but not as clean. His cauliflower ear and deep scar under his eye spoke of his life of brutality. He had no emotion in his eyes but impatience, and no sympathy. He was doing a job and waiting to get paid.

Such men would kill Marianne if we didn't hurry. They'd not stopped at striking down the son of one of the wealthiest gentlemen in London, or committing murder in Sir Gideon's drawing room. They'd thought nothing of roughing up Grenville, a famous and influential man, and they'd think nothing of killing an actress from the Drury Lane chorus. Someone in the shadows did not care for wealth or status in their victims. They simply struck and took what they wanted.

The ruffian rode on top of the coach to Covent Garden, until Jackson let us out at the entrance to Grimpen Lane. The tough jumped down and joined us when we descended, following us into the cul-de-sac.

All was quiet as we made our way toward the bakeshop, dusk settling over the city. Mrs. Beltan was still inside cleaning for the next day. She and her assistant had their heads in mobcaps down, concentrating on their tasks.

Grenville and I went up the stairs, the tough falling in behind us. The door on my landing opened, and a tall man peered out.

"Better have the book, guv," he said in a South London accent, "or your ladybird is done."

"He has it," Grenville snapped.

I climbed slowly, as though every step pained me, and

halted out of the man's reach. I took the small book from my pocket and held it close to my chest.

"Send Miss Simmons out," I said. "I want to see she's unhurt before I part with this."

The big man grinned. He was bulky, like Brewster. Greasy black hair clung to his head, and tufts of hair on his upper chest peeped around the cloth tied carelessly around his throat. He looked like a man used to wrestling beasts, a hostler perhaps, or a farm hand.

This man knew he could simply knock me down the stairs and take the book from me when I landed at the bottom. I wanted him to think that.

"Miss Simmons, please," I said, making sure my voice was not as robust as usual.

Grenville said nothing, did nothing. In the carriage, he'd loaded and primed one of the pistols he always kept there, and shoved it into his pocket before descending from the coach. The activity, and our quiet discussion on what we'd do, had put paid to his usual motion sickness, and the darkness in the stairwell now hid the bulk in his pocket.

The man called back into the rooms without turning his head. "Make 'er come out."

I heard Marianne before I saw her, nothing wrong with her voice. I could tell by her tone that she was frightened, but she cursed and threatened dire retribution as the men inside pulled her forward.

The first man opened the door wider, and Marianne, struggling, blond curls falling into her eyes, was shoved around to face us. The man who held her was shorter than the others, but he had a barrel-like chest and beefy arms.

I didn't glance at Grenville, but I sensed him tense, ready.

"Let her walk downstairs," I said.

The black-haired man, clearly the leader, shook his head. "Give us the book first, guv." He held out a broad hand.

"Who wants it so much?" I asked, not moving. "Who would go to all this trouble to obtain it?"

"That's our business," the first man said. "It's someone as pays, innit?"

"Why didn't he come directly to me? If he knew I had the book?"

The head man obviously did not know or care. "Just hand it over."

I held up the book in one hand, stretching the other toward Marianne. "At the same time," I said. "And don't you dare hurt her."

A problem was that Grenville and I and the ruffian behind us blocked the way downstairs. We'd have to descend surrounded by the men, and it was a long stretch between my door and Russel Street, where Jackson and the coach waited. They could box us in and simply kill us.

The lead man gave me a nod. He grabbed Marianne by the wrist and shoved her at me, simultaneously taking the book from my hand.

Marianne stumbled into me, her eyes round in rage and fear. I righted her and swung her behind me at the same time. "Take her out," I ordered Grenville.

Both Marianne and Grenville hesitated. I was momentarily flattered that my friends did not want to leave me to the mercy of the toughs, but their action was not sensible at the moment.

"Go," I said sternly. I would defend their escape. There was not much else I could do.

Marianne gave me a worried look but let Grenville slide a hand to her waist and pull her down the stairs with him. The man below us moved to let them pass, and I held my breath until Grenville and Marianne safely reached the bottom of the stairs, and went out.

CHAPTER 29

ell me who hired you," I said to the lead man as the man on the stairs below me closed the door behind Grenville. "I can make it worth your while."

"No chance," the first man said. "Best you be off with your friends, guv."

"These are my rooms," I said, jaw tightening. "*You* be off."

"Don't tempt me, duckie; I'm spoiling for a fight." He came down a few steps. "Your toffy friend there was too easy for me. He was mother naked, and worried about the actress. More fool him. I know you'll have sent for help, so we'll be gone. If this is the right book, I get paid, and you'll never have to worry about me. If it's the wrong one, I'll come for you, don't think I won't. All your toff friends won't be able to stop me having a go at you, and your missus."

My red-hot temper stirred at the mention of Donata, but I knew better than to let him goad me into rashness. I folded my arms and leaned against the worn wallpaper, a faded shepherdess smiling at me from the opposite wall.

The first man's face hardened. "If that's what you want." He jerked his chin at his partners. "Put him down."

At his signal, the man behind me rushed my back. Though

he had to move up several steps, he came fast. I shifted my weight to my good leg, brought my substantial cane up and whacked him in the middle.

The man doubled over. I hit him again, getting around him and down a few steps, but he was strong. He came to his feet, roaring, his fists already moving.

I had retreated far enough from him to draw the sword from my walking stick. The repaired sword was firmer than ever, and I had just enough room in the stairwell to bring it to bear on the man who swung to fight me.

Swords were old-fashioned nowadays, but I'd been trained to use one—several different bladed weapons in fact. I was also good at firearms. I took from my left pocket the *other* pistol from Grenville's carriage and pointed it into the man's face.

My attacker backpedaled away from the sword and the pistol. "Bleedin' 'ell," he said before scrambling up the stairs past the others and into my front room.

"You can only get one of us with that," the lead man said. He sounded unworried that it would be him. "But I brought my own." I found myself facing the round opening of a black-powder pistol that looked as though it had seen plenty of use. "Say your prayers, guv. Last words you'll ever speak, I'm thinking."

Withdrawal was prudent, but I stood my ground. "I'm a dead shot, at any distance." I aimed my pistol to hit him between the eyes.

A few weeks ago, I'd stood in a similar position, facing another opponent, waiting for him to shoot me. But the duel I'd fought with Stubbins had been like a play—exact lines and rehearsed moves, a formal dance. That had been a staged battle; this was a real one, deadly, final. There, I'd been in the fresh green of the park, surrounded by cool mist. Here, the sour odor of sweat filled the close air of the stairwell.

The man's eyes widened slightly, and his finger moved on the trigger. I dropped to the stairs just as the pistol blasted.

The ball whizzed over my head. It struck the wall with a crash of plaster, passing clean through the neck of a wallpaper shepherd.

I brought up my pistol and fired. The man above me bellowed in pain and fell toward me. I caught him, his shoulder bleeding fiercely, his eyes full of hatred as he tried to get his hands around my throat.

We stumbled and slammed into the wall, me fighting his giant hands. He was slow, the wound weakening him. He could have chided me about my boasting of being a dead shot, though I'd hit him exactly where I'd meant to. I wasn't a murderer.

He was one, unfortunately, and fought me with silent ruthlessness. This was the man, I knew, who'd struck Gareth his fatal blow.

The two other men clattered down to help their friend. I fought, losing my footing, but I used the momentum to carry us both down the stairs. I needed to get them out into the open, where others would see, and help would come.

It did come, in the form of Brewster, who yanked open the door at the bottom of the stairs. He shouted as he charged upward, and I heard the roar of another pistol.

Brewster's shout changed to one of pain, but he kept coming. If he'd been hit by a bullet, he did not let it slow him. He had the lead man off me, wrestling him down the stairs. The lead man smacked into the door frame and stumbled outside, straight into the arms of Milton Pomeroy.

"Jared Draper, as I live and breathe," Pomeroy said cheerfully. "Been looking for you a long time. How about I arrest you now?"

"Fuck you," Draper said, and he tried to run.

I could have told him it would make no difference. Pomeroy was on him in two strides. I made it out the door to the street, panting, to see Pomeroy grab Draper by the injured shoulder and swing him, face-first, into the nearest wall.

Draper yelled in pain and rage, and Pomeroy had shackles on him with speed. Two other patrollers, large lads, jogged in to help me. Brewster had already grabbed a second man, and the patrollers swarmed up the stairs for the third.

Grenville hurried back toward the bakeshop, with Marianne behind him. I leaned against the wall of the shop as Mrs. Beltan popped out to see what was happening, her eyes wide.

"It's all right, Mrs. Beltan," I said struggling to catch my breath. "Just another evening in the life of your tenants."

BY THE TIME I HAD CONVEYED TO POMEROY THAT I believed Draper to be the killer of Gareth and Mackay, and asked a boon of him—one which would catch Draper's employer—the street around my door had emptied. The curious followed Pomeroy and his patrollers with the three villains out of Grimpen Lane, and I returned upstairs.

My front room was a mess. Draper and his fellows had knocked over my writing table with its meager contents, and strewn my books across the room. As I started to pick them up, I glimpsed movement in my bedchamber, and looked in through the half-open door.

Grenville and Marianne stood in the middle of the room, on the new rug Donata had bought for the chamber. Grenville touched Marianne's face with gentle fingers, then he made a raw sound and pulled her into his arms. He held Marianne close, tumbling her hair.

Neither saw me. Marianne laid her head on Grenville's shoulder, eyes closing, her fingers curling on his back.

I closed the door silently and left them to it.

Brewster lumbered up the stairs not long after that. He had blood on his sleeve, but it was a small patch, already drying, and he did not behave as though he were hurt. "Your Mr. Pomeroy dragged everyone off to Bow Street," he said. "But you took a chance, guv. I might not have got here in time."

"I knew you would," I said. "Denis enjoys looking after me, and he has as much curiosity in him as I do, in his own way." I straightened up from putting my bookshelves to rights, and faced him. "Did you bring it?"

Brewster flushed dark red. This was the first time I'd seen the man truly disconcerted.

"How'd you know?" he asked.

"I did not, until today. Once I ran through all possibilities, I realized there could be only one solution."

"Huh," Brewster said. "No worry. I brought it."

I wondered what Denis's reaction had been when he'd read the note I'd directed Bartholomew to deliver. Anger? Amusement? Indifference?

I'd written, imitating Denis's abrupt style, only two lines.

Send the book Brewster took from my rooms back to me. I need it to catch a killer. Lacey.

"You stood here," I said, indicating the spot in front of my small bookcase, "going through my books, even sitting down to read one. When we left, you held up a book—I couldn't see which one, but I assumed the one you'd been perusing—and asked to borrow it. I told you to take it, paying no attention. But you switched it, didn't you? While I was seeing Marianne off, you switched it for the other book you'd found on my shelf, the one Mackay had left."

Brewster nodded, looking embarrassed to be caught but not ashamed he had done the theft. I remembered him standing in the ruined kitchen of my Norfolk house, holding up stolen silver he'd found there, and offering to split the take with me when he sold them. That had been one of the images that had poured through my head when I'd stood with Grenville in Donata's reception room.

"I saw what it was," Brewster said. "And I knew his nibs would be interested in it. He likes that sort of thing—art and old books, especially old books what have pictures."

"And he pays you a percentage when he sells them?"

"He does. Or gives me a fee just for bringing him the bloody things. I've learned over the years what he wants."

"You're a thief, Brewster."

Brewster shrugged. "Never pretended to be anything else, have I? Anyway, you didn't know nothing about the book. I found it shoved with the others, which ain't worth nothing, I have to tell you. Knew you didn't know a thing about it, or you'd never have let me get near it."

I gave him an impatient frown. "How the devil did you suppose the thing had gotten into my bookshelf in the first place?"

Another shrug. "Not my job to reason how a thing gets to where it is. I sees it, and if it's worth something, I take it to Mr. Denis. Your Mr. Grenville comes here all the time—I thought maybe he'd left it behind. He has so many, he'd never miss it."

I pointed a rigid finger at him. "That book is the key to the brutal death of one of my friends."

"Well, I wasn't to know, was I? You didn't know either, or you'd have kept it safe."

To be fair to Brewster, none of us had known about the damned thing until too late to save Gareth and Mackay. Even though Brewster had been with me when Freddie had started to talk of books, neither I nor he had realized its significance. Freddie had talked about erotica, but I now knew that the book was something quite different.

"Let me see it."

Brewster heaved an aggrieved sigh. "Hang about."

He walked past me without explanation, out the door, and down the stairs. I did not hurry to follow or doubt he'd be back. If Denis had told him to bring the book to me, Brewster would do so.

I tapped on the door of my bedchamber and went in when Grenville's baritone rumbled that I should. I found Marianne and Grenville sitting together on the edge of my bed—simply sitting, thighs touching.

"Are you all right?" I asked Marianne. "If Draper hurt you, I can tell Pomeroy to put his boot pretty hard up his backside."

Marianne dragged her loose hair from her face, and I saw that her cheek was dark with bruises. "No, I am fine," she said, her look daring me to contradict her. "He didn't let his men do anything too permanent. He truly only wanted that blasted book, whatever it was."

Grenville gestured to the small leather-bound book on my night table, the one we'd brought from Donata's library. "Pomeroy took it off Draper and gave it to me for you. Kind of him. But it doesn't matter. It did the trick, which was the point."

"Tell your wife I thank her," Marianne said.

"I will, if she ever speaks to me again for stealing a book from her house and running off to fight three villains," I said dryly. "How fortunate that I still have these rooms at my disposal."

"She will scold but forgive you in time," Marianne assured me. "I understand ladies of her character."

I hoped Marianne was right, but first I needed to find the instigator who had employed Draper in the first place.

"Both of you might want to remove yourselves," I said. "The danger is not yet past, and Marianne has been tangled in this enough."

"Agreed," Grenville said, his voice taking on a stern note.

Marianne gave him an almost fearful look. "Please do not take me back to that bloody house in Clarges Street."

Grenville gentled his tone. "You may stay wherever you

like," he said. "But for right now, Lacey is right. It's not safe here."

Marianne's eyes narrowed. "What about for you? *You're* going to stay, aren't you?"

Grenville gave her a nod. "I want to see this thing through."

Marianne flashed an irritated glance at me then one at Grenville. "Well, if you're staying, then I am too. I'm not one to sit wringing my hands, wondering if her man will return alive."

"That is indisputably obvious," Grenville said. "A compromise. You retreat upstairs to your rooms and lock yourself in. Then we'll leave together once Lacey and I see this thing to its conclusion."

"You know that Pomeroy can simply beat the name of the person out of Mr. Draper," Marianne pointed out. "I imagine he's already doing so."

"By the time Mr. Draper grows tired of holding out and gives him a name—providing it's the right one—that person can have fled London," I answered. "I do not wish to wait."

Marianne sighed, disentangled herself from Grenville, and rose. "Upstairs it is." She swayed on her feet, and Grenville was beside her in an instant, steadying her. "I don't want *you* up there," she said swiftly to him.

"That is unfortunate," Grenville said. "Because I am going."

He steered her past me and out of my rooms. It said much about Marianne's emotions of the moment that she argued with him only halfway up the stairs.

BREWSTER RETURNED IN A QUARTER OF AN HOUR. HE HAD the book with him, but he'd also brought James Denis.

It was fully dark now in Grimpen Lane, but I recognized Denis's tall silhouette in front of the bulk of Brewster as they turned in at my doorway. Two other of Denis's bullies blended into the shadows of the cul-de-sac.

Brewster opened the door of my rooms without bothering to knock and led Denis inside. Grenville, hearing them, came down from Marianne's chamber and in behind Denis, shutting the door.

"This was too valuable not to accompany," Denis said without greeting. He handed me a paper-wrapped, rectangular object. "I should not like to hunt it down again after a murderer takes it from your dead body."

I took the parcel to my writing table and unwrapped it. Grenville joined me, and as the paper fell away, he dragged in a breath.

"Good God," he whispered.

Grenville put out a hand and carefully opened the book's dark leather cover, worn bits of gold leaf clinging to it here and there. But if the cover was somewhat plain, the inside of the book was a different matter.

The first page Grenville turned over had a stylized capital *P* on one side, on the other an illustration of Christ on the cross. The sky above the scene was vivid blue, bringing out the deeper blues of the garb worn by the women surrounding the cross, which were just as bright as the reds, yellows, pinks, and whites of the tunics and robes of others in the background. The soldiers were in glorious red cloaks over plate armor, one holding his spear to Christ's side.

"Prayer book, Reverend Travers called it?" Grenville asked, awed. "Not a prayer book, a Book of Hours. Centuries old. Ones I've seen with illustrations this rich were done only for royalty." He touched the page with light fingers, and looked up at me, eyes shining. "Lacey, this is a treasure. Worth thousands and thousands. A man could live well on the price of this for decades."

CHAPTER 30

*D*enis knew its exact worth, I'd wager, down to the penny. Grenville caressed the thing as he would a lover.

"No wonder Mackay was anxious to have this back," Grenville said in a near whisper.

Denis remained still, not as enraptured as Grenville, but I knew he'd have the book in the end.

"Did you know Gareth Travers had this?" I asked Denis. "Did you tell Mackay to acquire it for you?"

"I did not." Denis frowned. "I had no idea he had come across it. As I say, Mr. Mackay did not only work for me." And he looked—for Denis—quite put out that Mackay hadn't come to him immediately upon discovering such a book was for sale.

Grenville was turning the pages, handling them with his fingertips. Some of the pages had only words on them, but as he leafed through, more and more beautiful illustrations revealed themselves to us. They depicted not only scenes from the New Testament, but from everyday life in fourteen-hundred something.

"You say poverty-stricken Reverend Travers had this, and

simply handed it over to Gareth?" Grenville asked me in amazement.

"That is what I understand."

"Think he stole it?" Brewster asked as he looked over our shoulders at the book. "The vicar, I mean?"

"Who knows?" I said. "Reverend Travers said it belonged to his family. I doubt he'd have the energy to steal the thing himself."

"Nah, *someone* stole it," Brewster said, confident. "If you say it were made for royalty ages ago, then someone nicked it from them. It's what happens."

"However the Travers family came into possession, it is exquisite," Grenville said reverently. "I can see a man killing for it."

"Stupid, when he can just steal it," Brewster said.

"Or purchase it," Denis said. "The killing was not necessary."

Denis, ever efficient, and Brewster, ever focused on what was important to him.

"Now it will catch a killer." I looked at Denis. "I was wondering how to put out word that I had it, but perhaps you can … ?"

"I could," Denis said, his dark blue eyes glinting. "As a favor."

Another mark in Captain Lacey's debit column, he was saying. Saving Denis's life, helping him track down a man who'd betrayed him, and preventing him from being blown up apparently had not cleared me.

"I will have to accept," I said. "I want to be able to tell Leland that his friend's murderer was brought to justice."

Denis did not much care about my reasons. He gave me a nod, signaled to Brewster, and walked out into the chilly stairwell with him.

Grenville remained at the writing table, transfixed by the book. "This is one of the most beautiful things I've ever seen.

The Limoges brothers made it, I am positive, though I'd get it authenticated. I wonder if Reverend Travers would consent to sell it to me."

"Only if Denis will release his hold on it." I watched Grenville as he continued to gaze at the book as though he could not have enough of it. "You were prepared to hand over this book to procure Marianne's release when you did not know what it was," I said. "Would you have handed it over now that you do?"

Grenville drew a breath, still taking in the book, then he looked up at me sharply. "Yes," he said. "I would."

I believed him.

DENIS HAD A NETWORK THAT RIVALED ANY SECRET POLICE'S in any country on the Continent. Within an hour, one of his men trundled up the stairs, spoke to him on the landing, and departed.

Denis reentered my front room where Grenville had returned to admiring the book, while I paced moodily.

"We have a bite, gentleman," Denis announced. "I will retire here." He indicated the open door to my bedchamber. "I doubt your murderer will come in if he sees me waiting."

Without further speech, he went into the smaller room, taking Brewster with him, and closed the door.

Grenville and I waited another twenty-five minutes. Marianne stayed upstairs, Denis in my bedchamber. Neither Grenville nor I speculated on who would turn up—I had my suspicions, and whether I'd be proved right or wrong was no matter. Whoever had given the order to kill Gareth would not escape me this night.

At last, we heard the unlocked door at the bottom of the staircase open, and a heavy tread ascend.

A man. Well, if he was who I thought he'd be, that fit with

one of my theories, but not the other. I was crossing to the door, ready to open it, when another set of footsteps came scurrying with him. This one was lighter and swifter, and then I heard the shrill sound of a woman's voice—confirming my second theory.

Grenville and I exchanged a glance of surprise before I moved to the door and flung it open. Two of Denis's men stepped into the stairwell at the bottom, cutting off retreat, while another stood on the steps leading to Marianne's flat, preventing any escape that way.

"Please come in," I said to the man and woman, who were both red-faced with anger. "We have much to discuss."

The pair looked down the stairs and up, realizing they were trapped. Resigned, Lord Percy Saunders walked inside, giving Grenville a cold bow. The woman did not want to follow, but when I reached to haul her in, Mrs. Travers snatched her arm from my grasp and marched in unassisted.

"Captain Lacey," Mrs. Travers began before any of us could speak. "I have come for my husband's property." Her gaze fell on the book Grenville stood over like a guardian. "That is it. Give it to me."

She held out her hand, angry and imperious.

I regarded her calmly. "How do you suppose it came to be here?" I asked.

"I can only assume that Leland Derwent stole it from Gareth and for some reason gave it to you," Mrs. Travers snapped. "What do you want for its return, Captain? Money?"

I switched my gaze to Lord Percy. "What is your interest, sir?"

Lord Percy raised his light-brown brows. "The Book of Hours, of course. I paid for it."

Mrs. Travers bristled. "*Paid*, did you? It's mine. My husband's. Stolen from us."

I moved myself in front of the book. Grenville stood at his ease, giving Lord Percy a cool stare.

I heard a shout from below, and the door to the street banged open again. "Here, you, get out of the way," a voice floated up.

Grenville lifted his brows then went out into the landing. I remained where I was, recognizing the voice—and this time, I admit I was surprised. The man went on angrily to Denis's men as he ascended and entered.

He was the Honorable Mr. Henry Lawrence, the man we'd interviewed at Brooks's, who'd first put us on to both Lord Percy and the Bull and Hen. Lawrence halted when he entered, his hazel eyes taking in me, Mrs. Travers, and Lord Percy Saunders waiting for him. He recognized Saunders, of course, but he frowned in perplexity at Mrs. Travers.

"Good afternoon, Mr. Lawrence," Grenville said, giving the man a little bow. "And what brings you to this quiet lane?"

Lawrence swept his gaze around the room again. "The summons did. Told me that ... Ah ..." He saw the Book of Hours lying open on my writing table and fixed upon it. "The transaction is taking place here, now, is it?"

"Transaction?" Lord Percy asked in irritation. "What the devil are you on about Lawrence?"

"My purchase of the Book of Hours, of course."

Grenville and I exchanged a glance. I had not expected Mr. Lawrence. Denis had not told us whom he'd ensnared, and I hadn't expected him to catch more than one bird.

I could not continue without knowing the lay of the land. "Your purchase?" I asked Lawrence. "Mr. Mackay tried to sell the book to you as well?"

Lawrence frowned. "Mackay? Never heard him. This was set up through my man of business. He knew a Book of Hours had come on the market, and told me of it. This evening I received a note that said I should arrive here to complete the purchase."

"I see."

"*My* man of business sent me notice to come here, blast

you," Lord Percy said. "He was in contact with this Mr. Mackay. Where is *he* by the way?"

"Dead," I said.

Both men gaped at me, their expressions so nearly identical I wanted to laugh. Grenville broke in.

"Do you mean, Lacey, that Mackay was busily selling this Book of Hours to Saunders *and* Lawrence at the same time?"

"Possibly more," I said. "But Saunders and Lawrence bit. I have to wonder how he would produce two books. Maybe he was having forgeries made, one for each of you? While he kept the real book and sold it to another?"

Saunders glanced at the tome open on the writing table. "Is that real?"

"An excellent point," Lawrence added. "You're an expert, Grenville. You'd know if it were a true Limoges."

"Oh, it is," Grenville said. "Perfectly beautiful and more than four hundred years old."

"I have no doubt you would be showed the real one," I said. "What you got after you handed over the money might have been different. But now Mackay is dead, and the authentic book lies there, waiting to be purchased."

"No, it does not," Mrs. Travers, who'd stood in silent shock throughout the conversation, exclaimed. "The book belongs to my husband. Gareth had no right to try to sell it to you—nor did this Mr. Mackay, whoever he is."

"Your husband gave the book to his son," I said. "However it came to be in the possession of the Travers family in the past, it is their property now. Reverend Travers gave it to Gareth, which means it was Gareth's to do with as he pleased."

"Gareth was a foolish young man who wanted money to impress those Derwents," Mrs. Travers said testily. "They taunted him for his poverty, made him desperate and dependent on them."

Both Saunders and Lawrence looked surprised at this characterization of the Derwent family.

"Whatever Gareth's motives," I said, cutting her off, "Reverend Travers gave *him* the book. It belonged to him, and if he chose to sell it ..." I spread my hands.

"It was *not* his." Mrs. Travers's voice rose. "But Gareth is dead, so the book belongs back with his father. I will take it home with me."

"The devil you will," Lord Percy said. "I already paid Mackay a handsome deposit for it. The book belongs to me."

"Steady on," Lawrence said. "*I* made a deposit on the thing through my man of business."

Mrs. Travers rounded on both of them. "Mr. Mackay had no business taking money for it at all. It is *ours*."

"Captain," Lawrence said, looking at me with a troubled expression. "I had no idea this book had anything at all to do with Mr. Travers. Are you telling us this is why young Gareth was killed?"

"Yes," I said, my voice quiet. "When Gareth realized how valuable the book his father had given him was, he contacted Mr. Mackay, a dealer, to ask him to sell it for him. He'd planned to meet Mackay at the Bull and Hen the night you saw him at Brooks's, Lawrence, the same night Lord Percy enticed them to the Nines. I imagine Lord Percy wanted to sweeten up Travers, so that if Travers found out who Mackay had approached to buy the book, Travers would look more favorably upon him."

"Bloody hell," Lord Percy said. He drew out a handkerchief with far more lace on it than the one Freddie had used and dabbed his lips.

"A moment," Grenville asked. "Why did Travers use Mr. Mackay at all? Why not offer the book himself?"

"To get a better price," I said. "Mackay is known to art collectors, a go-between who can haggle, so gentlemen do not have to soil their hands and ruin friendships over a transaction. Besides, Mackay could feel out the market, find the highest price without Travers having to bestir himself. Travers only wanted the money from the sale, to gain some independence."

Lord Percy finished bitterly. "And Mr. Mackay played us against each other. Bloody man."

"Leland kicked up a fuss about the cheating he saw at the Nines," I continued, "and he and Travers were taken away. You faded into the woodwork, Saunders, distancing yourself from them, which I am certain was not the way to make friends with Mr. Travers."

"Possibly not," Lord Percy said. "But I was a bit terrified at the moment, and I would have made it up to him."

I went on. "Leland and Gareth were dragged to Mr. Forge, who owned the Nines, and given to his toughs to frighten them then toss them out." Everyone listened to me now, including Mrs. Travers, wondering where I was leading them. "They took a hired coach to the Bull and Hen in Seven Dials, where Gareth had made an appointment to meet Mackay. Leland does not remember what the appointment was about, and he might have known nothing about the book itself, but he was not pleased that Gareth wanted to cease being dependent on him and Sir Gideon for his living. From what I understand, he and Leland argued about it quite a bit."

"I don't believe you," Mrs. Travers said indignantly. "It must have been Leland who put the idea of selling the book into Gareth's head."

I sent her a severe look. "I do not know why you are so angry at the Derwent family, but I and everyone else believe you read them wrong. You are simply annoyed that Gareth was about to take the only thing the Traverses had that was worth any money, sell it, and keep the funds for himself. Gareth was not an unkind young man, however. I imagine he'd have shared the proceeds with his father."

"I doubt it," Mrs. Travers said in a hard voice.

"You wrong him. But let me continue. Mackay did not make the meeting with Gareth at the Bull, for what reason, I do not know. Perhaps he was so busy setting up buyers for this very expensive book that he was late. Or had other irons in the fire—I have heard he served several masters. When he was late, Leland persuaded Gareth away. They walked from the Bull and Hen to find a hackney stand to hire a coach home."

"This is all fascinating, Captain," Lawrence broke in. "But what does it mean?"

"It means they were followed. Gareth had the book with him, or so the killer thought. Perhaps Gareth had already given it to Mackay and was waiting for payment; who knows? Gareth and Leland were followed, and when they reached a likely spot—Seven Dials is full of them—they were attacked."

"So, it was a robbery?" Lawrence asked. He watched me with the most interest, his eyes clear and shrewd.

"It was. The killer had hired a man called Draper and his friends to set upon Leland and Gareth, beat them, and steal the book. Possibly also to arrange them so they'd be found in a position that left the world in no doubt of their relationship with each other. But men like Draper are not very subtle. They struck too hard, killing Gareth and nearly killing Leland. They dragged the bodies into the passage, quickly searching them. I believe they were interrupted, or heard Mackay coming, or some such. For whatever reason, they retreated. I am not certain of all the details."

Percy touched his lips again with his delicate handkerchief. "Then what happened to the book?"

"I believe Mackay found it on Gareth—or else, as I say, he might already have had it. Or Draper missed it, or they were interrupted, or Draper was not asked to search the bodies for a book. Draper half stripped Leland and tossed his clothes aside, where they were found by a destitute man of the area. Draper likely pocketed Leland's money and watch, because the destitute man found nothing in the coat and waistcoat. Imagine Mackay's shock when, hurrying late toward the Bull and Hen, he finds the two lads lying in their own blood, looking as though they'd been engaging in buggery and killed by someone such an act enraged.

"Leland, who was just sensible enough to speak, begged Mackay to run to me for help. Mackay, while he was a thief, a cheat, and possibly a blackmailer, had enough compassion to obey. After all, he had the book, he'd not struck the lads down, and he was truly horrified by the crime, at least he was when he found me. I'm certain that fear for his own skin was a part of it. He returned here with instructions to tell Marianne to send for Grenville. In the commotion, he slid the book into my bookshelf, knowing he could return when the rooms were empty and take it. But the killers were still out there, and he had no idea if they'd try to beat and rob him. He decided to lie low until things settled, and then retrieve the book."

"A risk," Lawrence pointed out. "You might have found it."

"I spend most of my time in South Audley Street these days," I said. "News of my wedding to Lady Breckenridge has been in all the newspapers. I believe Mackay returned for the book when I was at my new home and Marianne out. When he didn't find it, it must have been a great blow to him. But I have the reputation for being an honorable man. Mackay no doubt assumed I'd taken the book to Sir Gideon or Leland, two honest men who would be certain to return it to Reverend Travers."

"And did you?" Lawrence asked, watching me with intensity. "Take it to Sir Gideon?"

"I did not, but Mackay could not have known that. He went to the Derwents', slipping in through the front door during an unguarded moment or up through the scullery. He enters covertly to search—if he is found he can pretend he came to inquire about Leland. The killer, who had followed him, gained entrance through the kitchens, where food was being handed out, discovered Mackay in the drawing room and struck him down. However, the book was nowhere to be found, and the killer realizes that perhaps Sir Gideon never had it. Which meant I might still have it. The killer had to depart or chance being caught, and left either via the kitchen or the front door when it was unattended."

"This Mr. Draper again?" Lawrence asked.

I shook my head. "Upon reflection I do not believe Draper killed Mackay. Draper is distinctive, and I believe Sir Gideon's household would have noticed him. The staff are well paid and careful about protecting their unworldly employers. No, this killer was unremarkable, able to blend in with the down-trodden poor come for charity. I imagine you were once down-trodden yourself, Mrs. Travers. The thought of all that money simply walking away from your grasp was too much to bear."

CHAPTER 31

$\mathcal{M}$rs. Travers's mouth opened to reveal her fairly even teeth. "I have no idea what the devil you mean."

"Good Lord," Lawrence said, with a mock start. "Such language. And you a vicar's wife."

I went on, ignoring Lawrence. "I mean that you entered the Derwents' house in Grosvenor Square," I said to Mrs. Travers, while Grenville surreptitiously stepped between her and the door. "You went there to find the book. If anyone saw you in the family's private rooms, like Mackay, you had an excuse to be there—you would have come to look in on your stepson's dear friend Leland. You found Mackay there. Whether you argued with him or demanded he hand you the book, you lost your temper. The poker was at hand. And so, he died."

Mrs. Travers stared at me, her blue eyes wide. "You assume much."

"When I came to you and told you Gareth was dead, you were surprised," I said. "Genuinely, I imagine. Your shock was real. You had hired Draper to rob Gareth and Leland, not murder them. But you discovered with Mackay, did you not, that it is easier to kill than one might think. One moment, the person is alive. The next ... Nothing."

The distress in Mrs. Travers's eyes told me I had the right of it. She had never intended death. She'd wanted the book, and the money it would bring. That was all.

Still, she tried. "You don't know," she said swiftly. "You were not there. You can know nothing."

I lost my sympathy for her. "You killed your husband's son, and Leland might die. Likewise, you murdered Mackay, who was only interested in the same thing you were—the damned book."

"Which is mine, by rights," Lord Percy broke in, still angry. "Have this woman arrested, do, Lacey. I'll take the book and go."

"The devil you will, old boy," Lawrence said. "As I say, I've already made a payment for it."

"If you want it, you can give me what I gave Mackay," Lord Percy said heatedly. "Fifteen hundred pounds."

Mrs. Travers's mouth hung open. "*Fifteen hundred?* You are lying, sir. Gareth did not have that money. Mr. Mackay never had so much either."

She condemned herself. She couldn't have known what Mackay had if she hadn't had him followed or searched him after she'd killed him.

Saunders flashed her a dangerous look, not used to impertinence from the lower classes. "I will have the book, or the money for it, madam."

"I haven't got the money," Mrs. Travers said desperately.

"No, you never got anything for it," I said, cutting over them. "All that death and violence, and you still have neither the book nor the price of it."

Mrs. Travers glared at me again for a long moment, then her hauteur vanished. "Bleedin' upstart," she shouted, her cultured voice giving way to the long vowels of South London.

"Trumped up, worthless piece of dung, friend to bloody mollies."

She came at me, the same rage in her eyes Mackay must have seen when she'd lifted the poker and gone for him. She had no weapon now; she only lunged at me, her fingers curved, ready to gouge out my eyes.

She found herself held back by the strong arms of Brewster. Mrs. Travers struggled, trying to reach me. "You're a liar," she spat.

"Your ruffian for hire, Mr. Draper, is even now in the hands of Bow Street," I told her. "I imagine Pomeroy or Spendlove are promising to spare him the noose if he tells who hired him."

Mrs. Travers hesitated at my words, then she screamed and renewed her efforts to attack me.

Lord Percy stepped away from her, his handkerchief at his mouth. "Good heavens," he said. "What a varlet."

Lawrence only regarded her with disapproval. "I thought it was too good to be true. Do compose yourself, woman. You've lost. The bloody mollies, as you call them, have defeated you."

I HAD SUMMONED SPENDLOVE AND POMEROY TO BE ON hand to arrest the culprit when identified, to prevent Denis meting out justice of his own. The fact that Mrs. Travers was a woman would not deter him from taking his vengeance for the death of one of his agents.

Pomeroy came through the door first, with his cheerfulness that had struck fear into the hearts of many a criminal. "Mrs. Travers, I arrest you in the king's name for willful murder against your stepson Gareth Travers and the man called Nelson Mackay. Come along with me now, won't you?"

"It were an accident," she shouted, tears starting from her eyes.

"I was only trying to get him to *listen*." She fought again, but Brewster held her hard. "It should have been Leland that was killed, not our Gareth. That family made a bloody sodomite out of him. I will tell everyone what the Derwents are, and *Leland* will hang. Unnatural acts are against the law, and they will pay for corrupting him."

"That's as may be," Pomeroy said in his good-natured way. "But first, I need you to come with us to the magistrate. You can turn her loose now, sir. I have her."

Brewster, at a nod from me, relinquished his prisoner to Pomeroy. He watched Pomeroy take the woman out, she quivering with fury and terror, Brewster's dismissive look saying all. He thought her a fool, and well he might. Of everyone interested in the book, only Brewster had managed to actually get hold of the thing.

Spendlove remained, his light blue gaze sweeping the room. Lord Percy turned away, as though he did not wish to be recognized. Henry Lawrence remained straight-backed and unashamed. Grenville and I presented a solid wall between Spendlove and the priceless book behind us, and Brewster blocked Spendlove's way to the bedchamber.

"This will be an interesting trial," Spendlove said. "A woman killing her stepson for the sake of a valuable book that could keep the family fed. And the stepson a sodomite. The jury's sympathy might be with her, if they believe her."

I acknowledged this with a nod. "Possibly."

"Might help if the book never turned up," Spendlove said. "If the jury thinks she simply had a bee in her bonnet, we might have our conviction."

"True," I conceded.

Spendlove knew damn well I had the book. I also wagered he knew exactly who was in my bedchamber, listening to every word.

Spendlove settled his tall hat on his head. "Pomeroy will thank you for the arrest," he said, "but next time you have a killer, Captain, just bring her to Bow Street and never mind the dramatics."

"She might not have confessed to you," I said without rancor. "And I needed the satisfaction of hearing it myself. Gareth Travers was my friend."

Spendlove fixed me with a hard stare. "I waste my breath pointing out that you take too much on yourself." He gave Grenville, Percy, and Lawrence a nod. "Gentlemen."

He cast one more look at Brewster and the closed bedchamber door, and then finally turned and walked out.

None of us spoke until we heard him bang the door at the bottom of the steps, then his steady footfalls on the cobbles outside.

"Well," Lord Percy said. He brought out a tiny, round snuffbox, opened it, inhaled a pinch, and politely offered some to Grenville, who just as politely declined. Percy tucked the box away and sneezed into his handkerchief. "I'll take the book now and go," he said, wiping his nose. "Do not worry, I will keep it under lock and key. I already have a place in my cabinet arranged for it."

"Have you been in the same room with us all, my dear?" Lawrence asked. "I equally have paid for this book."

"Which belongs to Gareth's father," I said firmly. "He's lost his son and is about to lose his wife. Must he lose his treasure, as well?"

Lord Percy blinked. "But I paid for it, man."

Grenville came forward. "I am certain we can all come to some arrangement," he said smoothly. "You know I have some manuscripts in my collection that interest you both. Call round, and we'll discuss things."

Percy's eyes narrowed, but he must have read in my face how angry I was. He studied me, studied Grenville, with the silent Brewster hovering, and understood his options.

He let out a sigh. "Very well." He took up his hat, which he'd left on a table by the door. "I will send word, Grenville,

and call on you. You must already know what I have my
eye on."

Another polite bow between the two, and Lord Percy
departed.

Lawrence bestirred himself, likewise taking up his hat. "I
will call on you as well, Grenville. I adore your collection.
We'll natter the day away." He bowed to me. "Thank you,
Captain Lacey, for a most entertaining evening."

Giving me a smile that said many things, he turned and
made his exit.

Once both gentlemen had gone, Lawrence's voice floating
after Percy, Brewster opened the bedchamber door.

I slanted Grenville a look, feeling the need for a large glass
of brandy. "Was that innuendo from Lord Percy?" I asked.
"When he said you must know what he had his eye on?
Meaning Marianne?"

Grenville shook his head. "Percy is not that witty. Unlike
me, Percy would give up an *inamorata* for a manuscript in the
blink of an eye. No, he wants a medieval psalter I purchased a
few years ago. I outbid him for it, and he's never forgiven me."

Denis had not emerged from the bedchamber during this
speech. Even Brewster was surprised, and called a puzzled,
"Sir?"

I looked in. Denis reposed in a chair next to my bed, one of
the journals I'd begun to keep about my adventures in London
open on his lap. He glanced up as we pushed in, marking his
place with one finger.

"Remarkable reading, Captain," he said. "I commend you. I
believe I will continue to enjoy this accounting until its end,
then I will retire. With the Book of Hours, which you will
leave with Brewster. Do not worry," Denis said in a sterner
tone when I opened my mouth to argue. "I will compensate the
reverend. In fact, he will do quite handsomely from this. You
may go, Captain. I will see myself out."

CHAPTER 32

I traveled back across London with Grenville and Marianne, she having clattered down the stairs as soon as she heard the Runners leaving.

Grenville held her hand all the way from Covent Garden, while he told her what had transpired below. She'd listened in the stairwell, she said — she would never have stayed meekly in her rooms — but complained that she missed much when we kept our voices down.

I did not care for talking at the moment. I'd exposed Travers's killer, but I'd solved nothing. Gareth was still dead. If Leland survived, he would grieve. He had lost the other half of his whole, and it would take him a long time to recover from that, if he ever did.

Grenville took Marianne to his own house. Or so he said was his destination when I descended in South Audley Street.

"He's taken leave of his senses, hasn't he, Lacey?" Marianne called to me from the carriage. "Inviting an actress and his ladybird to his home, of all places. What will the neighbors think?"

"Damn what they think," Grenville said. "They will concede to me this boon."

Marianne gave me a mock amazed look, but I could see she was stunned and touched.

When I entered the house, Donata banged swiftly out of an upstairs room and started down the stairs for me. Lady Aline and Gabriella were nowhere in sight—I assumed the one gone home, the other in bed.

Bartholomew took my coat from my tired body, the light in his eyes telling me he was eager to know all that had happened. Barnstable headed for the backstairs, ordering the scattering staff to draw a bath for me, as the lady of the house came down to the foyer.

"Go to bed, Bartholomew," she ordered crisply.

Bartholomew looked disappointed, but he only bowed and obeyed. Donata waited until he'd taken my things away before she faced me, on the exact spot Grenville had hours before.

"Now who is reckless and a damn fool?" she said, not bothering to lower her voice. "Bartholomew told me everything, and then he and the rest of my servants barred the door to me. Locking me in my own house. On your orders, I was told."

Her blue eyes blazed, her rage making her shake.

She was the most beautiful woman I had ever known.

I put my hands on her shoulders, unable to speak. Donata gazed back at me, her anger high, but I read stark fear in the depths of her eyes.

"I'm home," I said. "And whole."

"Damn you." Tears filled her eyes, and she thumped her fists to my chest. "Don't you ever ..."

I caught her hands. I kissed each tense fist, then I put my arms around her and held her close.

"Damn you," she whispered.

I rested my face in her neck, breathed her scent, and became myself again.

I ONLY LEARNED WHAT HAD BECOME OF THE BOOK OF Hours much later. Denis did indeed pay Reverend Travers a handsome sum for it, though I never heard how much. What Denis did with it after that—kept it, sold it on—I never knew. The Nines did close, both Sir Montague and Sir Gideon made certain. Not long later, it opened again, and became all the rage.

The morning after the arrest, I went to see Leland. Donata—I had told her all as we'd lain in bed in the early hours—journeyed the short distance with me in the Breckenridge carriage, and we visited the sick room.

Leland's color was better, and I let myself put aside fears he wouldn't live. Life was never certain, I knew, but he was being well looked after.

"I wish Gareth had never seen the book," Leland said after I'd finished my tale, his hands loose on the covers. "Why could he not believe we cared for him as he was? That he did not have to have *money* to be worthy of notice?"

I had no answer, but Donata did. "Sometimes we find it difficult to believe that we measure up to those we love. That we could possibly be cherished only for ourselves."

She shot a look at me, and I wondered if she were admonishing me or admitting to the fault within herself.

Leland was not comforted. "I'm glad Mr. Denis has the book. It only brought misery to us all—Gareth, his father, his stepmother, me, and my family. It is ironic, is it not, that a book meant for prayer and devotion should be the heart of so much evil?"

A poetic way of looking at it. I was about to make the point that it was, in the end, only a book, but Donata again spoke first.

"It was a book meant for vanity, not devotion," she said decidedly. "A prince or a duke paid a high sum to have it made for him so he could look at pretty pictures when he was supposed to be listening to sermons and meditating on his sins. I am certain that the gold leafing on the pages alone could have fed a village for a winter. But that is royalty for you." She dismissed the dukes and princes with a wave of her elegant hand.

"Those who are not royalty spend plenty of money on frivolous things," I said, my spirits rising a little. Bantering with Donata was good for the humors.

"I never said they did not," she returned. "But Leland is right. I imagine the book was the source of much trouble from the time it was commissioned."

And yet, it was so very beautiful. Denis, a man who recognized beauty, had immediately taken possession. Even Brewster, who'd run hungry in the rookeries as a youth, had known how much such a book would be treasured.

"It has cost me too much," Leland said, a sadness in his eyes that might never vanish. "Gareth could be such a fool about many things, but I miss him, Captain."

He let his eyes drift closed, his lashes wet. Donata and I quietly took our leave.

"He is young," Donata said as we journeyed home. "He has everything of life before him."

"True." Leland might not appreciate that now, however. I threaded my fingers through Donata's gloved ones. "I lost much in my young life, but what I have gained pleases me."

Donata gave me a little smile, without her usual archness. "I like now, too."

I agreed without words that now was quite a fine time.

DONATA HOSTED A SUPPER FOR FAMILY AND FRIENDS A FEW weeks later, in preparation for Gabriella's come-out. The double doors had been thrown open between the three ground-floor rooms to create as large a space as possible for the guests, which included a smattering of appropriate young men. Donata's idea of "private" meant fifty people.

I'd seen Leland Derwent several times as he'd healed, the last walking slowly with Mrs. Danbury and his sister in Hyde Park. Leland had tottered along, leaning on a walking stick, the ladies on either side of him. I'd stopped to inquire about his health, and Leland had given me a faint smile, emptiness in his eyes.

While we'd stood thus, Grenville's famous high-stepping horses pulling his equally famous phaeton came toward us. Grenville drove, and on the seat beside him was none other than Freddie Hilliard.

Grenville halted and descended when he drew alongside us, giving his horses to his tiger, the lad who rode on the back of the phaeton for that purpose.

I professed my pleasure at renewing acquaintance with Mr. Hilliard, and Grenville presented him to the Derwent ladies, and Leland, who acknowledged that they'd met once before.

Freddie tipped his hat politely. Then his expression of wry amusement at his fellow human beings vanished as he enclosed Leland's weak hand in his large and strong one. "Mr. Derwent," he said, his voice holding quietness and compassion. "My condolences for your loss."

Leland started to answer with his customary politeness, then he caught something in Freddie's dark eyes and faltered. I watched him realize that Freddie did indeed understand everything Leland was feeling. "Oh," Leland said. "Thank you."

The sinews of Freddie's hand moved as he tightened his grip, then released Leland. "May we walk with you a spell, ladies? Mr. Derwent?" Freddie asked. "As you know, riding with Mr. Grenville can be an alarming experience."

Leland smiled at his jest—Grenville was reputed to be one of the best drivers in the *ton*—while Grenville raised his brows,

and Mrs. Danbury laughed. Mrs. Danbury, with a swift glance
at me, said she'd take Melissa home and let the gentlemen
enjoy one another's company.

Shy Melissa had looked relieved, Mrs. Danbury flashed a
smile at me, and took Melissa away. I walked with the others a
while longer before I departed for home. Freddie had done
most of the talking, pulling Leland into the conversation, but
not so forcefully as to tire him.

Grenville dropped behind to say good-bye to me when I
left them. "Perhaps Leland will make a full recovery," he said,
watching the tall actor and the smaller young man walking
close together.

"Perhaps he will," I agreed. "Fine chance that you and Mr.
Hilliard happened to be strolling this way today."

"Is it?" Grenville's eyes twinkled, his spirits high. I pictured
him and Marianne planning the encounter at length. "Yes, it
was most fortunate."

"Give my regards to Marianne," I said.

Grenville tipped his hat. "Of course. Good day, Lacey." He
walked away to catch up to the other two, his walking stick
swinging.

"SHE WILL TAKE, I AM CERTAIN OF IT."

Donata's voice startled me from my thoughts. She stood at
my elbow, clad in a silk gown of light peach that clung to her
curves, the gossamer sleeves mere puffs on her shoulders.

I watched Gabriella in her pristine white muslin as she
spoke in her friendly way to Colonel and Louisa Brandon.
Colonel Brandon watched her closely, no doubt remembering
her babyhood, and her mother, Carlotta, and our whirlwind
life at that time.

I saw only my daughter's loveliness, and felt a cold qualm.

"I know I should be happy for her, but why do I want to lock her into the attic until she is five and thirty?"

Donata squeezed my arm. "Do not worry overmuch, Gabriel. Aline is no fool—she and I will watch Gabriella like hawks, and only young gentlemen we have rigorously vetted will be allowed to even speak to her."

"I am the father of a beautiful daughter," I said in a resigned voice. "I worry. It is ingrained, I think."

"So you should," Donata said. Another squeeze. "And while we are speaking on the subject, perhaps now is as good a time as any to tell you that I am increasing."

I did not register the words at first. I heard only conversing and well-bred laughter from Donata's guests, the soft strains of the pianoforte as the newly married daughter of one of Donata's friends played. I saw Bartholomew, who'd conceded to help out as a footman tonight, pass by me in a blur of dark blue footman's livery and blond hair.

"Ah," Donata said as I began to seek air. "Yes, it was quite worth the wait, that look on your face."

I found my voice. "Bloody hell, Donata. You could not prepare me more carefully than that?"

She lifted one peach-clad shoulder in a shrug. "You and I share a bed quite often. We have done so for nearly a year now, I will remind you. I would think you well prepared. The news can hardly come as a shock."

My qualms turned into full-blown fear. Childbirth was dangerous. So many things could go wrong.

At the same time, rapture came over me. A child. One I could watch grow up, as I had not been able to do with Gabriella.

I looked into the eyes of my wife, seeing my fears and excitement reflected there.

"On second thought," I said, striving to make my voice light. "I believe I had better lock *you* in the attic for the next year."

Donata's smile warmed me, and I knew I had been waiting all my life for this woman.

"Only if you lock yourself into it with me," she said. "I know we'd have a fine time."

"Done." I took her hand, and raised it to my lips.

EXCERPT: THE THAMES RIVER MURDERS

CAPTAIN LACEY REGENCY MYSTERIES
BOOK 10

June, 1818

*T*he letter, neatly folded at my plate, looked innocuous enough, but I had a sense of disquiet about it.

The letter had come through the post, my name and direction carefully printed by hand. *Captain Gabriel Lacey, South Audley Street, Mayfair.*

An auspicious address, though not my original. I'd married it. Six months ago, I had been living in straitened circumstances in rooms above a Covent Garden bakeshop. At New Year's I had married Donata Breckenridge, a young widow, and moved into tasteful splendor.

The previous master of this house, Lord Breckenridge, had been a brute of a man, and a boor. Did I feel a sense of triumph that I had awakened with the beautiful Donata half an hour ago, while the foul Breckenridge was dead?

I did, I am very much afraid.

I breakfasted alone. Donata slept on upstairs, weary from her social engagements of the previous night. Her small son from her first marriage, Peter—the current Viscount Breckenridge—took his breakfast in the nursery, and my daughter had not yet woken. In the family, Peter and I were the early risers.

I eyed the letter for some time, filled with a sense of foreboding. I'd received two rather nasty missives in the last weeks, unsigned, purporting me to be an imposter—in fact *not* the Gabriel Lacey who had left my Norfolk country estate more than twenty years ago with a regiment posted to India. I was a blackguard who'd come to cheat Lady Breckenridge out of her money and leave her destitute. If I did not heed the writer's warning, leave a substantial sum for him in a yet-to-be determined meeting place, and disappear again, he would denounce me.

I, of course, showed these letters to my wife at once. Donata had great fun with them, and was busy trying to decipher the handwriting. A jealous suitor, she proclaimed, though she had no idea which one. Could be dozens, she'd said, which unnerved me a bit, though I should not have been surprised. Donata had been quite a diamond of the first water in her Season.

I finished my ham and slice of bread, toasted to near blackness as I liked it, and took a long draught of coffee before I lifted the letter and broke the seal with my knife.

I make so bold to write to you, Captain, to beg a favor. I have a problem I have been pondering for some time, and would like another opinion. Sir Montague Harris, magistrate at Whitechapel, suggested I put the affair before you and see what you make of it. You would, unfortunately, have to travel to Wapping, but there is no way around that. If you would prefer to discuss the matter first, I am happy to meet you in a place more convenient to explain.

Yours sincerely,

Peter Thompson

Thames River Police

"Barnstable," I said to the butler, who hovered nearby, waiting to serve me. "Please send for a hackney. I am off to Wapping this morning."

BARNSTABLE, WHO WAS A STICKLER FOR APPEARANCES, wanted to rouse the coachman to have me driven across London in the Breckenridge landau. I forestalled him, seeing no reason to wake the man, Hagen, who'd been out until four driving my wife from place to place. Nor did I wish to roll into the seamier parts of London in a luxurious coach with the Breckenridge crest on its side.

A hackney would do. Barnstable made sure one halted at our front door, a plain black coach, shining with rain. I asked Barnstable to convey to Donata where I'd gone, in case she woke before my return, and I was off.

The coach had only reached the end of South Audley Street when the door was flung open again. The vehicle listed sharply as a large man climbed inside, slammed the door, and fell onto the seat opposite me. He gave me a nod.

"Mornin', Captain."

"Mr. Brewster." My hand relaxed on my walking stick, which had a stout sword inside it. "I would have hoped Mr. Denis had ceased sending a minder after me."

Brewster folded his thick hands across his belly and returned my look blandly. "Mr. Denis pays me to follow you. When you dart out of your house at nine in the morning and leap into a hackney, I can't but help wondering where you're off to. If I didn't find out, Mr. Denis would not be pleased."

James Denis was not forgiving of those who disobeyed his orders. I had to concede Brewster's dilemma.

"I am going to visit a man of the River Police," I said. "Perhaps not an errand you'd wish to take."

Brewster made a slight shrug. "I go where you go, Captain."

Brewster was a criminal, a thief and possibly a murderer. James Denis, an even greater criminal, ever plotted to have me under his thumb. The association between us, however, had become much more complicated than that. My ideas about Denis had changed, though I had no illusions about exactly what sort of man he was.

The journey across London was tedious, its streets clogged with vehicles, animals, and humanity living as hard as they could under the cloud of smoke twined with mist from the river.

We moved along the Strand, then Cheapside, then through the heart of the City's financial prowess at Cornhill and Leadenhall. We turned southward around Tower Hill and so to the docklands.

Wapping was in the midst of these, with tall ships lining the wharves, the forest of masts and yardarms stretching down the river. The bare rigging moved as the ships rocked, the vessels straining to be released to the freedom of the sea.

I'd sailed plenty myself in such ships, my longest voyage being to India when I'd been young and in the army, to fight in Mysore. I'd dragged my delicate first wife across the ocean with me. That she would not have the eagerness to see an exotic part of the world at my side had never occurred to me.

A similar ship had taken me to Norway, then to France, and finally to Iberia, to fight battle after battle in the unceasing wars. Since I'd returned to England in 1814, an injury denying me the glory of Waterloo, I'd been land-bound. The sight of the tall ships stirred in me a longing to explore parts unknown.

For now, I turned my back on the ships and descended from the coach in front of the narrow house that was an office for the Thames River Police.

Formed by merchants and ship owners tired of cargo being stolen from the holds of moored ships, the Thames River Police patrolled the river, watch over the ships and docks, and apprehend thieves. While the river was their jurisdiction, they did sometimes help the magistrates and Runners throughout London with investigations.

I entered the house to find a small room filled with desks, maps of the river, and pigeonholes crammed with scraps of paper. A wiry young man scampered into the back when I removed my hat and gave my name.

Brewster did not enter the house behind me. He remained outside next to the hackney, leaning on its wheel and narrowly watching anyone who passed. He had no intention of letting the hired driver leave, he'd said, in case I needed a quick departure, but neither had he any intention of voluntarily walking into a house full of patrollers.

Peter Thompson came through a door in the rear of the room and held out his hand to me. He was a tall, bony man with lively eyes in a thin face, wearing a frock coat and breeches that hung loosely on his limbs. So he'd looked every time I'd seen him. He was only minus his frayed gloves this morning, clasping my hand with a bare, callused one.

I'd been in the office to which Thompson ushered me before, long ago, when I'd investigated the affair of the Glass House. I'd met Thompson not long before that, when his men had pulled the body of a young woman out of the water and asked my help identifying it.

Thompson's room hadn't changed. He had a desk and chair for himself, a stool for any visitor. I remained standing, remembering that the stool was less comfortable than leaning on my walking stick.

"Thank you for coming, Captain." Thompson also remained standing, a man who disliked to be still. "I hesitated to write to you, but this has been weighing on my mind for some time. Puzzles intrigue you, so I decided to ask your opinion."

While I'd gained something of a reputation for ferreting out things that were none of my business, I had to wonder why a man of Thompson's repute would ask for *my* help. He had plenty of young, sturdy men at his disposal to assist him in investigations.

"It is an old mystery, I'm afraid," Thompson said. "I must not lie to you—my superiors have told me to let it be. If no one has come forward in all this time, we are to make a mark through it and continue with more pressing matters. But I dislike leaving a thing unsolved."

"And you recalled that neither did I," I supplied.

The corners of Thompson's lips twitched. "You have a tenacity I admire, Captain. I believe you are the exact man for this little problem."

"You've piqued my interest," I said. "As you knew you would with your cryptic letter. Now I cannot leave here without knowing the whole of it."

"For that, I must show you." Thompson took up his hat and gestured for me to follow him out of the office. He led me from the house entirely, and around a narrow path between buildings to a yard in the back.

Brewster was not having me walk through tiny, dim passages with only a man from the River Police to protect me. He fell into step behind me, his stride even.

Thompson opened the door to another gray stone house, its bricks crumbling from years of exposure to damp, mist, and rain. A light rain was falling now, fog thickening until we stood in a ghostly atmosphere, the air gray-white around us.

Inside the door was a set of steps leading into a cellar. Thompson took us down these into clinging chill.

Candles burned in the darkness to light our way. Crates and boxes were piled in the room below, in front of open cupboards of filled pigeonholes. In spite of the cold, it was somewhat dry down here, no windows to let in the outside air.

Two young men stood in front of tall desks, making notes in ledgers. When they saw Thompson, they stood upright, at attention.

"Take some air, lads," Thompson told them. "Stretch your legs."

The two patrollers looked grateful and wasted no time hurrying up the stairs.

"They catalog things here," Thompson said, waving his hand at the ledgers. "Things we find in the river, goods seized from smugglers, evidence in cases, that sort of thing."

I glanced at Brewster. I wasn't certain that information about goods taken from smugglers was a wise thing to pass on to a known thief, but Brewster did not comment or even look interested.

"They catalog things more gruesome as well," Thompson said. He moved to a heavy, bolted door, and when he opened it, my breath fogged in the air that came out.

We looked into a chamber with a very low stone ceiling and thick walls, as though it had been carved into the banks of the river. The cold was enough to make my throat raw.

Shelves held wooden and metal crates and boxes, though not as many as in the outer room. Thompson lifted a crate from only a step inside the door and brought it out.

He set down the crate to close and lock the door again then carried it to a long table at the back of the main room. Brewster helped him lift the crate to this table, then Thompson used a long piece of metal to pry off its top. Thompson reached inside, lifting out a rolled piece of canvas.

"Will you move the crate for me, sir?" Thompson asked Brewster. Brewster lifted it down, clearing the table, now as intrigued as I was.

Thompson laid the canvas bundle on the table and carefully unrolled it.

"'Struth," Brewster breathed.

On the dark, stained canvas was a collection of bones. Human bones, clean and preserved.

Thompson started laying them out, one by one, until we gazed down at a near-perfect skeleton of a human being lying before us. The skull, which was mostly intact, bore a large gouge from the top of the head down to the right eye socket.

Someone had smashed a cudgel into this poor creature long ago and left him to die.

"Here we are, Captain," Thompson said. "I want you to help me discover who she is and what villain out there killed her."

ALSO BY ASHLEY GARDNER

Leonidas the Gladiator Mysteries

Blood of a Gladiator

Blood Debts

A Gladiator's Tale

Captain Lacey Regency Mystery Series

The Hanover Square Affair

A Regimental Murder

The Glass House

The Sudbury School Murders

The Necklace Affair

A Body in Berkeley Square

A Covent Garden Mystery

A Death in Norfolk

A Disappearance in Drury Lane

Murder in Grosvenor Square

The Thames River Murders

The Alexandria Affair

A Mystery at Carlton House

Murder in St. Giles

Death at Brighton Pavilion

The Custom House Murders

The Gentleman's Walking Stick

(short stories: in print in

The Necklace Affair and Other Stories)

ABOUT THE AUTHOR

USA Today Bestselling author Ashley Gardner is a pseudonym for *New York Times* bestselling author Jennifer Ashley. Under both names—and a third, Allyson James—Ashley has written more than 100 published novels and novellas in mystery, romance, fantasy, and historical fiction. Ashley's books have been translated into more than a dozen different languages and have earned starred reviews in *Publisher's Weekly* and *Booklist*. When she isn't writing, she indulges her love for history by researching and building miniature houses and furniture from many periods, and playing classical guitar and piano.

More about the Captain Lacey series can be found at the website: www.gardnermysteries.com. Stay up to date on new releases by joining her email alerts here: http://eepurl.com/5n7rz

Follow Ashley Gardner
www.gardnermysteries.com

Printed in Great Britain
by Amazon

42517495R00172